WHAT HAPPENED AT THE LAKE

BY

PHIL M. WILLIAMS

Printed in the United States of America.
First Printing, 2018.

Phil W Books.
www.PhilWBooks.com

ISBN: 978-1-943894-38-3

Cover design and formatting by Tugboat Design

Dedicated to my big brother, Chris.

A NOTE FROM PHIL

Dear Reader,

If you're interested in receiving my novel *Against the Grain* for free, and/or reading my other titles for free or discounted, go to the following link: http://www.PhilWBooks.com.

You're probably thinking, *What's the catch?* There is no catch.

Sincerely,
Phil M. Williams

CONTENTS

PROLOGUE

Ghazni Province, Afghanistan

"Sergeant Wilson, leave us," the captain said. "Help the men secure the perimeter."

The sergeant glanced at the three trembling figures—one man and two burka-clad women. "Yes, sir," Sergeant Wilson said and left the mud brick house.

The captain removed the Beretta 92 from his holster. He held the handgun at his side, pointing to the sandy floor. He stood for a few minutes, still and dead silent. The Afghani man's gaze was locked on the Beretta. He was bearded and dark-haired, as they all were, but his eyes were blue. He had thick lips, deep grooves in his forehead, and a long thin nose. The captain approached, and the man put up his hands. The women shrieked as the captain aimed his gun at the man's forehead.

The man begged in his native tongue—Dari. The captain didn't waiver. The begging only served to whet his appetite. The begging turned to praying, and the captain squeezed the trigger. The crack reverberated through the tiny room. Blood and brain matter splattered the mud wall. The two women fell to the floor in concert with the man. The women huddled in the corner, clinging to each other.

Their burkas were light blue and covered the women from head to toe. Even their eyes were obscured by a woven screen. One of the women crawled to the man, crying and praying while his blood stained the sand. The captain approached her and pointed his Beretta at her head. She looked up. Even with the screen, he saw the crow's feet. She wasn't the one he wanted. He squeezed the trigger. Another shot, another body.

He holstered his weapon and approached the woman cowering in the corner. He grabbed her under her armpits and hoisted her to her feet. She jerked at his touch but otherwise complied. The captain gazed into her woven screen. Her eyes were blue like a Florida swimming pool. No crow's feet. She whimpered as he removed her veil.

Her skin was olive and even. Big pleading eyes, her chin pointy and small, but her nose a little large. She closed her eyes and prayed in Dari. He removed the rest of her burka. The young woman was compliant but not present. Underneath, she dressed like a child. Colorful shorts and a ratty T-shirt—no bra. Her legs were hairy. She was probably in her mid- to late teens. *Perfect.*

Removing the shorts and T-shirt proved a little more difficult. She shook violently and offered some resistance—holding her arms at her side as he tried to pull her T-shirt over her head. The resistance only increased his arousal. He easily overpowered her. She stood naked, hugging herself, her eyes on the floor.

The captain removed his knife from his scabbard and dropped his pants and underwear to midthigh. He knew she saw it. She flinched backward, not at the knife exiting the scabbard but at his erection exiting his skivvies. He wondered if it was the first penis she'd ever seen. He moved closer, his body and bulge pressed against her—the blade against her neck. Her breathing was short and shallow. Her eyes were wide circles, showing plenty of white.

"Beg," he said in Dari.

CHAPTER 1

Alex and the Grudge

Alex gripped the steering wheel, trees whipping past, an amalgamation of green alongside Route 40 East. He was in a trance, his knuckles white.

"Sweetie, … sweetie, are you okay?" Emma asked.

Alex blinked and glanced at his wife.

Emma Palmer looked like a southern belle—tall, blonde, blue-eyed, and attractive. The only things she lacked were pedigree and youth.

Alex forced a smile and focused back on the highway. "I'm fine."

Emma turned her body in the passenger's seat of the Ford F-150 toward Alex. "How long have we been married?"

"Almost twenty years," Alex replied.

"Almost twenty-one."

"Time flies when you're having fun."

"Good save. Now, are you gonna tell me why you've been gripping that steering wheel so dang tight?"

Alex exhaled and took one hand off the wheel. "I still can't believe we're letting Brett come on this vacation."

"We've been through this. It was the best option. We weren't gonna leave Kristin home alone with him. And, if we didn't let her bring him, she would've been miserable the whole week."

"Did you know that Brett drives her car?"

"Yes."

"That's not a problem for you?"

"No. Should it be?"

"We buy her a car for her sixteenth birthday, and her boyfriend drives it more than she does."

"He's a good driver."

"Something's wrong with that kid. And Kristin's too damn nice. She only sees the good in people."

"Because we raised a good Christian."

Alex, suddenly chilly, closed the AC vent blowing in his face. He gripped the steering wheel again. "I'm telling you, that kid's bad news."

"All I know is, she's happy," Emma said. "If Brett's no good, she'll figure it out sooner or later."

Alex frowned. "It's already later."

"It's only been five months."

"Feels like forever. And how do you know it's been five months? That's oddly specific."

"Because I pay attention. They started dating on Valentine's Day. Remember? She came home with those beautiful roses."

Alex sighed. "This is gonna end badly. Better it happens sooner."

"You worry too much."

"I worry too much? You worried about her before she was even born. Our miracle baby."

She grinned. "I didn't think you'd want me because I couldn't have children."

"You were wrong."

"So were the doctors."

"Now I'm the one worrying." He peeked into the back seat of the extended cab. Buster, their black-and-white Boston terrier slept in a tight circle. "Brett had something to do with Charlie."

"We don't know that."

"No, we can't *prove* it."

"Why don't we focus on having a relaxing family vacation? I can't remember the last time your family's been together. It'll be nice to see everybody on your father's side. I am surprised Matt agreed to come. Especially after what happened at Jeff and Gwen's wedding."

Alex winced, almost imperceptibly.

Emma sat up straight. "You didn't tell him that Harvey and Jeff are gonna be there?"

Alex rubbed the back of his neck. "I want everyone to be together. I think I can fix this … rift between them."

"Matt's gonna be fit to be tied. You need to call him."

"You're right."

Emma smirked. "And don't you forget it."

Alex grabbed his phone from the center console and tapped the Matt icon from his Contacts list.

"Hey, Alex," Matt said.

"Hey, bro," Alex replied. "Where are you? Have you left yet?"

"I'm still at work. I'll be there late tonight."

"We're looking forward to seeing you. Kristin was going on and on about seeing her favorite uncle."

Emma shook her head at Alex's exaggeration.

"I'm looking forward to seeing you guys too," Matt said. "By the way, how much do I owe you for my room?"

"Thanks for the offer, but don't worry about it. I rented the house for the whole family—my treat."

"The *whole* family?"

Alex took a deep breath. "I hope you don't mind, but I invited Harvey and Jeff and Rachel."

The line went silent.

"Don't worry. You're upstairs, and they're in the basement," Alex said, breaking the silence.

"I wish you would've told me," Matt replied. "You know how I feel about them—especially Harvey and Jeff."

"I should've told you. Sorry about that." Alex paused for a moment. "There'll be plenty of people around to provide a buffer if you don't wanna talk to them. And the house is pretty big, so you'll have your space. You *are* still coming, right?"

Matt paused. "I'll be there."

"How's the book?" Alex asked, eager to change the subject.

"Very slow. No idea if what I'm writing is good or total crap."

"I really liked the chapters you sent me."

"To be honest, I don't know what the hell I'm doing," Matt said.

"You could ask Dad for help," Alex said.

"He's the last person I'd ask. And I'd appreciate it if you didn't tell Harvey or anyone who might tell Harvey about my book. You know how competitive he is."

"All right. You know, he's not that bad anymore."

Matt didn't reply.

"Oh, one other thing," Alex said. "Cell service is spotty to nonexistent on the lake, and the house doesn't have internet. There is cable and a landline. It's like going back to 1990. I wanted everyone to be together, not on their phone. I hope that's okay."

"That's fine. It might be good for my writing to unplug."

"Sounds good, bro. I'll let you go, so you can get back to work."

"See ya later tonight."

Alex disconnected the call and set his phone on the center console. "He's fine." Alex glanced at Emma.

Emma's blond brows were arched "You didn't really give him much choice."

"I love my brother, but he needs to let this shit go. It's been three years."

"I think this goes deeper than what happened at the wedding."

"You're right. Like everything, it goes back to our childhood. But it's not Dad's fault. I can't imagine being married to our mother. No wonder he left."

"It takes two to tango."

"Matt's problem is he's too sensitive for his own good."

"What's wrong with being sensitive?"

"Nothing. But he's sensitive to the wrong things. And insensitive to the wrong things. That's why he got kicked out of the army. That's why he can't get along with Dad and Jeff. That's why he's divorced, and that's why his life's a mess. Life's not fair. Our dad's a dick sometimes. So what? Move on. That's life."

"Harvey has some serious issues, and Matt's entitled to his feelings. The wedding *was* bad."

"Again, the wedding was Matt being insensitive and oversensitive at the same time. Don't forget. He called Harvey and Jeff murderers. Technically, he was also calling me a murderer."

"That's not exactly true. He said, 'We're all murderers.'"

"Yeah, in reference to soldiers. And he said that at Jeff's wedding, and Jeff was just back from Afghanistan. Matt can't be that stupid not to know what kinda reaction he'd get."

"Matt was just back from Afghanistan too."

"But he was out on a dishonorable discharge."

"And Harvey called him the p-word and a coward. That's what started the whole thing."

"Harvey shouldn't have said that, but, like I said, 'Our dad's a dick sometimes.' Matt needs to let it go. Blood's thicker than water."

"Then Jeff tried to beat up Matt. He would've too, if you hadn't stepped in."

Alex exhaled. "I don't know what you want me to say. I love my brothers and my dad. I just want everyone to get along."

"Did you ever ask Matt why he refused to go on that mission?"

"No. I assume he was afraid. I get it. When I was in Iraq, I was afraid all the time. But you can't refuse to go on a mission. It puts your entire team in danger."

"It's not like that was his first mission."

"Sometimes guys hit a breaking point. What's done is done. If Matt's ever gonna find any peace and happiness, he's gonna have to learn to let things go."

CHAPTER 2

Kristin and Blue Balls

Kristin sat in the passenger seat of her car, dancing to the pop tune on the radio. Brett drove the Ford Fiesta nearly eighty, in and out of the sparse highway traffic. He flashed a grin her way. He had dark soft hair, a thin but athletic build, and a boyish face.

Brett turned down the radio. "You're such a dork."

Kristin pouted. "Am not."

Brett put his hand on her bare knee. "You are, ... but I love that about you."

Kristin's face felt hot. "You do?"

He slid his hand up her thigh, fingers reaching under the hem of her shorts. "I do." Brett ventured closer to his goal.

Kristin giggled, grabbed his hand, and wiggled from his touch. "Stop it."

Brett frowned. "You're no fun."

Kristin stuck out her tongue. Her gaze dropped to his neck and the gold crucifix that hung from his gold necklace. "Do you like your birthday present?"

"I'm wearing it, ain't I?"

She scowled. "Ugh, you're way too smart to say *ain't*."

"Lots of smart people say *ain't*."

"A whole bunch more dumb people do."

He laughed.

Kristin touched her gold crucifix hanging from her neck. "I never take off my cross. Not since I did a few years ago when we were at the beach, and I was sucked under by a riptide and pulled away from the shore. My dad saved my life. God's been protecting me ever since. Now He'll protect you too."

Brett glanced at Kristin with a crooked grin, then back to the road.

"We're so blessed," Kristin said.

They traveled on Route 40 East, the Tennessee countryside zipping past. Kristin looked up information on Norris Lake. "It says here that the lake's 33,840 acres, with an average depth of seventy-five feet. Wow, that's huge, huh?" Kristin looked from her phone to Brett.

He pursed his soft lips. "Yeah, I guess. So who's gonna be at this family reunion thing again?"

"It's not really a family reunion. Not like a formal one. More like a family vacation."

"What difference does it make?"

"I'm just saying." Kristin smiled at Brett. "Papaw Harvey and Mamaw Cathy'll be there. My real mamaw is Mamaw Crystal, but we don't see her very much. I think she cheated on Papaw Harvey when my dad was young. She always says she's gonna come see us, but she never does. But Mamaw Cathy's real nice."

"And Harvey?"

"He's nice. He just takes a little getting used to. Uncle Jeff and his wife, my aunt Gwen, will be there. They're nice. They look like they could be models or movie stars. And Aunt Rachel and Seth will be there. They're engaged, so Seth's not my uncle yet."

"What's Rachel look like?"

"She's real pretty. Maybe not as pretty as Gwen but prettier than me."

Brett glanced at Kristin, then back to the road. "You shouldn't say stuff like that."

Kristin looked away. "It's true."

A moment of silence passed before Brett asked, "Is that it?"

Kristin looked back to Brett. "There's my parents of course and Uncle Matt."

"He's the one who got kicked out of the army, right?"

"Yes, but don't talk about it, okay?"

"Yeah, sure."

"I have to pee. Can we stop at this rest stop?" Kristin asked, pointing at the sign.

Brett exited the highway and parked the Ford Fiesta in the lot with only a few other cars there. They held hands as they walked to the one-story building. It was hot and humid, heat waves rising from the asphalt parking lot. Inside were bathrooms and vending machines and air conditioning. Kristin went to the ladies' room, peed, and checked herself in the mirror. Her straight blond hair flowed to the middle of her back. Her face was bright and clear without makeup.

Brett waited by the vending machines.

Kristin joined him and reached into her purse. "I'm gonna get a sweet tea. You wanna Coke or something? My treat."

"I'll have a Sprite," Brett replied.

With their drinks in hand, they exited the building.

"My butt hurts from riding in the car so long," Kristin said.

"I could rub it for you." Brett grabbed her backside.

Kristin twisted from his grasp and smacked his hand, not hard. "Stop it. People can see."

Brett looked around at the empty lot. "What people?"

"I just need to walk a bit. They have a sidewalk." Kristin pointed to a sidewalk that snaked through the wooded area next to the building.

They strolled on the path, sipping their drinks, the rush of cars and trucks still audible from the highway. Picnic tables sat under the trees along the path. The sidewalk meandered around oaks, maples, and yellow poplars. The highway traffic was muted now, and the couple was shaded and concealed by the trees.

Brett took her hand and led her to a picnic table. He took her tea and placed his drink and hers on the table. They stood next to the table and the path. She pursed her lips, looking up at her six-foot-tall boyfriend. He placed his hand under her chin and tilted her face toward his. He put his hands on her hips, bent down, and pressed his lips to hers.

Her stomach flipped. She reciprocated, opening her mouth for his tongue.

Brett moved his hands from her hips to her backside. He pulled her tight to his body.

She felt his erection against her stomach.

He unbuttoned the top button of her shorts and slipped his hand down the front, beneath her underwear.

She gasped as he curled his fingers upward. Kristin was in an endorphin-induced haze as Brett touched her. He moved her hand from his lower back to his crotch. She gripped his erection over his athletic shorts.

He groaned.

"Mom!" a child said, the voice carrying from the parking area.

"What?" a woman replied.

Kristin let go and stepped back, the spell broken.

Brett looked toward the voices. "They can't see us," Brett said, his breath elevated, and his shorts tented.

"What if they come down here?" Kristin asked, buttoning her shorts.

"They won't."

"We shouldn't be doing this."

"Why not?"

Kristin frowned as if the answer were obvious. "Because we're not married."

"We're gonna get married when we're older, so what's the difference if we fool around a little?"

"I promised God."

"You got me all horny—"

"Ugh, I hate *that* word."

"How else would you like me to refer to this?" He pointed to his erection.

"I'm going back to the car." She turned, but he grabbed her wrist.

"What am I supposed to do?"

"About what?"

"You know what. You want me to get blue balls?"

"Stop being gross. That's not even a thing."

"I'm not being gross. You're being a prude, like always."

Kristin snatched her wrist from his grasp and crossed her arms over her chest. "Don't call me that."

"You're right. I'm sorry. It won't take long. I just need you to touch me a little. Come on."

"You're just trying to get as far as you can with me before you go to UT."

"I love you, Kristin. I'd marry you now if your parents wouldn't freak out. I just wanna show you how I feel."

Kristin sighed and moved closer to Brett. He hiked one leg of his athletic shorts and pulled out his penis. Kristin clamped her hand around his erection. Brett moved his hips.

"Find a table," the woman said, now much closer.

Kristin's eyes widened.

"It's fine," Brett said. "Don't stop."

The pitter-patter of little feet sounded on the concrete sidewalk. "It's like a maze," the boy said.

Kristin let go and turned toward the footsteps.

"No, I'm almost there," Brett said, his voice strained.

A young boy ran around the corner and stopped at the sight of Kristin and Brett. "Hi," the boy said.

Kristin glanced back at Brett, praying that his penis was back in his pants. It was. He held his T-shirt down to obscure his tented shorts.

"Hi," Kristin replied, her face on fire.

"What are y'all doin'?" the boy asked.

Brett laughed.

"Nothing." Kristin glared at Brett and turned back to the boy. "We were just leaving."

CHAPTER 3

Kristin and the Townie

Kristin and Brett floated on doughnut-shaped floaties, held together by their intertwined hands. The lake sparkled in the summer sun. Rachel and Seth were on the dock, sitting on camping chairs, only ten feet away. Two lemon-yellow kayaks were tied to the dock. Rachel shoved her fashion magazine in her beach bag and stood from her chair.

"I'm gonna get in," Rachel said to Seth.

Seth tapped on his phone. "I can't get a signal."

"Cell phones don't work here," Kristin said.

"That sucks." Seth stood from his chair. He was pasty white, chubby, and short. "I'm gonna go up to the house and check my email."

"There's no internet either," Brett said with a frown.

"No internet?" Seth looked at Rachel with a furrowed brow.

Rachel glared back at her fiancé. "I told you that."

"You said it was spotty, not nonexistent."

"Whatever. I'd like to have my phone too you know."

Seth shook his head. "I have to check in with work. I'm gonna ask Alex about it."

"My parents are at the grocery store with Papaw and Mamaw," Kristin said. "There's a Starbucks like half an hour from here if you need the internet."

Seth started for the lake house.

"Where are you going?" Rachel asked.

"Starbucks, I guess." Seth trudged up the steep hill toward the rental house.

Rachel removed her tight T-shirt, exposing her bikini top. She stepped from her flip-flops and slid her short-shorts down her toned legs. She was petite like Kristin, but she had subtle curves in the right places.

I'm so flat, Kristin thought as she spied Rachel's nipples poking through her blue bikini top.

Brett let go of Kristin's hand, their floaties drifting apart.

Kristin glanced at Brett as he stared openmouthed at her aunt Rachel. Kristin pursed her lips.

Rachel brushed her hair and tied it back in a ponytail. She was tan, blonde, and blue-eyed because of a tanning bed, hair dye, and colored contacts.

I wish she'd just get in the gosh darn water.

Rachel strutted to the dock ladder, turned around, and stepped down the short ladder into the water.

Brett seemed to enjoy a nice view of her butt.

"Let's go kayaking," Kristin whispered to Brett, not wanting Rachel to hear.

Brett shrugged, his eyes still on Rachel. "I'd rather relax here."

"This feels so good," Rachel said, sidestroking closer to the couple.

"Do you know when Jeff and Gwen are coming?" Kristin asked Rachel.

"They're already here."

"Are they coming down to the dock?"

"I don't know. I think they're, like, unpacking." Rachel submerged for a moment to wet her hair. She surfaced and brushed her wet hair back with her hand. "So, what do y'all have planned this week?"

"I don't know." Kristin glanced at Brett.

"I wanna relax," Brett said, leaning back in his floatie, his hands behind his head, and his abs in full eight-pack revelry. "I've been train-ing real hard. I need a break. I'm going to UT on a soccer scholarship in the fall."

"Wow, that's awesome," Rachel replied, her eyes sweeping over his body, then to Kristin. "How many years of high school do *you* have left?"

"I'll be a junior, so unfortunately two," Kristin replied. "I'll take some college classes my senior year though."

"Are y'all planning to, like, do the long-distance thing?"

"Knoxville's not that far," Kristin said. "And I've got my car."

Rachel raised her dark eyebrows. "It's, like, real hard. I know from experience."

"We'll be fine." Kristin looked at Brett. "Right?"

"Yeah, we'll be fine," Brett replied.

"Y'all are young," Rachel said. "Y'all should be, like, having fun."

"We are having fun," Kristin said, her words coming out more like a plea than a statement.

"God doesn't let us have much fun," Brett said with a smirk.

Rachel laughed.

Kristin glared at Brett.

Brett showed his palms. "What? I'm just saying."

Kristin looked at her aunt. "Do you wanna go kayaking?"

"Maybe later," Rachel replied.

Kristin dismounted her floatie with a splash.

"I'll take that," Rachel said, grabbing Kristin's floatie.

Kristin climbed the ladder to the deck, looking over her shoulder as she did so. Brett wasn't looking at *her* butt. She stepped into the kayak, untied it from the dock, and grabbed the paddle.

"Have fun," Rachel said, as Kristin paddled away.

Kristin cut through the glassy blue water with each stroke. She paddled hard and fast, ignoring the burn in her shoulders. She stayed near the forested shoreline to her left, passing docks and coves. To her right, the spacious lake was a wide thoroughfare for the sporadic boat traffic. The occasional speedboat or pontoon or Jet Ski motored past, their wake mostly dissipating before reaching Kristin, but still strong enough to reach the shore as tiny waves.

She slowed her pace and steered her kayak into a deep cove. More docks and still water, no people. The cove turned to the right. She steered around the corner. A man held a sprayer and sprayed a dock with his shirtless back facing Kristin. His tan muscular back was covered with a crucifix tattoo that stretched to both shoulders and from his neck to his shorts and beyond. The man turned and smiled at Kristin, his mustache and soul patch stretching across his face.

"How you doin'?" the man asked, as Kristin paddled near his dock.

Kristin stopped paddling, the kayak floating within ten feet of the dock and the man. "I'm fine, thank you. How are you?"

The man nodded his head. He had faint acne scaring on his cheeks. "The sun's shinin'. I'm workin' in paradise. I can't complain."

His muscles were lean and sinewy. His ears were pointy and elf-like. His thinning hair was cut tight to his scalp. He had an amalgamation of ink on his arms, calves, and upper body—many unrecognizable, except for the snake slithering around a naked lady prominently displayed on his chest.

"It was nice to meet you. I should get going." Kristin dipped her paddle in the water and turned around the kayak.

"So soon? Why don't you come over here for a minute?"

Kristin gripped the paddle and peered at the man over her shoulder. "Why?"

The man grinned. "No reason. Ain't nothin' to be afraid of. I just wanna talk, that's all. I get bored workin' by myself all day. Ain't nobody to talk to but God. I'm Danny by the way. What's your name?"

Kristin thought about Brett and Rachel. She turned the kayak around, facing Danny again. "I'm Kristin."

"*Kristin.* I like that. That's a nice name for a pretty girl."

She blushed. "Thanks."

"You here on vacation?"

"My parents rented a house. My whole family's here."

"That's real nice. I live here full time. I gotta house just over there." He pointed in the direction Kristin had come, exposing a mat of dark underarm hair. "I gotta dock and a kayak kinda like yours. Who knows? We might be neighbors."

"This isn't your house?" Kristin pointed to the house beyond the dock.

"No. I do construction work around the lake. I'm what you might call a jack-of-all-trades."

"I like your tattoo."

He grinned from ear-to-ear. "Oh, yeah. Which one?"

"The cross on your back."

"My cross to bear."

"Did it hurt?"

He shrugged. "Not really. I'm used to gettin' tattoos."

"I wanna get a cross on my ankle, but I'm afraid of the pain."

"You'll be fine, girl. It ain't that bad."

"My parents would never let me."

"If you're eighteen, you don't need permission."

Kristin frowned. "I'm only sixteen."

"Really? That's surprisin'." He licked his lips. "I figured you was a college girl. It's hard to tell these days."

"I should get going." Kristin dipped her paddle into the water.

"I'd love to take you out kayakin' sometime. I know all the secret spots 'round here."

"Oh, I don't know. My boyfriend, um …"

He chuckled. "I didn't mean it like that. Don't get me wrong. You're a beautiful woman and all, but I ain't like that. Your boyfriend's welcome to come along. Hell, your whole family can come along."

"Oh, okay, maybe. I'll think about it."

"See ya around, pretty lady. You have a blessed day."

Kristin blushed again. "You too. Have a blessed day."

CHAPTER 4

Alex and Suspicion

Alex sat on the leather couch, Buster in his lap, a paperback in hand. Kristin and Brett were on opposite ends of the love seat, a large space between them, watching some house-flipping show. *Trouble in paradise already? I sure hope so.*

The doorbell chimed.

Alex moved Buster from his lap and stood. "That's your uncle Matt. You should come say hello."

"In a minute," Kristin said, her eyes never leaving the television.

Alex stepped to the front door and opened it with a big smile. "Hey, bro."

Matt stood, bleary-eyed and rumpled from the long car ride. He had a backpack slung over one shoulder and held on to an army duffel bag. "Hey, Alex. Sorry I'm so late."

"It's fine. I was worried you got lost. Come in." Alex stepped to the side. "I'm glad you made it."

"Thank you for inviting me."

"Of course. How was the trip?"

"Long," Matt replied.

"Let me take that," Alex said, grabbing his large duffel bag and setting it on the hardwood floor. Alex hugged his younger brother. "It's good to see you."

Matt smiled as they disengaged. He was two inches shorter than Alex at 5'8". He had a full beard and wavy brown hair nearly to his shoulders.

Kristin and Brett approached. "Uncle Matt," Kristin said with a wide grin. "Your hair's getting long."

"Not as long as yours," Matt replied, giving his niece a hug.

"This is my boyfriend, Brett," Kristin said, motioning to Brett.

"Nice to meet you," Matt said to Brett, shaking his hand.

The teens returned to the living room.

Alex picked up Matt's duffel bag and pointed to the stairwell. "Your room's upstairs." He led Matt upstairs. "Unfortunately, there's only one bathroom up here, so you'll have to share with Brett. His room's down the hall from you. I hope that's not a problem."

"That's fine," Matt replied.

Matt's room had a queen-size bed, a dresser, and a small table with two chairs. It was nicely decorated with framed prints of lakes and mountains. Matt dumped his backpack on the bed, and Alex set the duffel bag there as well.

"We're gonna have a great week," Alex said. He clapped Matt on the back. "I'm glad you're here, bro."

"Me too."

Matt and Alex looked like brothers. They both had wavy brown hair, small blue eyes, strong chins, and pointy noses. The major difference was Alex's hair was shorter, a lighter shade of brown, and he was normally clean-shaven. Alex did have a five-o'clock shadow at the moment. Alex was also a little bigger and more athletic than his younger brother, but they were both in decent shape for men past their prime at forty and thirty-six.

"I need to talk to you about something important," Alex said. "It can wait until tomorrow though. I know you're probably wiped out."

"I'm all right."

"Let's take a walk down to the lake. I don't want anyone to hear."

They stepped out the back door to find it still warm and humid. Moths fluttered around the outdoor lights attached to the house and the deck overhead. A picnic table and a concrete patio sat under the deck. The backyard sloped for a hundred yards or so to the dock. They stepped carefully down the steep embankment to the dock. The moonlight reflected off the lake, and a few nearby docks had illuminated light posts. An elderly man stood on the next dock over, smoking a cigarette, the ember brightening as he sucked in the nicotine.

"How are you doing?" Alex said, waving.

The old man flicked his cigarette into the lake and walked back toward his house.

"Was it something I said?" Alex asked Matt.

Matt shrugged.

They stood on the dock, overlooking the moonlit lake.

"What do you think?" Alex asked.

"It's nice," Matt replied.

"Check out that Jet Ski," Alex said, pointing at the small watercraft across the inlet. "It looks like the keys are in the ignition."

Matt squinted at the Jet Ski, illuminated by a dock light, the keys and leash hanging from the ignition. Norris Lake Watercraft Rentals was written across the side in vinyl lettering. "I think you're right. Good eye. We should take it out for a joyride."

Alex chuckled. "It's a rental. I doubt they'd give a shit. I was actually gonna rent a pontoon boat tomorrow. It'll be fun to motor around the lake."

"I can give you some money for the boat," Matt said.

"No, I got it. I could use a ride to the marina in the morning though."

"Yeah, no problem. But seriously you gotta let me give you some money. You shouldn't have to pay for everything."

"We'll see," Alex replied. "Not to change the subject on you, but I wanted to talk to you about Brett."

"He seems like a nice kid."

"I think he might be a psychopath."

Matt laughed, but Alex was stone-faced. "Seriously?"

Alex nodded. "I need your help watching him. Kristin's a smart girl, but she's too trusting. She only sees the good in people."

"Why do you think he's a psychopath?"

Alex took a deep breath. "Did I tell you about the puppy we got for Kristin?"

"No," Matt said.

"Kristin wanted a puppy, another Boston like Buster. I told her, if she kept her 4.0, we'd get her the puppy, but she had to take care of it."

"Did you get her the dog?"

"Yeah, we did," Alex replied. "His name was Charlie. He died about a month ago."

"Shit, how did it die?"

"I think Brett had something to do with it."

"Really?"

"I think so. Kristin had this church retreat. Charlie was still a puppy and needed constant care, so she left him with Brett. When she got back, Charlie was listless and woozy. We took him to the vet the next day, but he died on the way there."

"Shit, I'm sorry," Matt said.

Alex nodded again. "I was suspicious, so I paid for an autopsy."

"What did the vet say?"

"He died from head trauma. I think Brett kicked Charlie in the head."

"What did Brett say?"

"He said Charlie fell down the stairs, but the dog seemed fine. That's why he didn't do anything or say anything about it."

"You don't think that's true?" Matt asked.

"No, but I don't have proof that he's lying."

"What does Kristin think?"

"She thinks it was an accident. She thinks Brett's the love of her life. She told Emma that she's gonna marry him after college. I'm hoping that they'll break up when he goes to UT in the fall."

"You sure you're not overreacting?" Matt asked.

Alex shook his head, his jaw set tight. "I'm telling you, there's something wrong with that kid."

CHAPTER 5

Kristin and Ephesians 5:3

The bedroom door creaked and then clicked. Kristin stirred in her bed and blinked. A dark, blurry form approached.

"It's just me," Brett whispered. The room was barely lit by blind-filtered moonlight. Brett sat on the bed next to her.

Kristin sat up in bed, rubbing her eyes. "What are you doing?" She wore shorts and a T-shirt—no bra.

"I'm sorry about today. I'm really not interested in Rachel."

Kristin crossed her arms over her chest. "You sure seemed interested in her."

"First of all, she's way too old. What is she, like, thirty?"

Kristin narrowed her eyes. "Twenty-eight."

"Whatever. It doesn't matter. What matters is I love *you*."

"Promise?"

"I swear to God." He leaned over and pressed his lips to hers.

She smiled as they separated.

"Can I get in with you?"

Kristin frowned. "My dad would kill you if he knew you were in here."

He grinned. "Then don't tell him." He slipped under the covers. "I just wanna hold you."

Brett kissed her on the cheek. He lay flat on his back, his head on her pillow. He wore baggy shorts and a T-shirt. Kristin laid her head on his thin chest, her arm hugging him. He reciprocated, holding her tight.

"You feel good against me," Brett said.

"This is nice, huh?" She tilted her head up.

He kissed her forehead.

She pulled back, searching his neck. "What happened to your cross?"

He touched the void that once housed the gold necklace and crucifix Kristin had given him. "I, uh, ... took it off to swim earlier." He cleared his throat. "I don't know where it is."

"What?" Kristin sat up, her eyes wide.

"It'll turn up."

"Did you look for it?"

Brett sat up. "Yeah."

"Where?"

"Like, everywhere. My bag, my room, the kitchen, the dock. Everywhere."

Kristin frowned. "You probably lost it in the water."

Brett shook his head. "No, I'm like 99 percent sure I left it in my room."

"We have to find it."

"What do you want me to do? I already looked everywhere."

"It's your protection."

"It's a necklace."

Kristin glared.

"Which I love, but it's not the end of the world. It'll turn up." Brett pulled her into an embrace. "You'll have to be my protection."

He pressed his lips to hers. Their mouths parted and tongues touched. Brett eased her to her back, their lips still locked. He was on his side, his hand exploring—her hip, her stomach, up her T-shirt, over her small breasts, his fingertips grazing her nipples.

Kristin gasped and kissed him deeper.

Brett moved his hand from her breasts downward, over her stomach, under the waistbands of her shorts and underwear, over her pubic hair, over her clitoris. He lingered there. His fingers moved over the vaginal opening, poised to enter.

Kristin clenched her legs together and pulled back. She removed his hand from her crotch and sat up again.

Brett didn't resist.

"We can't," Kristin said, breathless.

"Doesn't it feel good?" Brett asked, sitting up, the blanket falling away.

"Of course, but it's wrong."

"Kristin, you're killing me." His eyes flicked to his tented shorts. "Literally killing me."

"Ephesians 5:3."

"What?"

"Ephesians 5:3 says, 'But among you there must not be even a hint of sexual immorality or of any kind of impurity.' I think we're definitely having a hint of sex."

Brett ran his hand over his face. "You can't have a hint of sex. Either you're having sex or you're not. We're clearly not. I can't keep doing this. You can't expect me to go to UT and be faithful when we're barely more than friends."

"That's not fair."

"You're not being fair to me. I'm committed to you. I love you, and only you, but you treat me like my needs don't matter. It really hurts my feelings."

Kristin took his hand in both of hers. "I'm sorry. The last thing I wanna do is hurt you."

He snatched his hand back. "Then don't. Then show me you love me like I love you."

"What am I supposed to do?" Kristin showed her palms.

"Be my girlfriend, not just my friend." Brett hiked one leg of his baggy shorts and exposed his phallus. He wasn't wearing underpants. He placed his hand on the back of her neck and kissed her—soft and chaste. Brett pulled back, glanced at his penis, then back to Kristin. "Kiss it."

Kristin frowned.

"Come on. Just once." Before she answered, Brett pushed her head toward his crotch.

Kristin pecked the head of his penis, but he held her in place. "Let me up," she said.

"Put it in your mouth."

She squirmed, but he held her firm, his hand gripping the back of her neck. "Brett, stop."

"It won't take long," he said.

"No."

Brett squeezed her neck tighter.

"You're hurting me," Kristin said.

"You're hurting *me*," Brett replied through clenched teeth. He let go of her.

Kristin sat up, rubbing the back of her neck and scowling at Brett. "That hurt. Why did you do that?"

"This hurts." He pointed to his crotch. "I don't think you're ready for a love relationship."

"That's not true."

"Other guys aren't near as understanding as I am. Especially guys who can get girls."

"What are you saying?"

"I'm saying you gotta give me *something*."

He grabbed her hand and put it in his lap. She pursed her lips and gripped his erection. She moved her hand up and down. He groaned in appreciation; his breathing grew ragged.

Screams came from upstairs. It was a man. A terrified man. Kristin stopped and looked at the door.

Brett placed both hands around hers and said, "Don't stop." He forced her grip harder, the stroke faster. Brett moaned, finishing, as the man upstairs shouted, "No. Stop it."

CHAPTER 6

Alex and PTSD

"Alex, wake up," Emma said, shaking her husband. Alex groaned; his eyelids fluttered.

A man screamed upstairs. The man shouted, "No. Stop it. Lemme outta here."

"What's happening?" Alex asked, still dazed.

"I think Matt's having a nightmare," Emma said, sitting next to Alex in their bed. "You should check on him."

Alex sat up and kissed Emma on the cheek. "I'll be right back." He hurried upstairs, taking two steps at a time. He knocked on Matt's door. No answer. Matt was quiet now. Alex knocked harder. "Matt, are you okay?" Still no answer. Alex turned the doorknob and pushed into the room. "Matt?"

The queen-size bed was a disaster—covers and sheets swirled and partly on the floor. The bed was empty. Alex flipped on the light. No Matt. Alex rushed to the open window, his stomach in his throat. He moved the curtains and peered outside. Matt sat cross-legged on the roof overhang, just outside the window, his back against the house.

"You all right?" Alex asked.

Matt turned and looked up at Alex. "I'm fine. I just needed some fresh air. Did I wake you?"

"Yeah, you were shouting."

"Shit, I'm sorry. I didn't realize."

"Bad dream?"

"I don't remember."

Alex climbed through the window and sat next to his brother on the roof overhang. They stared at the steep gravel driveway, lit only by moonlight and ambient lighting from the porch lights.

"That's a helluva hill," Matt said.

"Does this happen a lot?" Alex asked, ignoring his brother's statement.

Matt rubbed his temples. "Yeah. Angela used to say it scared her because I'd always open the window. She was terrified that I was gonna kill myself. I doubt she'd give a shit now. You know she married some doctor? I heard she was pregnant."

"I know. Emma told me. She and Angela are Facebook friends." Alex took a deep breath. "I'm worried about you, bro."

"I'm fine."

"When I came back from Iraq, I had some problems with PTSD. I saw a shrink at the VA. It helped."

"I'm not gonna let some shrink drug me up. And, even if I wanted to, I can't go to the VA. Dishonorable discharge, remember?"

"You can still see someone in the private sector who specializes in PTSD."

"I'm fine. All right?"

Alex sighed. "You sure?"

"Yeah."

"You ever think about it?"

"Think about what?" Matt asked, his eyes still on the driveway.

"You know. … Killing yourself?"

Matt was quiet for a moment. He blinked. A tear slipped down his cheek. "Doesn't everybody?"

CHAPTER 7

Kristin and Norris Lake

Kristin knocked on Brett's bedroom door, holding her beach bag. "Are you coming?"

Brett opened the door. The morning sunlight shone through his bedroom window, giving him an angelic glow. "I gotta go to the bathroom."

"Don't you wanna go swimming?"

"Gimme a minute. Unless you got Depends for me to wear."

Kristin crinkled her nose. "Gross."

Brett laughed and went to the bathroom.

Kristin walked to the upstairs sitting room with two rocking chairs and a couch, but she doubted that anyone ever sat there. Sun streamed through the sliding glass door to her left. The stairs were on her right. Kristin heaved the sliding glass door open and stepped onto the deck. The morning sun warmed her skin. She set down her beach bag and leaned on the railing, mesmerized by the sparkling blue water in the distance.

Norris Lake was created by Norris Dam, the first project by the Tennessee Valley Authority and part of FDR's New Deal. Even when she didn't have to, Kristin did her homework.

The back door opened and shut below her. She thought about calling out with a "Hey, y'all," but she remained quiet and curious.

"I think you should let it go," Aunt Gwen said, standing on the patio below.

"He almost ruined our wedding," Uncle Jeff replied. "Do I have to remind you that he called me, Dad, and Alex murderers?"

"It's been three years. Maybe he's changed."

"He has serious problems, Gwen. You heard him screaming last night. He's crazy, like his mother."

"I think we should give him a chance."

"I'm not gonna do anything, if that's what you're worried about. He better not start anything though because I'll finish it."

Gwen sighed. "Be nice."

"I am nice. But I won't put up with any bullshit."

"He is your brother."

"Half brother."

"So is Alex."

"Alex is different. I tried with Matt. I really did."

"Okay."

"It's a beautiful day," Jeff said. "Let's enjoy it. I don't wanna rehash old grudges."

"You're right."

They stepped out from under the deck into the sun. Jeff wore a desert camo backpack and held a beach bag filled with towels, sunscreen, and other lake paraphernalia. Gwen was comparatively unburdened, holding only her sunglasses.

Gwen looked down the steep slope to the bright blue water. "The lake's gorgeous."

Jeff smiled at his wife. "You're gorgeous."

Gwen blushed and kissed him on the lips.

Kristin felt a pang of jealousy. She wished Brett was as romantic as Jeff. Brett was mostly interested in joking around or getting off. She alternately felt like a platonic buddy and a piece of meat. Kristin sighed involuntarily.

Jeff turned and looked up, catching a glimpse of Kristin.

Kristin blushed, metaphorically caught with her hand in the cookie jar. "Hey, y'all." Kristin waved.

Gwen turned and looked up. "Hi, Kristin. I didn't know you were up there."

"I just stepped out," Kristin replied. "I'm waiting for Brett to get ready."

"We're going down to the dock," Gwen said. "You want to walk with us?"

Kristin glanced over her shoulder, thinking about Brett. "Sure, but lemme tell Brett real quick."

"We'll be here waiting."

Kristin went inside and knocked on the upstairs bathroom door. "You almost ready?"

"Can't a guy go to the bathroom in peace?" Brett replied.

"I'm going down to the dock with Jeff and Gwen."

"Okay, I'll be down in a few minutes."

Kristin returned to the deck, picked up her beach bag, and walked down the deck steps, meeting Jeff and a smiling Gwen on the lawn.

Uncle Jeff was right. She *was* gorgeous. She wore a light-blue beach cover-up, but it didn't hide her athletic build. Her face was symmetrical, her skin tan and even, and her wavy hair flowed over her shoulders. Aunt Gwen looked much younger than her twenty-eight years. Kristin felt ugly by comparison.

Gwen and Jeff walked hand in hand down the slope toward the dock. Kristin walked next to Gwen, feeling like the third wheel. The neighbor to their right started a hedge trimmer. Bird chirps were replaced by the roar of the two-cycle motor. The old man glared at them as they passed.

They stepped onto the dock. Kristin set her beach bag under a camping chair and sat down.

Jeff glanced at the two yellow kayaks, each with a Miami Dolphins' sticker on the side. "Are those Alex's kayaks?"

"Y'all can take them out," Kristin replied. "My dad brought the kayaks for everyone to use."

"I could use a workout."

"Brett said he was gonna kayak after we go out on the pontoon."

"Your dad's still cleaning up from breakfast. It might be a couple of hours before we get the boat. Maybe I'll take a quick paddle before the boat gets here." Jeff set down his beach bag and backpack next to two empty camping chairs.

Across the inlet, a man with two young boys approached a docked Jet Ski. The man checked their life preservers and helped the boys onto the watercraft.

"That's sweet," Gwen said, gesturing across the inlet. "You'll be a dad like that."

Jeff smiled at his wife.

Gwen rose to her tippy-toes and kissed Jeff on the cheek. She grabbed her novel from the beach bag, adjusted her sun hat, and sat in a camping chair, content to escape with a good psychological thriller. The man across the inlet started the Jet Ski and drove slowly with his sons.

Jeff removed his T-shirt, exposing an upper body worthy of a *Men's Fitness* magazine. Jeff grabbed his backpack, stepped to the edge of the dock, and placed it in the kayak's rear storage compartment, although his pack was too big to shut the hatch. Jeff picked up the kayak paddle, eased into the kayak from a sitting position on the dock, and shoved off. "I'll be back," he said.

Gwen waved to her husband.

"Have fun," Kristin said, watching her uncle.

Jeff cut through the still blue water with little effort, his powerful arms propelling him forward with each stroke.

Gwen settled into her novel, and Kristin enjoyed the view. The watercraft traffic was minimal. The occasional pontoon or speedboat or Jet Ski went by, but just as many kayaks, standup paddle boards, and canoes were on the lake too.

Two girls on Jet Skis whipped past at full throttle—at least two hundred feet away but still close enough that their wake rocked the dock.

They're probably in college. That looks fun, Kristin thought. The girls played, zipping around each other and jumping each other's wakes. Kristin stared at them—envious of their unbridled enthusiasm.

CHAPTER 8

Alex and the Ne'er-Do-Well

Alex stood over the sink, rinsing the dishes from breakfast. Alex's father, Harvey, and stepmother, Cathy, sat at the kitchen table with their adult daughter, Rachel, and her fiancé, Seth. They talked and enjoyed their morning coffee.

"My dad's been through three heart attacks," Harvey said. "The other day he told me that he wanted to die. I told him that, for a man who wished for death, he was quite the survivalist."

"Don't talk like that, Daddy," Rachel replied.

Harvey placed his hand on Rachel's bare thigh and flashed her a crooked grin. Harvey wore a tank top, showing off his guns. *Sun's out, guns out*, as they say. He did have an impressive physique for a sixty-six-year-old. Above the neck, his age showed. He had a grayish white crew cut, wire-rimmed glasses, and a craggy face with thin lips.

"What time did Matt get here last night?" Cathy asked.

Alex shut off the water and turned from the sink. "Around eleven." He loaded dishes into the dishwasher.

Cathy was sixteen years younger than Harvey. She was once young and voluptuous, Harvey's trophy wife to add to his successful military-thriller-novelist persona, but now she was overweight, burdened by three decades of gravity, motherhood, and an abundance of unhealthy food.

"What's Matt doing now?" Harvey asked. "Last I heard, he was working for some landscaping company."

Seth scratched himself under the table. From Alex's vantage point across the kitchen, he had a decent view below the table. Alex raised his gaze. Between Harvey's hand high up on Rachel's thigh and Seth's scratching, he'd seen enough under-the-table shenanigans.

"He works in a warehouse," Alex replied.

"Doing what?" Harvey asked.

"I assume warehouse work."

Harvey huffed. "He's a ne'er-do-well."

"A what?" Rachel asked, giggling.

"It's a contraction for 'never-do-well.' It originated in Scotland, the first citation in the early 1700s—1737 to be exact."

"Wow, Mr. Palmer. You're like a human Wikipedia," Seth said.

"Dad, you gotta stop with this stuff," Alex said. "This's why Matt feels so alienated."

"I won't blow smoke up his ass like your mother does. That clearly doesn't help. Anyone with a pulse can work in a warehouse. That goddamn dishonorable discharge has ruined his life and disgraced this family. He takes after his mother. Crazy and impulsive."

"Dad, stop," Alex said.

"Let me finish."

Alex wagged his head and went back to the dishes.

"Nobody likes war. But, if you join the military, war's part of the deal. Did you ever disobey a direct order from your CO?"

Alex turned to his dad, holding a plate. "No, but if I was given an unlawful order, I would've."

"But he wasn't given an unlawful order. He was a coward. He was afraid to fight."

"Dad, come on. This isn't the time or the place."

"What about you, Seth. Did you ever disobey your CO?"

"No, sir," Seth replied.

"What branch were you in?" Alex asked Seth.

"Army. I was an intelligence officer."

Alex nodded to Seth and looked at Harvey. "Matt's had a rough time. I'd appreciate it if y'all didn't talk about it."

"He brought it on himself," Harvey said.

"Matt had his reasons. Leave it alone."

Harvey crossed his arms over his muscular pecs. "I might buy that if it were you or Jeff, but, like I said, 'Matt's a ne'er-do-well.' Name one thing he's done well in his life."

"He's writing a novel. It's pretty good too." Alex paused, his error sinking in. "Don't mention it to Matt. He wants it to be a surprise."

As if on cue, Matt walked down the stairs and into the kitchen.

"It looks like someone had a visit from the hair fairy," Alex said.

Matt smiled at the *Meet the Parents* reference and ran a hand through his disheveled brown hair. "Good morning, everybody."

"Good morning," Cathy and Seth said in unison.

"Have you met my fiancé, Seth?" Rachel gestured to the pale chubby man sitting across from her.

"We met at Jeff's wedding. Nice to see you again, Seth," Matt said, but not venturing close enough to the table to shake his hand.

"Yeah, nice to see you," Seth replied.

"Did you want some eggs?" Alex asked Matt. "I have some pancake batter left too."

"You don't need to make me breakfast," Matt said. "You're already cleaning up. I'll figure it out."

"It's no big deal." Alex grabbed the frying pan from the drying rack and placed it on the stove top.

"I hear you're writing a novel," Harvey said, his face expressionless.

Matt turned to his father and cleared his throat. "I'm trying."

"*Trying*? If you were a cabbie, would you say that you were trying to drive the damn car? Is this your first novel?"

"Yes."

"Then finish the damn thing and burn it, because it'll be garbage. Then write three more—at least half-a-million words—and burn those too. Then you *might* be ready to write something that isn't dreadful."

"It's really good," Alex said.

"I don't know if it's good or … dreadful," Matt said, "but I'll get an editor, do the best job I can, and let the readers decide."

"It'll never be published. You're wasting your time. Put in the work, learn the craft, then get an agent and a publisher."

"I'm gonna self-publish it."

Harvey cackled. "We used to call it vanity publishing. At least *that* required a sizable cash investment. Self-publishers are ruining the book business. The amount of drivel dumped on Amazon every day is criminal. Free books all over the place, ninety-nine cent books. It used to be that agents and publishers served as gatekeepers and kept this garbage in desk drawers where it belonged. Now every idiot with an internet connection thinks he's an author."

"Excuse me," Matt said and walked out the front door.

"Was that necessary?" Alex asked Harvey.

"I won't blow smoke," Harvey replied. "You know that. Better he knows what he's in for."

Alex left the kitchen and followed Matt out the front door where he stood in the morning sun, his fists clenched. A motor whizzed in the background. A Weed eater maybe.

"Why did you tell him?" Matt asked.

"I'm sorry," Alex replied. "It slipped out because I'm excited for you. It's really good, man. You gotta finish it."

Matt exhaled, his hands relaxing "Thanks, but I don't know if I can."

"Why not?"

Matt shrugged. "What if Dad's right? He knows what he's talking about. He *is* a best-selling author."

"Get it right," Alex said with a smirk, then perfectly mimicked their father's pompous baritone. "I'm a New York Times and international best selling author with fifteen military thrillers, all of which hit the best seller list."

Matt laughed. "Actually, his last one missed the New York Times list."

"Really? Maybe that's why he's being such a dick."

"I know he thinks I'm a loser."

"He doesn't. I think in his weird way, he thinks he's helping you. I know he has some issues, but deep down he loves us."

"Must be really deep down."

Alex chuckled. "Let's go get a boat."

CHAPTER 9

Alex and Danger in Paradise

Matt gazed up the gravel driveway. It was extremely steep—steep enough that walking up would be a challenge. "Has anyone tried getting out of here yet?" Matt asked.

Alex grinned with his hands on his hips. "I did it yesterday."

"I should've left my car at the top. It's front-wheel drive."

"My truck's not four-by-four. Rear-wheel-drive's probably worse. It'll be fine. You'll need to get a good head start though."

Matt unlocked the doors to his old Hyundai Elantra. He sat in the driver's seat, Alex in the passenger's seat. Matt turned around his car and backed up close to the house. He pressed the clutch and put it in first. He glanced at Alex, then back to the driveway. He mashed the accelerator and let off the clutch. The little sedan shot forward, the front tire gripping the gravel. They reached the top, the gravel driveway transitioning to asphalt road.

Matt stopped at the top with a wide smile. "That was like a rally race."

"Piece of cake," Alex said.

"It *was* easier than I thought, but can you imagine what it would be like in the rain?"

"Forecast's clear and sunny."

They drove the twisty mountain road alongside a forest of oaks and short-leaf pines. Kudzu was rampant in places, the ivy-like plant forming dense mats and snaking upward, using massive trees as elevators to the sun.

"Have you talked to Jeff?" Alex asked.

"I haven't seen him yet," Matt replied, glancing from the road to Alex. "Shit, I haven't spoken to him since the wedding."

"I can try to mediate. You know, to make it less awkward."

"I really don't give a shit anymore. I won't be rude, but I'm not here to hang out with him—or Harvey for that matter."

"He is our brother."

"You gonna tell me how blood's thicker than water?"

"It is."

"Blood and family ties, … it's all bullshit. I like people or dislike people for who they are."

"Is that what happened with Angela?"

Matt swallowed. "Yeah, she dislikes me for who I am."

⁎ ⁎ ⁎

After half an hour of slow, windy driving, they arrived at the Norris Lake Marina—home to Norris Lake Watercraft Rentals.

"You can just drop me off," Alex said.

Matt drove down the steep parking lot toward the marina. Norris Lake Marina was nearly a floating town. The dock looked like a wooden road system to access the houseboats, speedboats, fishing boats, Jet Skis, and pontoons. The shopping was dead center in the form of a mini-mart complete with milk for breakfast and crickets for bait. The marina even provided sewage removal.

Matt parked and removed his wallet from the center console. "I'd like to give you some money for the boat."

"I got it. Seriously," Alex replied, as he stepped from the car. He shut the door and leaned through the window. "I'll see you back at the house."

Alex walked on the floating dock toward the mini-mart and waved as Matt drove off. The marina smelled fishy, with a hint of urine. Inside the mini-mart, a thin gray-haired man stood behind the counter.

"Good mornin'," the man said.

"Morning. I called yesterday to rent a pontoon for the week. Alex Palmer. Actually, it'll be five days, because I'll bring it back on Sunday morning."

"Still cheaper to do the week rental."

"Yeah, that's what you said when I called."

"Lemme see here." The man opened a manila folder and flipped through the papers. "Here it is."

Alex signed the waiver and the contract for a week of sun and fun on the pontoon boat. He paid the man for the rental and the insurance.

"It's all gassed up. The man outside'll give you the rundown."

"Thanks. Any local secrets we should know about the lake? Good fishing spots? Rope swings?"

The old man took a pamphlet from the rack on the counter. He opened it to a map of Norris Lake. "Now I don't know if these are secrets." The man marked a couple of inlets and coves in pencil. "These marks are places where you might find a rope swing. I say *might* because they sometimes get taken down or moved. Make sure you check 'em before usin' 'em. They been known to break on occasion." He made an *X* on a bridge. "If you're lookin' for a real thrill, the locals like to jump off this here bridge. You gotta be careful when the lake's low. There's a rusty fence at the bottom. A kid got cut up pretty bad during a drought a few years ago. The lake's a little low but prob'ly not too low to be an issue."

"Probably?"

The old man grinned, exposing yellow teeth. "Ain't nothin' for sure."

Alex laughed. "Any good fishing spots?"

"Truth be told, the lake's not the best for fishin'. There's bass and crapple and walleye. Might find some sunfish too. But I wouldn't eat 'em, unless you like mercury."

"The water looks clean."

The man folded the map back into a pamphlet. "Looks can be deceivin.'" He handed the map to Alex.

"Thanks for the information." Alex started toward the door.

"Another thing."

Alex turned back to the man.

The man was stone-faced. "Stay off the islands at night. Some folks campin' on them islands are a sandwich short of a picnic, if you know what I mean. And I don't know where you're stayin', but I'd make sure to lock the doors. We've had some burglaries 'round here the past few months."

CHAPTER 10

Alex and the Island

Nearly everyone was present for the maiden voyage. Alex and Matt loaded gear onto the pontoon boat. Emma and Rachel sat near the front, talking under their sun hats. Harvey, Cathy, and Seth sat in the rear, under the canopy. Brett and Kristin sat in the sun, talking in hushed whispers. Buster the Boston terrier trotted from person to person, wagging his tail in search of treats.

Jeff and Gwen walked hand in hand down the hill toward the dock. They could pass for models. Gwen, slender and youthful, wearing a white beach cover-up. Jeff, six feet tall, wearing board shorts and a faded T that emphasized his broad shoulders and trim waist. Jeff and Gwen were greeted with smiles and invitations as they boarded. Jeff nodded to Matt. He nodded back.

Progress, Alex thought.

"Come sit with us," Emma said to Gwen.

"Need a hand?" Jeff asked Alex.

"You wanna get the rope and shove us off?" Alex replied.

With the gear loaded and everyone aboard, Jeff untied the pontoon, pushed off from the dock, and stepped onto the boat in one graceful motion. Alex started the motor and exited the inlet slowly, observing the no-wake rule.

Alex steered the boat, but he watched Brett through his shades.

Brett wore orange board shorts, showing off the tan and fit body of a future UT soccer player. Kristin wore a light-blue bikini, her lithe body sun-kissed from the day before. Brett placed his hand on Kristin's thigh. She removed it, flashing a frown toward Brett. He shrugged and leaned back. Brett's eyes swept over the women and settled on Rachel and her string bikini. It was hard to tell with Rachel's sunglasses, but the gazes didn't appear one-sided.

Once outside the wake zone, Alex accelerated the pontoon to full throttle. The front end rose from the bright-blue water and bounced against small swells. The sunlight reflected off the lake in glistening crystals. Much of the shoreline was wooded, but interspersed were lake houses. Some were mansions, covered in glass to soak up the view and perched on hills with endless staircases to the water. Others were more modest versions of the same equation.

Brett scooped up Buster and put the dog in his lap. He palmed the dog's skull and jerked his head back and forth. Buster growled and tried to nip at Brett's hand, but Brett had control, laughing at the little dog's impotent attacks.

"Stop," Kristin said, taking Buster into her lap.

"I'm just playing with him," Brett replied.

"You play too rough."

Two young women on Jet Skis passed them, traveling in the opposite direction. They turned and jumped the pontoon's wake. Then they were gone.

Occasional islands of varying sizes dotted the lake, most with beaches of coarse sand and sparse boulders to navigate. The outcroppings and stones mostly congregated along the cliffs of the mainland. Alex beached the pontoon on an island about half the size of a football field.

Harvey, Cathy, and Seth remained planted under the canopy. The women, without Cathy, took off their cover-ups and went swimming. Matt grabbed his fishing gear and his backpack and headed for the shore.

"Let's go explore the island," Brett said to Kristin.

"I said I was going swimming," Kristin replied.

"Aren't you getting in?" Rachel called out to Seth from the water.

"I guess," Seth replied, standing.

Seth took off his shirt to reveal pale skin, a spare tire around his midsection, and a breast cup similar to Kristin's. He jumped in the water, eager to cover himself with the lake. Nobody commented, laughed, or stared at his physique. In this time of corn-syrup addiction, it wasn't abnormal for a twentysomething man to be overweight.

Brett exited the pontoon from the front. Alex and Jeff were right behind him.

"You gonna check out the island?" Jeff asked.

"I have to piss," Alex replied.

"Me too."

Brett skipped rocks off the beach. Matt searched the shore for a good fishing spot. Alex and Jeff walked into the island's interior along an informal pathway of compacted sand, created by repeated trampling. Jeff stopped after he was screened by the trees. Alex continued down the path a polite distance from Jeff. Alex peed on a tree, the relief instant. Afterward he tied his board shorts, and Jeff approached.

"Where does this go?" Jeff asked.

"I don't know," Alex replied.

They continued down the path, deeper into the interior. The path turned left. Around the bend was a tent, a fire pit, and clothes hanging on a line strung between two trees. A one-man kayak was next to the tent. Beer cans and snack wrappers littered the ground. It smelled like urine and fish. A rod and reel leaned against a tree with a tackle box nearby. A skinning knife stuck out of a stump.

The tent was open on both sides, allowing the breeze to pass through. Alex peeked inside. A heavily tatted man slept shirtless, the smell of alcohol and BO emanating from his pores. A few porn magazines were strewn about the tent.

Alex put his finger to his lips and motioned to Jeff who crept to the tent and peered inside. Alex pointed to the trail and mouthed *We should go.*

They returned to the shore. Brett still skipped rocks. Matt was fifty yards away, casting from the shore.

"We should get out of here," Alex said to Jeff. "Can you get everyone on the boat?"

"Yeah." Jeff walked toward the boat and the swimmers.

Brett was laser-focused as he skipped rocks with a sidearm motion.

Alex approached. "You doing all right?"

Brett shrugged. "I'm fine." He threw another rock. This one skipping five times before dying.

"I'm gonna be brutally honest with you for a minute."

Brett turned to Alex and swallowed.

"Kristin's a nice girl. I think you know that."

Brett nodded.

"She's a trusting person."

Brett nodded again.

"I'm gonna tell you this once. Don't abuse that trust, and don't take advantage of her kindness." Alex glared at Brett. "You understand me?"

"Mr. Palmer, I wouldn't—"

"It's a yes or no question, Brett. Do you understand me?"

"Yes."

"Good. We should get going. There's a homeless guy in the woods, and he has a knife."

"For real?"

"Yeah, he lives at the end of that trail," Alex said, pointing to the footpath.

Brett hurried to the boat.

Alex motioned for Matt who slung his backpack over his shoulder and approached with his rod and reel in hand.

"What's going on?" Matt asked.

"We're leaving," Alex replied. "We saw a homeless dude in the woods with a knife."

"It's probably just for cleaning fish."

"The guy at the rental shop told me to be careful of people camping on these islands. He said some of them are crazy."

Alex and Matt walked onto the pontoon boat. Harvey and Cathy remained seated under the pontoon canopy. The old couple perspired despite the shade. Emma, Rachel, Gwen, Kristin, and Seth sat on the boat with towels wrapped around them. Brett sat with Kristin and Jeff with Gwen.

"Everyone ready to go?" Alex asked.

"Is there really, like, a crazy homeless person in the woods with a knife?" Rachel asked.

"You think I'd make that up?" Jeff said.

"I don't know if he's crazy or not," Alex said, "but I'd rather not find out."

CHAPTER 11

Alex and the Rope Swing

Alex steered the pontoon away from the island. Everyone was seated except for Brett. Back in open water, Alex gunned the motor, and Brett fell to the deck.

"Sorry," Alex called out above the roar of the engine. One side of Alex's mouth was raised in contempt.

Brett nodded and sat next to Kristin.

"Hey, Matt," Alex called out and motioned for his brother.

Matt stepped with a wide base toward the captain. He held on to a bar next to the helm. "What's up?"

Alex handed Matt the map from the marina. "The marked areas are rope swings. Can you figure out how to get to the nearest one? The buoys have numbers on them that correspond to the map."

Matt took the map and sat next to the helm. He found a buoy, oriented them on the map, then helped navigate to the nearest rope swing. At Matt's direction, Alex turned into an inlet. They motored along the shore of the cove, searching for a hanging rope.

Matt pointed. "There it is."

Alex cut the engine in open water, thirty yards from shore. Matt threw the anchor. The rope swing was attached to a decrepit branch and hung over the water, only ten feet or so from a shoreline littered with boulders.

Alex stepped out from the helm. "Who wants to go first?"

"Honey, that doesn't look safe," Emma said. "How deep is it?"

"I'll check it out first," Alex said and kissed his wife on the cheek.

"No way I'm getting on that thing," Cathy said.

Alex, Jeff, Brett, Kristin, and Matt dove into the water and swam ashore. Alex brought the rope swing with him. Two-by-twos were nailed into the tree to form a makeshift ladder.

Jeff dove off the shoreline, trying to find the bottom. After thirty seconds, he surfaced. "It's plenty deep," Jeff called out.

Alex pulled on the rope, the branch bending but sturdy. "I think the branch'll hold."

"That tree looks dead," Emma called out from the boat.

"It's fine," Alex called back to his wife. "It has a few leaves." Alex held the rope in his left hand as he climbed the rickety two-by-two ladder. Near the top of the ladder, Alex gripped the rope with both hands.

Everyone watched in anticipation. Rachel videoed from the boat with her phone.

Alex swung out from the tree, over the water. At the apex, he let go, free-falling fifteen feet. Alex crashed into the lake feet first, his momentum taking him into the depths. He looked up, the sunlight dissipating above him. He swam toward the light, his head breaking the surface, a wide smile on his face. The audience on shore and on the boat hooted and hollered.

After Alex had blazed the metaphorical trail, everyone took a turn. Everyone except Cathy. She sat on the boat as the group had a blast, swinging and diving. Alex ventured a headfirst dive, Jeff a flip. Even Buster made it ashore. He ran around, barking and wagging his tail at the excitement.

"Mamaw Cathy, you should try. It's fun," Kristin called out to the boat.

"No thanks, sugar," Cathy called back. "Your mamaw's too old to be swinging like Tarzan."

"You're way younger than Papaw."

Cathy didn't respond.

"But I'm in good shape," Harvey said, loud enough that Cathy probably heard. "She's too heavy to hold on to the rope."

Cathy buried her nose in her paperback.

"Dad, come on. That's rude," Alex said.

Harvey shrugged. "It's the truth."

Cathy wasn't huge. She was naturally curvy—and overweight for sure—but she didn't look abnormal for a fifty-year-old woman in a first-world country.

"Who's next?" Harvey asked.

"You are," Jeff replied, handing the rope to Harvey.

The branch creaked a little when Harvey swung out and plunged into the lake. Or was it a crack?

"Did you hear that?" Alex asked Matt.

"Hear what?" Matt replied.

"I thought I heard the branch cracking. Did anyone hear the branch cracking?"

Nobody did, but that was enough to scare off most.

"I think I'll quit while I'm ahead," Emma said.

"Me too," Gwen said.

"Me three," Rachel said.

Jeff caught the rope as it swung back from Harvey's plunge. He started up the makeshift ladder.

"That branch might be cracking," Alex said.

"It's fine," Jeff said, continuing up the ladder. "I'm gonna try one-handed."

Jeff swung out from the tree, one muscled arm holding the rope like Tarzan. The branch held, but Jeff let go too early and plunged precariously close to the boulders along the shoreline. There was a collective gasp. He crashed into the water. Alex hurried to the shore. Gwen covered her mouth, her eyes bulging. Jeff surfaced.

"Are you okay?" Gwen asked.

"I twisted my ankle on a rock," Jeff replied, treading water.

"Can you swim to the boat, or do you need help?" Alex asked.

"I got it."

Jeff sidestroked to the rear of the pontoon boat. Alex swam ahead with the intention of examining Jeff's ankle once on board. Gwen was right behind him. Deflated, the rest of the crew swam back to the boat behind Jeff.

Jeff climbed the pontoon ladder using his upper body and his good leg. Alex helped him to a seat, propping up his leg. Jeff winced as Alex removed his water shoe. Alex examined his ankle, with Gwen hovering over the scene.

"Your ankle looks fine. Probably just a sprain," Alex said.

Gwen breathed a sigh of relief. "You need to be more careful, sweetheart." She looked at Alex. "He's such a daredevil."

"Always been that way," Harvey said, dripping wet, his hands on his hips.

Alex grabbed a Ziploc bag and filled it with ice from one of the coolers. He placed it on Jeff's propped-up ankle. "Ice for fifteen minutes every couple of hours for the next two days."

"We should take you to the hospital," Gwen said, her arms crossed over her bikini top.

Jeff shook his head. "I'll be fine. I've had much worse jumping out of airplanes. I just need to stay off it for a few days. Maybe we can get some crutches and Aleve from the drugstore."

CHAPTER 12

Kristin and Pressure

Kristin leaned on the kitchen counter and stared toward the living room. Rachel and Harvey cuddled on the love seat, watching HGTV, while their significant others, Cathy and Seth, sat on opposite ends of the leather couch.

"Hey, girl," Gwen said, entering the kitchen.

"Hi, Aunt Gwen," Kristin replied.

"How are you? I feel like we haven't had a chance to chat."

"I'm fine." Kristin was blank-faced.

Gwen narrowed her eyes for a split second. "Why don't we go down to the dock and catch up?"

"Good idea," Kristin replied.

It was dark outside when Kristin and Gwen headed out the back door, save for the lights on the deck and on the dock below. They walked down the steep hill.

"Did you see Rachel in Papaw's lap?" Kristin asked.

Gwen nodded. "I don't know what that's about. I guess they're just really close."

"I think it's kinda weird. The other day I saw Papaw with his hand on her leg. I love my dad and all, but I do *not* wanna cuddle with him."

"Me neither. I think that's just how they are. I don't think it means anything."

They continued their careful trek down the darkened hill.

"I'm surprised Rachel got together with Seth," Kristin said. "He seems nice but ..."

"But what?" Gwen asked.

"This is gonna sound kinda mean, but he's just not as attractive as Rachel—bless his heart."

"Seth may not be as good-looking as Rachel, but I think he's good for her. I think he calms her down."

"I didn't know Rachel was hyperactive."

Gwen giggled. "That's not what I meant. Rachel's had some issues."

"Like what?"

"I really shouldn't say."

"Come on, Aunt Gwen. I won't tell anyone."

Gwen stopped walking and put her hands on her hips. "You have to promise not to breathe a word of this to anyone, not even Brett."

Kristin stopped and turned to Gwen. "I promise."

"She had sex with two of Jeff's groomsmen at our wedding."

Kristin's eyes widened. "*Eww.* Was she with Seth then?"

"Yes. You don't remember? Seth was at the wedding too."

"That's gross."

Gwen nodded. "Not one of her finer moments."

Kristin sucked in a breath and put her hand over her chest. "I think she kinda likes Brett. She was staring at him today without his shirt. You don't think she'd try something with him?"

"No. I think that's too far even for her."

Kristin breathed a sigh of relief.

They continued down the hill and stepped onto the dock. Brett and Matt fished off opposite sides.

"Hey, guys," Kristin said.

"What's up?" Brett replied.

Matt gave a little wave. Kristin approached Brett.

"I'm going to sit on the boat," Gwen said.

Kristin looked over her shoulder to Gwen. "I'll be right there."

Gwen stepped toward the docked pontoon.

"Catch anything?" Kristin asked Brett.

Brett shook his head. "I just like to cast and reel."

"How does this not bore you to death?"

Brett shrugged. "I don't know. It's relaxing."

"I'm gonna hang out with Gwen."

"Okay."

Kristin walked to the end of the dock and climbed into the pontoon boat. She sat next to Gwen, under the stars.

"So, how are things with Brett?" Gwen whispered.

Kristin raised one shoulder and matched Gwen's low volume. "Okay I guess."

"That doesn't sound good."

Kristin sighed. "It's fine."

"What's fine?"

"It's just …"

"Are you guys … intimate?"

"No, no, of course not."

"Is he pressuring you?"

Kristin looked down for a moment and nodded.

Gwen sighed and took Kristin's hand in hers. "If he really cares about you, he won't pressure you. What you decide to do or not do is entirely up to you."

"I know." Kristin thought about last night. "Can we talk about something else?"

"Did you find Brett's necklace?"

"No." Kristin frowned. "I looked everywhere. I think Brett lost it in the water."

"That's too bad."

"The cross was his protection." Kristin touched the gold crucifix around her neck. "When I took mine off at the beach, I nearly drowned."

"Thank God you didn't."

Kristin nodded. "I think God looks out for us. Do you think that's true?"

"I don't know. I hope so."

They were quiet. Kristin looked up, the sky dotted with stars. Boots clomped on a neighboring dock. The ladies turned. An older man walked on his dock, smoking a cigarette, looking in their direction. Gwen waved at the man. The man continued to stare and smoke. Gwen waved again. Still no reaction.

"Hello," Gwen called out.

The old man flicked his cigarette into the water, turned, and walked back to his house.

"That was strange," Gwen said to Kristin.

CHAPTER 13

Alex and Indoor Plumbing

Alex was vaguely aware of the sunlight filtering through the shades. His eyes fluttered and opened. Emma was still asleep next to him. Alex rolled out of bed and staggered to the bathroom. He flicked on the light, leaned against the sink, and wiped the sleep from his eyes. One glance in the mirror confirmed he had a stubbly beard, bloodshot blue eyes, and disheveled brown hair.

The bathroom smelled like … shit. He looked in the toilet and found three offending turds. Old brownish-black turds. Waterlogged turds that had broken apart in flaky chunks.

He flushed the toilet, and the water level rose, the shit along for the ride. It took a second to register, but Alex rushed to his knees and reached behind the toilet, groping for the water shutoff valve. He found it and turned the valve to the right, stopping the flow of water. The brackish toilet water stopped millimeters from the crest of the bowl.

Alex stood, his heart rate returning to normal. He really had to pee now. He grabbed the plunger next to the toilet and waited for the water to recede, but it didn't move, not for a few minutes. Once the level was safe enough to plunge without fear of any overflow, Alex tried to unclog the toilet, but all he did was swirl the poop water. He removed the plunger, a hunk of shit stuck to the side. He shook the excess water and feces back into the bowl before setting the plunger on the tile floor.

Alex went upstairs and checked that toilet. The water was clear. He flushed. The water bubbled and lowered a little, but it wasn't a normal flush. *The pipes must be clogged.* Alex shook his head. *Shit, … literally.* He turned on the water in the sink for a moment. It was slow to drain. The basement toilet looked like his, with brackish water.

The urge to urinate was intense now. Alex stepped outside the front door, hurried across the street into the woods, and peed. He returned to the house and told everyone who was up not to use the toilets or the sinks. Alex snatched the rental info tacked on the fridge with a magnet. Emma and Kristin were in their pajamas, hands on hips, with full bladders. Alex went to the living room, grabbed the cordless phone, and dialed the landlord.

"Hello," Dorothy said.

"Hi, this is Alex Palmer. I'm renting your house on Norris Lake, and the toilets are clogged."

"You gotta plunger in the master bath."

"I know. It's not working. None of the toilets work."

She exhaled, emitting a gravelly breath. "I guess I could call the Roto-Rooter man."

"When will that happen?"

"I'll get 'round to it. I gotta few things to do yet, and it depends on what the man says."

Alex gripped the handset. "You have a houseful of people who need to use toilets that don't work. What would you like us to do while you *get around to it*? Maybe we can piss on the lawn and dig holes so we can shit."

"Ain't no reason to get all pissy, mister."

"Given the situation, I think *pissy's* perfectly appropriate. We can't stay here with toilets that don't work."

"I guess I could call now, but I ain't even had my coffee."

"Call me here at the house as soon as you know when the plumber will be here."

She exhaled again. "All right."

Alex slammed the cordless on the receiver. "Goddamnit."

"Don't take God's name in vain," Kristin said, eyes narrowed.

Alex frowned at his daughter, then softened his expression. "You're right. I'm sorry."

"Is she sending someone out?" Emma asked.

"She's calling Roto-Rooter. I have no idea when they'll actually come out."

"What are we supposed to do in the meantime? People need to use the bathroom."

"I peed in the woods across the street."

Kristin's eyes were wide. "What if people have to …"

"Shit?" Alex asked.

Kristin frowned. "Yes."

"I don't know. Dig a hole in the woods? Hold it? Drive to a gas station?"

"The nearest gas station's at least half an hour away," Emma said.

"What do you want me to do, Emma? Construct a bathroom in the next ten minutes so people have a place to shit?"

The phone rang. Alex picked up. "Hello."

"Roto-Rooter man'll be there in an hour," Dorothy said.

"Thank you."

"Uh-huh."

Alex hung up. "Plumber will be here in an hour."

In the meantime, most of the family peed in the woods. Even Jeff made it to the woods on his crutches. Kristin couldn't hold it, but she had to do more than pee. She put a trash bag on a five-gallon bucket and did her business. At Alex's instruction, Kristin took Buster down to the boat before the plumber arrived since they weren't allowed to have dogs in the house.

* * *

The Roto-Rooter man snaked the toilets, and the sewage flushed, to be replaced with crystal clear water. Everyone was thrilled to have indoor plumbing again. The plumber was just about finished when an old couple walked into the living room. The woman had a wide nose and a square jaw. She was short and stocky, wearing a flowered muumuu. Without the muumuu, she could pass for an ugly man. Her husband looked like he had just rolled out of bed. His remaining crescent of hair was white and wild, his eyes glassy. He wore pajama pants and a white T-shirt, his nipples visible.

Alex and Emma rose from the leather couch.

"Everything workin'?" Dorothy asked as she and her husband waltzed into the living room.

"Are you Dorothy?" Alex asked.

"You the man I talked to on the phone?" Dorothy asked.

"Alex Palmer." Alex held out his hand.

Dorothy shook his hand. "This is my husband, George."

Alex shook the old man's hand. "Nice to meet you, George. This is my wife, Emma." Alex gestured to his wife. More weak handshakes followed.

"All fixed now?" Dorothy asked.

"The plumber said he's almost done. The toilets are draining."

"You gotta lotta cars out front. How many people you got stayin' here?"

"Eleven."

"That's too many people for the septic," Dorothy said. "Max is nine."

"You didn't tell me there was a limit," Alex said.

"You didn't read the instructions."

"What are we supposed to do now?"

"It's an extra hundred bucks per person."

"This is bullshit. I don't believe two extra people clogged the septic."

"I ain't never had a problem with it before. We ain't never even had to pump it."

Alex clenched his fists. "You're really starting to—"

"Is this your son," Emma asked, interrupting her husband's eruption. Emma pointed to the pictures on the mantel over the fireplace.

"Yeah," Dorothy said.

They moved closer to the pictures. Most of the pictures portrayed the couple in their younger years with a thin smiling boy. One picture showed them a little older and the same boy, an acne-riddled teen forcing a smile that didn't reach his eyes. Another snapshot in time showed the couple much older, the teen now a man with neck tattoos and a scowl.

"That's Danny," George said. "He has problems."

Dorothy shot George a glare. "He's a hard worker."

"What does he do?" Emma asked.

"He don't do nuthin'," George said.

"Shut up, you old fool," Dorothy said, still glowering at her husband. She turned back to Alex and Emma. "My husband's a brick short of a load. Danny can fix just about anything. Works on houses 'round here."

Alex stared at the most recent picture. "I saw your son camping on an island not too far from here."

* * *

With the crisis averted and bowels emptied, Alex and Emma strolled down the slope toward the dock. Alex peered over his shoulder at the house next door. The neighbor was in the upstairs window, staring back at him. It was the same old man who had ignored Alex the first night at the dock.

"Have you noticed the neighbor staring at us?" Alex asked.

"No. Why?" Emma asked.

"Look back to the right. Upper right bedroom window."

Emma looked. "I don't see anything."

Alex looked again. The curtains were drawn. "He was there a second ago, staring at us."

"He's probably just wondering about us. He does have to live next to people like us, coming and going."

"True." Alex glanced over his shoulder at their rental house. "What did you think of our landlords?"

"They were interesting, bless their hearts."

"That's a nice way of putting it."

"I feel bad that their son's homeless," Emma said.

"We don't know that for certain. Maybe he was just camping out."

"From the way you described the camp, it seems like he's living there."

"That's what it looked like."

"Why wouldn't they let their son live with them? Can you imagine Kristin homeless?"

"We don't know their son's story. Maybe he's on drugs. Maybe he's an alcoholic. Who knows?"

At the dock, most of the adults were spread out on camping chairs, their mouths open and their heads craned toward Harvey and Matt, who stood in defensive postures. Kristin was in the water, hanging on a floatie, watching the scene from the water, her eyes wide. Jeff and Brett were the only ones missing. Buster stood next to Matt, looking up at Harvey, growling.

"You're a coward," Harvey said, his arms crossed.

Shit. "That's enough, Dad," Alex said as he approached.

"Stay out of it, Alex. I'm tired of tiptoeing around Matt's disgrace."

"It wasn't because I was afraid," Matt said.

"Then why ruin your life and disgrace this family?" Harvey asked.

"Because it was wrong! You ever been to a village bombed to shit? Fucking dead bodies everywhere. Kids. Women. Old men. People staggering around, all fucked up because of what we did."

"That's collateral damage. It happens."

"You write about war, but it's all fucking fiction. You don't know what it's really like. You were never on the ground in the shit."

"I served honorably. That's more than you can say."

"Fuck you."

Harvey moved closer, pointing a craggy finger in Matt's face. "You still had a duty."

"Duty to what? A piece of cloth? Lines drawn on a map?"

"To your family."

Matt clenched his fists, his arms twitched.

Buster barked at Harvey.

Alex stepped between the pair before they came to blows. He wrapped up Matt in an embrace and pushed him away from Harvey.

"Let him go," Harvey said to Alex. "If he wants a piece of me, I'm right here."

"I'm fine. Let me go," Matt said to Alex.

Alex released his brother.

Matt turned and marched up the hill toward the house.

Alex moved toward Harvey. "Jesus, Dad, was that necessary?"

"He needed to hear it."

"Let it go. It was five years ago. He can't go back and fix it."

"That's the problem. He can't let it go because he hasn't dealt with what he did. His life will always be a disaster until he faces facts. I'm trying to help him."

Alex put his hands on his hips. "You sure about that?"

Harvey scowled at Alex, sat down in his camping chair, and picked up his, literally *his*, novel—a bold-lettered thriller with a kitted-up soldier on the cover.

"Well that was entertaining," Rachel said, standing from her chair and mounting the dock ladder.

"Rachel," Cathy said, shaking her head.

"What? Matt's always been, like, weird." Rachel pushed off the ladder into the water.

Seth leaned over in his camping chair, his head in his hands, massaging his temples.

"Are you all right?" Cathy asked Seth.

Seth sat up and looked at Cathy. His nose and arms were sunburnt.

"My head is killing me, and my legs feel achy."

"Would you like some Aleve?" Emma asked, injecting herself into the conversation.

"Yeah, I need something," Seth replied, turning to Emma. "I feel like someone's pounding on my head with a hammer."

"I'll go up to the house and get you some Aleve."

"No. Don't bother." Seth groaned as he stood. "I'm gonna lie down. I need to get out of the sun anyway."

"The Aleve's on the counter in the kitchen."

"Thanks, Emma."

"Do you need anything else?"

"No, but thanks." Seth glowered at Rachel. She floated on an inflatable doughnut, soaking up the sun. "I'm going up to the house," Seth said to Rachel.

"See ya later," Rachel replied.

Emma and Cathy frowned at Rachel.

"I hope you feel better," Rachel added.

Seth trudged up the hill toward the house.

Emma sat in a camping chair next to Gwen.

"I'm assuming Jeff and Brett took the kayaks?" Alex asked, settling into a chair next to Emma and Gwen.

"They've been out all morning," Gwen said. "Jeff's doing one of his insane workouts, and Brett's just paddling around the lake, I guess."

CHAPTER 14

Menace

The island was wooded with a small beach. They stood on the shore, wearing bright bikinis, one red, the other yellow. They were both athletic, with tanned, toned bodies—probably college students. Red bikini was a brunette, yellow bikini a blonde.

"I'm Kate," the blonde said, shaking his gloved hand limply.

"I'm Whitney," the brunette said—no hand shake.

"I've seen you guys around," he said. "On your Jet Skis."

Kate pursed her lips. "Yeah, I think we've seen you around." She motioned with her chin to the kayak. "On your kayak." She narrowed her eyes at his gloves. "What's with the gloves?"

"I get blisters from the paddle if I don't wear gloves."

Kate nodded.

"What are you guys doing here anyway?" he asked.

"We're on summer break," Whitney said. "My parents have a house on the water."

"I meant, what are you doing here on this island?"

"We had to pee," Kate said.

Whitney blushed.

Kate crossed her arms over her chest. "What are *you* doing here?"

"Taking a break from paddling," he said. "I was gonna do some fishing."

Kate nodded, dropping her arms to her side.

He smiled. "You two should be careful. These islands are dangerous. Especially this one."

Whitney and Kate turned back to the island for a moment.

"Why?" Kate asked.

He said, "Sometimes the homeless camp out on the islands. A creepy guy lives here."

"Bullshit," Kate said with a smirk.

He pointed to the sandy path leading into the interior. "The guy has a camp at the end of that path."

"You're fucking with us," Kate said.

He shook his head. "I'm not."

"You can't live here. There's nothing here."

"If you say so."

"You're just trying to scare us," Whitney said.

"Prove it," Kate said.

He led them along the informal sandy pathway, created by repeated trampling. He stopped, the path ahead turning sharply left. He turned to Kate and Whitney with his finger to his lips. "He lives around this corner," he whispered.

They crept around the corner. There was a tent, fire pit, and clothes hanging on a line. Beer cans and snack wrappers littered the ground. A fishing pole leaned against a tree. A skinning and gutting knife stuck out of a stump. It smelled like rotten fish and urine.

He turned to the girls and put his finger to his lips again. They were wide-eyed and hesitant. He approached the tent. The girls stayed back, ready to bolt. He put his hand on the zipper. In one grand gesture, he unzipped the tent and peered inside. He pulled back. "Oh my God," he said.

"What?" Kate said.

He laughed. "Nothing. He's not here."

Kate and Whitney relaxed. They looked around the campsite. It was quite Spartan, given what they were probably used to.

"*Eww*, he has porn," Whitney said, peering into the tent.

"The pages are probably stuck together," Kate said.

"You're gross."

Kate laughed.

He removed the Ziploc bag from his pocket. He put the rubber swim cap on his head and shoved the condoms back into his pocket, careful to conceal them from the girls. He picked up the knife from the stump, holding it up for closer examination. The fixed blade was four inches long and curved with a gut hook on top. It was menacing with a black blade and black handle. The only thing that wasn't black was the silvery sharp cutting edge.

"What's that on your head?" Kate asked with a smirk.

"It's a swim cap," he replied. "I think I'll go for a swim soon."

Kate narrowed her eyes. "But why put it on now?"

He ignored the question, holding up the knife. "You two know what this is?"

"A fish knife?" Kate asked. "Like to take out the bones?"

He shook his head. "You're thinking of a fillet knife. This is for skinning and gutting. I wouldn't use this for fish." He grazed his wrist over the knife's edge. "It's sharp."

"What do you think he uses it for?" Whitney asked.

He deadpanned. "Skinning and gutting."

Whitney frowned. "We should get out of here." She walked toward the trail.

He stepped in front of Whitney, blocking her egress. He sliced her midsection from her xiphoid process to her pubic bone in one expert motion. Whitney looked at the straight red line, her eyes wide in disbelief. She screamed, shrill and high-pitched, as he plunged the blade into the incision, into her body. He grabbed her small intestines with the gut hook and pulled. A mass of the coiled pinkish-gray tubing spilled to the sand. Whitney fell to her knees, her hands groping her insides.

Kate stood by the tent, frozen like a deer in headlights. She sprinted past him for the trail. He chased her, catching her before she made it to the beach. He grabbed her ponytail, the force pulling her feet out from under her. She landed on her back. He straddled her. They heard a motorboat approaching.

"Help! Help!" Kate said.

He silenced her screams with a gloved hand over her mouth and the knife to her throat. "Scream again, bitch, and it'll be the last sound you ever make."

Moaning and mewling came from the interior of the island. It was Whitney.

Kate breathed through her nose, her chest rising and falling rapidly. The outboard motor noise was louder now, then quieter, then it was gone. Tears slipped down the sides of her face.

He smiled. "*Aww*, don't cry. If you do what I say, I won't hurt you. I'm gonna remove my hand, but, if you scream or fight, I *will* cut your throat from ear to ear." He removed his hand.

Her eyes were glassy and wide. "Please don't hurt me. I'll do whatever you want."

"I know you will." He sat back on his haunches, still straddling her, the knife off her throat. He slid the side of the blade under her bikini top.

She shook.

"I'd hold still if I were you." He turned the blade, the sharp side against the bikini. He pulled up, severing the bikini between the cups. He brushed aside the cups, fully exposing her small breasts. "That's better." He traced the blunt side of the knife over her body.

Kate followed the knife with her eyes, struggling to stop from shaking. Whitney still mewled in the background, like music to his ears. He scooted back, on Kate's legs now, and cut off her bikini bottoms.

He stood, pointing the knife at her. "Don't move." He stuck the knife into the sand next to him. He grabbed a condom from his pocket, untied his shorts, and stepped out of them. His pubic hairs were totally shaved, his penis flaccid. "Beg me not to do this."

Kate was quiet.

"I said, *beg*, you *fucking* cunt."

"Please don't," she said.

He touched himself. "You better beg, or I'll kill you."

"Please don't hurt me. Please, I'll do anything."

He grinned, his penis hardening in his gloved hand. He slid the condom on and grabbed the knife from the ground. He spread her legs with his knees and climbed on top of her. "Beg," he said, breathless.

"No, stop. Please don't hurt me."

He rammed his penis inside her, Kate shrieking at his insertion. He held the knife to her throat. Kate wasn't acting on his command anymore. She was begging of her own volition. Her begging was almost enough, but he wanted all of her for the climax. With two strong movements, one on each side of her neck, he cut her jugular veins and carotid arteries. He and Kate were covered in arterial blood spray. Kate's eyes faded, her body letting go. He pounded faster, groaning and climaxing as her body convulsed, her last gasp before death.

He stood, his chest heaving, his body and face covered in Kate's blood, and his condom filled with semen. Whitney's moaning was intermittent now. He took off his condom and dumped it in the Ziploc bag. He grabbed a fresh condom, the knife, and marched along the trail toward the camp.

Whitney sat on the ground, holding her stomach, some of her small intestines in her lap. Flies buzzed around her wound. Her head hung, with her chin resting on her chest.

He frowned at her intestines. *That's not very appealing.* He pushed her on her side, pulled her legs out, and rolled her on her stomach. Whitney didn't offer any resistance. *I can't look at that. I'm not an animal.*

He spread apart her legs. "Beg me not to do this."

Whitney didn't respond.

He held his flaccid penis in his gloved hand. He kicked her, but she didn't respond. He kicked her again, harder. Nothing. She was gone.

In a fit of rage, he sliced at the flesh on her buttocks, her back, and her neck. He worked on her neck for several minutes, the cuts deepening. He hacked at the gash as if cutting down a tree. The roar of an outboard motor broke the spell he was under. He stood, naked, covered in blood from head to toe. The motor got louder. He heard voices. *Fuck.*

He crept down the trail toward the beach. The motor was cut, but the voices were louder. He peered from the woods, shielded by the trees. A pontoon was beached. The dad and his fat fuck son were on the beach with fishing poles. The mom and daughter were in the boat. *It's a fucking fat family. Jesus fucking Christ. How can you let your kids get like that? I blame the parents. They're the ones who buy the food.*

The dad pointed at the Jet Skis and the kayak.

"Whose Jet Skis are those?" the mom called out from the boat.

"I don't know," the dad called back.

"Can we drive 'em?" the boy asked.

"No, they're not ours."

Fuck, fuck, fuck, fuck, fuck, fuuuuuck. If they come back here, I'll have to kill them.

If you kill one, you have to kill them all.

I know.

They saw the kayak.

What are the chances they'll even remember? They'll probably be out of here in a couple of days. And, if they do report it, big deal, there are plenty of kayaks.

People will care about those girls. Somebody's probably looking for them now. You were so sloppy and so rushed.

Shut the fuck up.

You're gonna get caught.

I said, shut the fuck up.

He dragged Kate by her feet down the trail to the camp. He returned to Kate's murder scene. The sand was blood-soaked. He tried kicking fresh sand over the blood, but the sand was compacted and not easily moved. He peered out from the woods. The fat family was still there. Fishing and laughing.

"Lunch is ready," the woman called out from the boat.

He stood there, watching and waiting.

* * *

Almost an hour later, the fat family shoved off. With the boat gone, the beach and the island were relatively secluded. He hurried back to the camp. He was still naked except for his gloves, swim cap, and too big water shoes. Flies swarmed the scene and the bodies. He went back to work on Whitney's neck with the knife, finally severing her head from her neck.

He posed Kate on her back, spread-eagled, with Whitney's head between her legs. He chuckled. *The cops'll probably think it's a lesbian hate crime.*

CHAPTER 15

Alex and the Shit Show

Alex woke to Emma shifting off the bed. He turned to her, wiping his eyes. She stood from the bed in a T-shirt and underwear. Her pale skin was sun-kissed despite her obsessive sunblocking. Emma's long legs were feminine. Her blond hair was sweaty and matted. He glanced at the clock—7:04 a.m.

"Where are you going?" Alex asked.

"I'm gonna take a shower," Emma replied. "I was hot last night."

"We can turn down the AC."

Emma shook her head. "It's my hormones. The joy of being forty." She padded to the bathroom.

Alex closed his eyes. Emma screamed, jolting Alex from the bed and into the bathroom. Emma stood back from the shower, the curtain open, her hand over her mouth and nose. The smell hit him like a ton of bricks—shit and sulfur. The floor of the shower had an inch of brackish water with stringy chunks of feces.

"I think the septic's full," Alex said, shaking his head and stepping back into the bedroom, his fists clenched.

Emma followed. "How do you know that?"

"Because the landlord's a dumb ass," Alex replied.

Emma frowned. "I don't understand."

"She said that she's never had the tank pumped. I should've said something to the plumber, but I figured he knew."

Emma informed those who were awake of the bathroom situation. Alex called Dorothy from the cordless phone to get someone to pump the septic immediately.

"Might take a day or two," Dorothy said.

"There's shit in my shower," Alex said, gripping the phone. "We can't bathe. We can't go to the bathroom. We can't even use the sinks."

"I can just give y'all a refund for the last four days."

"Are you going to refund the boat I rented? Are you going to pay the people who took off work to be here? Are you going to refund our ruined vacation? You do realize that septic tanks have to be pumped eventually. Instead, you tried to blame this mess on too many people in the house." The line went quiet. "Are you still there?"

"I'm here. Just wonderin' if you were finished hollerin'."

"If you can't get someone here today, I want a full refund."

"I'll see what I can do."

Alex hung up. Heated voices came from the other side of his bedroom door. Alex joined the small crowd of anguished faces in the living room. Emma stood in a circle with Rachel, Kristin, and Cathy. Buster the Boston terrier was in the center, looking up at each person as they talked.

"Seth's sick," Rachel said. "He threw up in the trash can. I can't even go in there. It's, like, so gross."

"What's wrong with him?" Alex asked.

"I think he has a stomach bug."

"We have some ginger ale," Emma said.

"Maybe *you* can take it to him," Rachel replied. "Throw up, like, makes me gag really bad."

"I can do that," Emma said, then turned to Alex. "What did Dorothy say?"

"She said she'll see what she can do," Alex replied.

"What does that mean?" Rachel asked with her hands on her hips.

Alex blew out a breath. "I don't know yet. I'm hoping they can pump the septic today."

"You hope? What are we supposed to do until then?"

"We'll do what we did yesterday. Pee in the woods. We have bottled water to use to brush our teeth."

"What about going number two?" Cathy asked, blushing.

"Put a garbage bag in a bucket and go in it," Kristin replied.

Rachel scrunched her face in disgust. "That's, like, so gross."

"It's way more gross to hold it in. If you don't get it out, you have the nastiest farts. Then, when you finally go, it stinks like something crawled up your butt and died."

Emma frowned at her daughter. "That's more than enough, Kristin."

"I'm just saying."

"I'm not going in a bag," Rachel said.

"The other option is to go to a gas station down the road," Alex said.

"That's almost as gross," Rachel replied. "I'm just not gonna eat anything."

"We can't stay here if we don't have a bathroom," Cathy said. "I'm sorry, Alex, but maybe we should go home."

"Can you at least give it until this afternoon?" Alex asked. "I'm hoping they can fix it today."

"Okay." Cathy nodded.

Most of the men and a few women went to the woods to pee, including Jeff who was still on crutches. Some washed and peed in the lake. Matt found a shovel in the shed out back. He took the shovel with a roll of toilet paper and shat in the woods. He said it was like Ranger school.

Alex peed in the woods and borrowed Matt's shovel. Upon returning, the phone rang. Alex hurried to the cordless phone and picked up. "Hello?"

"They're sendin' a truck in a few hours," Dorothy said in lieu of a greeting.

Alex breathed a sigh of relief. "Thank you."

"Uh-huh. Anything else I can do for y'all?"

"No."

Matt walked into the living room as Alex set the cordless phone on the charger. "I need to talk to you for a minute, … in private," Matt said.

The brothers went to the backyard.

"What's up?" Alex asked.

"When I went to the woods this morning," Matt said, "I saw Brett and Kristin. I was far away, but Brett pushed her against a tree, and he seemed to be … sexually aggressive. Kristin looked like she didn't want him all over her."

Alex clenched his jaw and grit his teeth. "I'm gonna kill him." Alex started for the house.

"Hold on." Matt grabbed Alex's arm. "You can't attack the kid. Nothing really happened. Kristin stopped it."

Alex faced his brother.

"I was gonna step in, but he stopped when she said no," Matt said. "She walked away, pissed off. If you come down on Brett, she'll defend him. You know how she is about protecting people. I think she'll figure out Brett on her own. I don't think she'll be with him after this vacation. I just thought you'd wanna know."

Alex relaxed. "Yeah. Thanks, bro. I still think we should keep our eye on him. There's something off about that kid."

"I agree."

"We're still going out on the boat today," Alex said. "I thought we'd find that bridge that everyone jumps off. You're coming, right?"

"Yeah, I guess."

CHAPTER 16

Alex and the Bridge

Alex drove the pontoon. Matt navigated with the map. It was another beautiful sunny day on the lake. The weather was the one thing that had been on their side. Most of the men opted to go on the excursion. Except Seth, who still wasn't feeling well. Emma, Gwen, and Cathy opted to stay home. A day of jumping off bridges was not appealing to them, and someone needed to be there for the plumbers. Only Rachel and Kristin made the trip with the guys.

The girls sat on either side of Brett—lean and tan—who talked and laughed with Rachel, no doubt as punishment for Kristin's rebuff in the woods earlier. Kristin looked out over the water, trying to suppress the green-eyed monster inside her.

"There it is," Matt said, pointing at the concrete-and-metal bridge in the distance.

Alex grinned, turning the pontoon in the right direction. "It looks high."

A few pontoons and speedboats anchored near the bridge. People swam and floated, but nobody jumped off the bridge. Alex cut the outboard motor twenty yards offshore. Matt dropped the anchor.

They looked up at the bridge. It was at least a thirty-foot drop. Haphazard amateur graffiti decorated the steel girders. Occasionally a car drove over the bridge. The supports were concrete, with water marks ten feet above the waterline.

"Who's first?" Alex asked, with a smirk.

Everyone remained quiet.

"Jeff?" Alex asked.

Jeff pointed to his bandaged ankle. "I told Gwen I wouldn't get hurt again."

Alex held out his palms. "What? Are you serious?"

Jeff nodded.

"I can't believe it. Jeff's actually whipped."

Jeff smiled.

"What about the rest of you?" Alex asked.

"The water level looks low," Matt said, pointing at the concrete supports on the bridge. "Look at the water marks."

"It's fine," Alex said. "What about you, Brett? You gonna wuss out?"

"Uh, … I'll do it, but I'm not going first," Brett replied.

"Dad?" Alex asked.

"I'm the oldest. I should go last," Harvey replied.

"Yeah, but you have the least amount of years left."

Harvey grinned. "Watch it."

"I'll go first," Kristin said.

Everyone turned to her, flabbergasted.

"I'll go first," Kristin repeated.

"No," Alex said. "I'll go first, and, if it's safe, you can go after me."

"Dad …"

"No." Alex gave her a look.

Everyone swam ashore, except for Jeff. A family played on the small beach—two boys, the dad and mom.

"Have you seen anyone jump?" Alex asked the dad and glanced up at the bridge.

"Not since we've been here," the dad said. "Supposedly there's a fence under the water. With the low water level, people aren't jumping."

"I could swim over there and check it," Matt said.

"That's a good idea," Alex replied.

Matt swam toward the bridge. The rest of the crew hiked up the sandy embankment to the road. A sign on the bridge read No Jumping or Diving Off Bridge per Ordinance 15.30.876.

"The sign says we're not supposed to jump," Kristin said.

"Don't believe everything you read," Alex replied.

"But I think it's illegal."

"Jesus was illegal."

Kristin stopped for a moment, the wheels turning in her brain. She continued with the group as they hiked along the roadside to the middle of the bridge. They stood behind the concrete barrier and looked down at the water. The bridge was high, very high.

"There's, like, no way," Rachel said, stepping away from the barrier.

Matt surfaced from the water below. "It's pretty deep," Matt called out. "I didn't find any fence."

Alex waved at Matt. "Good enough for me," Alex said to the group.

"Don't do it, Dad. I have a bad feeling," Kristin said, touching the gold crucifix around her neck.

"I thought you wanted to go first?"

"It looks really high from up here."

Alex sat on the concrete barrier, his legs dangling into the abyss. He waited for Matt to swim safely out of the way.

"I can't watch," Kristin said, her hands over her face.

"Do it, tough guy," Harvey said.

Alex pushed off the concrete barrier, gravity taking hold. He was in a free fall for less than half a second. He crossed his feet and blew a breath from his nose as he crashed into the water. He swam to the surface and raised both arms in triumph. Everyone on the bridge and the onlookers cheered.

Kristin, a young woman of her word, jumped next. Brett jumped after her, then Harvey. Rachel sat on the concrete barrier, her legs dangling. She sat there for a minute.

They chanted, "Jump, jump, jump, jump, jump."

She swung her legs back onto the bridge. Everyone booed.

"I can't do it," Rachel said, annoyed. She marched back to the beach.

Matt was the only one left. He sat on the concrete barrier, his legs dangling, a grin on his face.

They chanted again, "Jump, jump, jump, jump, jump."

A siren disturbed their chanting, followed by a rapidly approaching police car. Matt jumped as if he were Dr. Richard Kimble in *The Fugitive*. He crashed into the water. Everyone cheered.

A cop glared down at them from the bridge. "All of you, on the beach now," he called to them and pointed toward the shore.

They swam to the beach. As they swam, Alex told them not to say anything, to let him do the talking. The cop waited on the shore with his meaty arms crossed over his chest. He had a close crew cut and a mustache. They stood in front of the cop, dripping wet in their swimsuits.

"You folks know that jumpin' off this bridge is illegal?" the cop asked.

"No, we didn't," Alex replied.

"How many of you jumped?"

"Just me, officer," Alex replied. "They were all afraid. The low water level and all. They're a bunch of law-abiding wusses." Alex smiled.

The cop glared at Alex, then looked at the group. "Is that true?

"I jumped," Kristin said, her head down. "I'm sorry."

"I should arrest every one of you—"

"I really didn't jump," Rachel said. "Ask anyone."

The cop pointed at Rachel. "Don't interrupt me."

Rachel shrunk back.

The cop continued. "We had a kid almost die a couple years ago. It's stupid for y'all to be doin' this. Go find a rope swing. They're all over this lake."

"I really appreciate your service, Officer. My name's Harvey Palmer." Harvey thrust out his hand. "You may have heard of me. I write military thriller novels. *Last Man Standing, Dead Heat, Jungle Warfare*."

The police officer narrowed his eyes at Harvey, ignoring his hand. Harvey dropped his hand.

"We're sorry, Officer," Alex said. "We really didn't know."

"None of y'all saw the sign?" The cop's radio crackled. He listened for a moment. "Y'all are lucky," he said, already hurrying up the hill to his cruiser.

A moment later, the cruiser zipped across the bridge with its siren blaring and lights flashing.

"What was that about?" Kristin asked.

"Must've had an important call," Matt replied.

"More important than making sure people have no fun ever?" Brett asked.

Rachel laughed.

Two more cruisers zoomed over the bridge with sirens and lights working.

"Must be something big," Alex said.

CHAPTER 17

Kristin and the Crime Scene

From the bridge, they motored around the lake, sampling a few rope swings. Everyone had a blast. Everyone except Kristin. On the way back, she sat in the front of the pontoon, alone, staring out over the bright blue lake. Behind her, Brett and Rachel talked and flirted. *I thought you wanted me to get along with your family. I can't win with you.* That's what Brett had said when Kristin asked him what he was doing with Rachel—who was pretty and sexy and slightly trashy. She was a dyed blonde and had stunning blue eyes—when she wore her colored contacts. She was tan and petite, with the perfect bathing-suit body.

Kristin turned and scowled at Brett. He was too enthralled with Rachel to notice. *He's been an asshole all day.* Kristin shook her head. *I'm sorry, God. I know I shouldn't think such awful words. He's being such a jerk though. I know he's a good person deep down. Am I supposed to help him be a good person?*

Up ahead were turning lights and police activity on and around a small island. Police pontoon boats were beached, and speedboats surrounded the island about half the size of a football field.

That's the same island where that creepy guy lives.

Her dad slowed the pontoon to a crawl as they approached, maintaining a wide enough berth to stay out of the way. Kristin now heard conversations over the low idling outboard motor. Everyone pointed and talked about the scene. Two Jet Skis were beached at the heart of the activity. Kristin moved to the middle of the pontoon and sat next to Brett. Rachel sat on the other side of him, dangerously close. Their necks craned to see the police.

"That's the island we were on the other day," Alex said.

"Isn't that where the homeless dude camps? The one with the knife?" Brett asked.

"Yeah," Jeff replied.

"He must've been doing something illegal," Harvey said.

"Y'all think it was drugs?" Brett asked.

"I doubt he can afford enough drugs for *that* kind of attention," Jeff said.

"Whose Jet Skis are those?" Kristin asked.

"I don't know, but I doubt they're his," Alex said.

"Maybe he was doing drug deals with the Jet Skis," Brett said.

"Maybe the Jet Skis belong to his victims," Jeff said.

The group went deadly quiet.

Harvey broke the silence. "Maybe he stole the Jet Skis. According to Occam's razor, the simplest explanation is usually the correct one."

"But that doesn't explain all the cops," Jeff said.

"Jeff's right," Alex said. "It is a ton of cops. You guys know that our landlords are his parents, right?"

"Really?" Harvey asked.

"Yeah, his name's Danny," Alex replied. "There are pictures of him in our living room."

"Maybe Danny murdered whoever was driving those Jet Skis," Brett said with a twitchy half smile.

CHAPTER 18

Alex and the Shitter's Full

Alex steered the pontoon to their dock. They grabbed their coolers and gear, and trudged up the hill to the lake house. Alex smiled at the sight of the tanker truck parked in the driveway alongside the house. A hose snaked from the rig to the backyard. A wiry tanned man with a cigarette hanging from his mouth held the hose as raw sewage was pumped from the sewage tank. Emma talked to a heavyset man on the concrete patio. The man wore a T-shirt that read Super Septic.

"I'm glad to see you guys," Alex said as he approached.

Emma smiled at Alex, then turned to the man. "Ed, this is my husband, Alex."

"Good to meetcha," Ed said with a hearty handshake.

"Likewise," Alex replied.

"Ed said that the tank was full and needed to be pumped," Emma said.

"The homeowner told me that she had never pumped the tank," Alex said. "I don't think she even understood that septic tanks have to be pumped."

"I told her," Ed said.

"So when do you think we'll be able to use the bathrooms?" Alex asked.

"Should be able to use 'em now."

Alex nodded. "We really appreciate it. We were gonna cut our vacation short."

Ed smiled, his mustache stretching across his fat face. "We wouldn't want that."

"Do you think the man on that hose would mind if I took a picture with him?"

"Alex, let the man work," Emma said.

"He won't mind," Ed said.

Alex hurried into the house, grabbed a can of beer, and set down his backpack. He returned and handed Emma his phone. "Take the picture when I'm holding up the beer."

Emma smirked at her husband.

Alex approached the man as he worked, the job smelling like sulfur, but it wasn't unbearable. "How are you doing?" Alex spoke loudly to be heard over the noise from the tanker truck.

"Good, how you?" the tanned man replied, his cigarette defying gravity and holding on to his lower lip.

"You mind if my wife takes a picture of us together? I was gonna post it on Facebook with a caption that says Shitter's Full."

The man laughed. "Hell, nobody ever wants to take a picture with us. Go for it."

Alex stood next to the man, holding up his beer, as Emma snapped the picture.

"Thanks, man," Alex said.

"No problem," the man replied.

Alex approached his wife.

"You're ridiculous, you know that?" Emma said.

"I was gonna post the picture on Facebook," Alex replied.

"There's no internet or cell service, remember?"

"When we get home then."

Dorothy, the landlord, rounded the corner of the house, into Alex's line of sight.

"Where's Buster?" Alex whispered. "Dorothy's coming up behind you."

Emma's eyes widened. "I'll get him." Emma disappeared into the house as Dorothy approached.

Dorothy wore the same floral muumuu that she wore the last time he'd seen her. She had a cigarette between two fingers. Her face was craggy, with deep crevices, her mouth in a perpetual frown.

"All fixed?" Dorothy asked.

"I think so," Alex replied. "The septic was full."

"I suppose it was." She took a puff from her cigarette, turned her head, and exhaled.

"We've had nearly two days with toilets that don't function correctly."

Dorothy clenched her square jaw. "You ain't gettin' your money back."

"I'm not asking for my money back."

She took another puff from her cigarette, this time exhaling in Alex's direction. "Y'all can stay an extra day to make up for this mess."

"That would be great. I appreciate it."

She nodded, her eyes narrowed.

"Have you seen Danny lately?" Alex asked.

"How's that any of your business?" Dorothy replied.

"I'm not trying to be nosy. We saw him on an island the other day, and today police boats were all around that same island."

She took another puff on her cigarette. "He didn't do nuthin'."

"I didn't say he did."

Emma peeked from the back door, with Buster in her arms.

"Uh-huh. I should check the toilets." Dorothy turned toward the house.

"I have another question," Alex said abruptly.

When she turned back to Alex, Emma slipped past them, taking Buster down to the water.

"I was wondering if you knew anything about the neighbors here?"

"Which one?"

"That one." Alex pointed toward the house of the old man who had been watching them.

"That old man's got problems. Best you stay out of his way."

CHAPTER 19

Alex and Their Civic Duty

Each night during this vacation, one couple had the responsibility to make dinner for the house guests. This night was Rachel and Seth's responsibility, but Seth was sleeping and still recovering from his illness, and Rachel said she was too tired from being out on the lake to cook by herself. Alex and Emma took over by default, with help from Matt.

Alex walked inside, carrying a plate of grilled burgers. Jeff and Harvey were in the living room across from the kitchen. Father and son sat on the couch watching television. Jeff's crutches were propped within reaching distance.

"Smells great," Jeff said.

Alex smiled at his brother and set the burgers on the kitchen counter. Emma and Matt prepared the sides. Alex approached the television, standing behind the love seat. The local news began after the commercial break. Breaking News was scrawled across the bottom of the screen.

A serious-looking anchorwoman with plastered hair spoke. "Two bodies were discovered on a small island in the Mill Creek section of Norris Lake." The local news cut to footage of the island, surrounded by police, the Jet Skis in view. "Sheriff Franklin made a brief statement to our very own Chase Manning."

"A freaking double murder," Alex said, his eyes wide.

"We don't know that yet," Harvey said.

Matt and Emma approached from the kitchen.

The news cut to Chase Manning stalking the sheriff in the parking lot of the sheriff's station. "Sheriff Franklin, we've had reports that two bodies were discovered on an island in Mill Creek today. Has the cause of death been determined?"

Sheriff Franklin stopped. He was a big man—built like a linebacker. He had short whitish-gray hair and a matching mustache. "Look. We haven't ruled out homicide, but I can't release any details at this time, because this is an ongoing investigation."

The anchorwoman appeared again. "We'll keep you updated as information becomes available."

"We need to tell the police what we saw," Alex said, looking at Jeff. "Especially with Danny in that tent and the knife. That might've been the murder weapon."

Jeff nodded. "You're right. We probably should've gone to the police station right when we got back."

"This is awful," Emma said.

"Should I call 9-1-1?" Alex asked.

"It is an emergency," Jeff replied.

Alex grabbed the cordless from the charging station and dialed 9-1-1.

"Nine-one-one, what is your emergency?" the woman asked.

"I have information about the two bodies that were found today," Alex replied.

"Are you in any danger at the moment?"

"No."

"What is your name, sir?"

"Alex Palmer."

"Hold please."

Alex sat, waiting, with the cordless to his ear. Everyone stared at him. "I'm on hold."

Thirty seconds later, a deep voice boomed in his ear. "This is Sheriff Franklin."

"Hello, Sheriff. My name's Alex Palmer, and I have information about those bodies that were found today."

"What've you got for me, Alex?" Sheriff Franklin asked.

"I'm here on vacation with my family, and we were on that island on Tuesday, and I saw a man living there. He had a knife."

"Do you know this man?"

"No, sir, not personally. He's the son of the couple we're renting a lake house from. His name's Danny. I don't remember his last name, but I could find out."

"You must be at the Stafford house on Lakeshore Drive."

"We're on Lakeshore. Stafford sounds right. I wrote them a check. Lemme get my checkbook." Alex walked into his room, grabbed his checkbook from his duffel bag pocket, and verified the name. "Yes, it is Stafford."

Sheriff Franklin exhaled. "Can you come down to the station and make a statement?"

"Yes, sir."

"As soon as possible. Can you do that, Alex?"

"Yes, sir."

"If any of your kin have information that might be helpful, bring them along."

"My brother Jeff saw Danny and the knife too. I can bring him with me."

"Good. You know how to get here?"

"No, sir, but we have GPS."

The sheriff gave Alex the address to his office. Alex disconnected the call, stepped back into the living room, and replaced the cordless phone on the charger.

"The sheriff wants to talk to both of us," Alex said to Jeff.

"I'll go too," Harvey said, standing from the couch.

"That's not necessary, Dad," Jeff said, standing with the help of his crutches.

"I know how the legal system works."

"This isn't a novel."

Harvey narrowed his eyes at Jeff, deep creases erupting on his forehead. "I'm going."

* * *

Alex drove them to the sheriff's station, a one-story building with tinted windows. Inside, was a waiting area and a deputy behind thick glass. They signed in and gave the deputy their licenses. A few minutes later their licenses were returned. A few minutes after that, another deputy escorted Alex beyond the waiting area. Apparently, the sheriff wanted to take Alex's statement first. The office area was filled with cubicles. Deputies and administrative assistants sat at their desks, tapping on laptops and talking on phones. Alex was escorted to Sheriff Franklin's corner office. His door was open. The sheriff rose from his desk and approached.

"Alex Palmer?"

"Yes, sir," Alex replied, stepping forward.

"Thanks for comin' down so quickly," Sheriff Franklin said, shaking Alex's hand.

Alex sat across from Sheriff Franklin at his wooden desk. The walls were littered with framed pictures and plaques. Many portrayed the sheriff in desert camo. Some showed men jumping from an airplane. One showed off his Ranger tab.

"Are you a Ranger, sir?" Alex asked.

Sheriff Franklin nodded. "Served most of my career with the 82nd Airborne. If you cut me, I might bleed green."

"*HUA*, sir."

The sheriff grinned wide at the reference to the acronym: *heard, understood, acknowledged.* "You an airborne Ranger?"

"No, sir. My brothers and father were. I did go to air assault school. I spent most of my career with the First Cav out of Fort Hood as a combat medic."

"Well, I'll be. It's a helluva small world."

"Yes, sir, it is. I wish we were meeting under better circumstances."

Sheriff Franklin nodded. "You ready to get down to business?"

"Yes, sir."

"I'm gonna record this conversation. You okay with that?"

"Yes, sir."

The sheriff placed a mike between them and pressed Record on his laptop. "What makes you think Danny Stafford had somethin' to do with those bodies?"

"I saw on the news that they found those bodies on the same island where I saw Danny camped out. A knife was there too. Not sure if it was used on the ... bodies, but it was there."

"Anything else?" Sheriff Franklin asked.

"The other day we had some problems with the septic at the house, and I talked to Danny's parents. Danny's father said something about Danny having problems. I know that doesn't mean he did anything." Alex stroked his stubbly chin. "I also think he might be an alcoholic."

"What makes you think that?"

"Beer cans were all over his camp, and he was passed out in his tent and smelled like alcohol."

"I have a Google Earth image of the island. Do you think you could show me where his camp was?" Sheriff Franklin asked.

"Yes, sir."

The sheriff removed a letter-size color image from a manila folder and slid it across the desk to Alex with a pen. "Mark the spot with an X."

Alex studied the image. It was from the past winter. Even though the leaves were off the trees, the trail and the open area where Danny had his camp were still mostly obscured by branches. Alex did his best approximation and marked the picture with an X. "It's hard to see through the branches, but I think it was here. I could show you if someone took me to the island."

The sheriff checked the spot marked on the image. "That won't be necessary. Why did you go to Danny Stafford's camp?"

"I had to urinate. I saw the pathway that led into the woods. I went back there so I wouldn't be in the open. My brother Jeff had to go too. He was behind me on the path. After I urinated, he and I followed the path deeper. I wanted to see where it went. That's when we saw the camp."

"Can you describe Danny Stafford's camp?"

"A clothesline was strung between two trees. Like I said, beer cans were all over the place. He had a kayak—"

"What did the kayak look like?"

"It was small, a one-man kayak, lime green, pretty beat-up."

Sheriff Franklin frowned.

Alex paused.

"Go on with your description of the camp," Sheriff Franklin said.

"There was a tent, and both ends were open. I assume for the breeze. It was hot, like today. I looked into the tent, and Danny was in there, passed out. A knife was sticking out of a stump. It had a gut hook on top. The blade was about four inches long."

Sheriff Franklin slid a picture across the desk of a similar knife with a Mossy Oak camo handle. "Is this like the knife you saw?"

"That's really close, except the handle was black."

Sheriff Franklin retrieved the picture. "Is there anything else you can think of that might help our investigation?"

"No, sir," Alex replied.

The burly sheriff rubbed the back of his neck.

"I get the impression that you already knew that Danny Stafford was living on that island," Alex said.

Sheriff Franklin nodded, turned off the recorder, and moved the mike to the side. "Danny's an alcoholic and a drug addict. We think he's responsible for some break-ins we've been havin' around the lake. We were gonna bring him in when this mess dropped in my lap. And now we don't know where he is. It's a shit show." The sheriff shook his head. "There is somethin' I feel compelled to tell you."

Alex leaned in, his eyes wide open.

"I don't think he'd try anything, given that we're lookin' for him, but I'd make sure to lock your doors at all times. Be vigilant. You and your family are stayin' in his childhood home. It's the same home that his parents kicked him out of not long ago. When Danny got married, his parents bought a house not too far from here and let him rent the lake house for a small amount. If you talk to Danny, he'll tell you that his wife and daughter left him because his parents kicked him out. Of course the truth of the matter is, he was gettin' drunk and high, and his parents didn't want him doin' that shit in their house, especially in front of their granddaughter."

At the conclusion of the interview, Sheriff Franklin said, "Make sure to let me know before you leave town."

Sheriff Franklin escorted Alex back to the waiting area. He held the door open for Alex and looked at Jeff. "Jeff Palmer, come on back."

Jeff struggled to his feet, using his crutches for support. He followed Sheriff Franklin to his corner office.

CHAPTER 20

Alex and Bubba's Brews

Alex slipped on his cowboy boots and stepped into the living room. Jeff and Brett sat on the couch, watching television.

"They're gonna talk about the murders," Brett said.

The All State commercial ended and the local news returned with a tag at the bottom of the screen that read Murder in Mill Creek. A serious-looking anchorwoman with plastered hair spoke. "Yesterday, two bodies were discovered on a small island in the Mill Creek section of Norris Lake." The local news cut to footage of the island, surrounded by police, the Jet Skis in view. "Earlier today, Sheriff Franklin made the following statement."

Alex, Jeff, and Brett watched the newscast with open mouths and wide eyes.

The local news showed Sheriff Franklin standing behind a podium. "On Wednesday, July 18, 2018 two female college students were murdered on an island in the Mill Creek section of Norris Lake. We have several leads that we're investigating, and we're confident that the perpetrator or perpetrators will be brought to justice. If anyone has information that might help our investigation, please call our nonemergency hotline at (865) 555-4211." The number flashed at the bottom of the screen. "Again, that number is (865) 555-4211. Thank you." Sheriff Franklin stepped away from the podium and off camera despite the volley of questions served his way.

The local news cut back to their anchorwoman. "That was Sheriff Franklin of the Norris Lake Sheriff's Department. We'll keep you updated as information becomes available."

"Jesus," Alex said.

"It really is a double murder," Brett said, practically giddy.

"This place'll never be the same," Jeff said.

Alex exhaled. "I'm going down to the boat."

"I'll see you down there," Jeff replied.

Alex walked down the slope toward their dock. He turned and shouted to his family behind him. "Make sure the last person locks the door."

Emma waved in response.

"Hey, you," a man said.

Alex turned to the right. It was the next-door neighbor—the old man who had been watching them. He had a scrunched-up face and held a shovel.

"Can I help you?" Alex asked as he approached the man.

The man narrowed his eyes, and deep creases erupted on his forehead. "Yeah, you can help me." He raised his shovel to show Alex the dog shit on the spade. "You can keep that mutt of yours on your own goddamn property." The old man tossed the dog shit over the property line into the Staffords' backyard.

Alex clenched his jaw. "You've been watching us all week. I don't know what your problem is but—"

"Keep your mutt off my property." The old man walked away.

"Fucking asshole," Alex muttered under his breath as he continued to the pontoon boat.

He was the first aboard. He sat in the captain's chair, enjoying the view. Another gorgeous cloudless day. It was still warm, but there was a nice breeze. Across the inlet, the two-man Jet Ski was docked with the keys dangling. The same watercraft he'd seen their first night here. A father with his two young sons boarded the Jet Ski. The dad waved as he motored past, observing the no-wake rule of the inlet. Alex waved back with a smile.

Alex's entire family packed into the pontoon boat. Everyone except Kristin. This time they weren't dressed in swimsuits. The women wore sundresses and makeup. The men were either cowboy-chic in jeans and boots or frat-boy-laid-back in khaki shorts and sandals. Matt was the only outlier with jeans and sneakers—or tennis shoes as they said in Tennessee.

Everyone had been touched by the sun. Some, like Rachel and Jeff, had nice tans; others, like Emma and Cathy, had mild burns despite extensive sunblock usage. Even though Seth had spent time indoors because of his illness, his lack of sunblocking when he was outside led to a lobster-red nose and peeling skin.

Kristin hurried down the hill. Her long hair was silky smooth and slightly wavy. Those waves would fall back to straight in no time. Her curling iron could make waves, but her hair never held them for very long.

"Hurry up," Alex shouted to his daughter.

"I'm coming," Kristin called back.

"Did you lock the door?" Alex asked as Kristin boarded.

"Yes, … I'm pretty sure."

Alex frowned. "*Pretty sure* implies that you might not've."

"Now you're making me think I left it unlocked."

"Run up the hill and check."

Kristin glanced down at her wedged heels. "I can't in these shoes."

"Take them off."

Kristin frowned. "Dad, come on. I'll get dirty."

"Leave her alone," Emma said.

"Let's go," Rachel said. "I'm starving."

It was still warm and sunny as Alex steered the boat toward the restaurant for dinner. The ladies complained about their hair as the wind destroyed their hard work. Upon arrival at Bubba's Brews, the lakeside restaurant, Alex steered the pontoon toward a dock next to the gas pump. Matt insisted on paying for the fuel, which was nearly twice the rate as the same stuff that goes in cars.

The dock worker pumped the gas and parked the pontoon near the eatery's entrance, as if the boat were the lake equivalent of a Ferrari in front of a fancy restaurant. Bubba's Brews wasn't fancy, but that was just how they liked it in rural Tennessee. Most of the sports bar and grill was under an open-air pavilion. A smaller section of seating was on the deck along the water.

The women went to the bathroom to fix their hair. The men were seated at a large picnic table on the deck. The women returned, and the waitress approached with a "Hey, y'all." Everyone ordered drinks. Gwen and Rachel ordered Big Bubba's Punch—a massive concoction of liquor and sugar. The guys mostly ordered beer, except for Matt who ordered water. Jeff and Harvey snickered at his less-than-manly choice.

Kristin put her hand over her mouth. "I think I left my curling iron on."

"You're gonna burn down the house," Brett said.

"Shut up. I am not."

"Doesn't it have one of those automatic shut-off thingies?" Gwen asked.

"I don't know," Kristin replied.

"Where did you leave it?"

"I think on the chair in my room." Kristin sucked in a breath, her eyes wide. "The chair's wooden."

"It would have to be touching the chair," Gwen said. "Don't you have the cover on it?"

"I don't know." Kristin turned to Alex, talking rapidly now. "Dad, I think I left my curling iron on. The house might burn down. We have to go back and turn it off."

With a crooked grin, Alex shook his head at his daughter. "It'll be fine. We're not going back. We just got here."

"But—"

"You worry too much."

Alex stood from the table and spoke to Emma. "If the waitress comes back, can you order me the frog legs?"

Emma wrinkled her nose. "You're not ordering that, are you?"

Alex smiled. "No. I want the pulled pork and fries." Alex stepped through the open-air pavilion toward the bathroom, passing an empty stage and a bar filled with flat screens. It wasn't crowded for a Friday evening, but it was only 6:10 p.m. Alex stepped into the men's room. It was cramped but clean. Seth was at a urinal, his pelvis pushed forward and his hand on his penis. His neck was red. Seth had opted for the frat-boy look of khaki shorts and a tight polo. His legs were skinny, which might've looked normal, but his midsection had a spare tire. He had Dunlap's Disease—his belly done lapped over his belt. He didn't have a bad face. He might've been a six—in the winter when he could hide his flaws—but, in the summer, he dipped below the mean.

Alex stepped up to the urinal next to Seth. He would've preferred at least one urinal gap between him and the next person, but Seth chose the middle urinal, and there were only three.

"Hey, Seth," Alex said, without looking at him.

"Oh, hey." Seth grunted as if he were in pain. He zipped up and went to the sink.

Alex peed and then washed his hands in the sink. Seth dried his hands under the dryer. When the dryer stopped, Seth adjusted his crotch.

"You all right?" Alex asked, shaking his hands over the sink.

Seth turned, his face bright red in the fluorescent light. "I'm okay."

"Emma has some aloe, if you want some for your sunburn."

"Thanks."

Back at the table, the family made small talk. Despite the ugliness of the murders, everyone seemed to be having a good time. It helped that Matt was at one end of the table, and Jeff and Harvey were at the other. Alex and Emma were in the middle, enjoying everyone's company.

Jeff spoiled it by talking about the murders. "Do you guys think Danny did it?" he asked the table.

Harvey narrowed his eyes at Jeff.

"This isn't polite dinner conversation," Gwen said to her husband.

"I don't even wanna think about it," Cathy said.

"Me either," Kristin said.

"I sure hope he didn't do it," Emma said.

"I bet he did," Rachel said.

"I think he did it too," Brett said. "That island's small, and he lives there. What are the chances that some other creepy homeless dude did it?"

"Often the simplest explanation is correct," Harvey said.

"When I went to the police station, the sheriff told me that Danny's the prime suspect," Jeff said. "Apparently, he was living in the house we're renting, and his parents kicked him out because he was getting drunk and high. The sheriff told me that Danny was living there with his wife and daughter, and they left him when he was kicked out. The sheriff thinks he might have an ax to grind."

"Did you know about that?" Kristin asked her dad.

Alex frowned at Jeff and nodded to Kristin.

"Maybe he, like, wants us out of his house," Rachel said.

"If he killed before, he'll do it again," Brett said with a grin. "Maybe we're next."

"That's stupid," Kristin said.

"Maybe."

"First of all, we don't know if Danny did anything," Alex said. "Second of all, whoever murdered those poor girls is probably long gone by now."

CHAPTER 21

Kristin and the Brewing Storm

After dinner, Rachel stood from the picnic table. "Anyone wanna play me in cornhole?" Cornhole targets were set up on the deck. Brett practically jumped to his feet. "I'll play."

Brett and Rachel played their game, while Kristin and Seth sat at the table, angry and alone. Alex and Matt talked at the water's edge. Emma and Gwen tossed pieces of Texas toast to the geese and ducks begging from the water. Everyone else leaned over the railing, talking and enjoying the lakeside view. Even Jeff limped over to the railing, his first foray without his crutches.

On the boat ride home, nobody worried about their hair. The family members were full and relaxed, except for Kristin. She was agitated.

"The house might be on fire," Kristin said, loud enough to be heard over the motor noise.

"I'm sure it's fine," Alex replied.

Kristin sat on the pontoon, across from Brett, scowling as he bantered with Rachel. Kristin hugged herself, rubbing her arms—a chill causing goose bumps. It was cooling off—the sun bloodred and low on the horizon. Clouds clustered in the darkening sky. *Brett didn't even notice me at dinner. I wore this dress. I even wore makeup but still nothing. He barely looked at me. He was too busy looking at Rachel.* Kristin narrowed her eyes at Rachel. Seth sat on the other side of

Rachel, his lobster-red arms crossed over his chest.

Alex steered the pontoon alongside the dock, and Matt tied it to the dock. Kristin got the house key from her dad. She slipped off her wedged heels, hopped from the boat, and bolted up the hill. Kristin ran, partly to get away from Brett and Rachel, and partly from worry that her curling iron was on fire.

As she neared the house, she knew something was wrong. Buster stood on the patio, barking. The back door was open. Her stomach dropped at the sight. *I left the door unlocked.* Buster calmed as she approached. She entered the house, Buster right behind her, his nails click-clacking on the hardwood. She stopped just inside. Buster stopped. It was dead quiet. She took a whiff, expecting to smell smoke. Nothing. Kristin hurried to her room. The curling iron was on the chair, just where she had left it. It was unplugged. She breathed a sigh of relief.

Kristin looked around the room, a wave of fear covering her like a blanket. Her suitcase was open; some of her clothes were scattered over the floor. A few dresser drawers were open. Her iPad was gone. *Did I leave it somewhere? No, I was charging it.* The charger was still there, plugged into the wall but no iPad. *Someone stole it.*

Kristin ran from her room to the back door. Emma and Gwen came inside, followed by Alex and Jeff.

"Someone was here," Kristin said, her hands shaky. "They stole my iPad and went through my clothes."

The rest of the family entered the scene.

"We've been robbed," Emma said.

"What?" Matt said.

"Someone stole my iPad and went through my clothes," Kristin said.

"Was the door locked?" Alex asked.

Kristin wagged her head.

"You were supposed to lock the door."

"I know. I'm sorry, Dad."

Alex frowned and shook his head. "Don't apologize to me. Whoever broke in probably stole from everyone here."

Tears slipped down Kristin's cheeks. "I'm sorry, everybody."

"He might still be here," Jeff said.

"Jeff's right," Alex said. "Everyone outside. We need to search the house."

Alex forced everyone into the backyard, while Jeff, Harvey, and Matt searched the house. Shortly thereafter, with the house deemed safe, everyone checked their belongings, and Alex called the police. Some of the women were missing underwear and jewelry. Electronic devices were missing—cell phones, iPads, laptops.

Alex and Matt and Kristin stood in the living room. Harvey was on the couch, unmolested. He'd left his laptop at his home, and his cell was in his pocket.

Alex hung up the cordless phone. "Police should be here in an hour."

"An hour?" Kristin asked. "Why so long?"

"I don't know. I guess this isn't an emergency."

"My laptop's gone," Matt said to Alex, shaking his head, his hands on his hips. "My novel was on there."

"I'm sorry," Kristin said for about the fiftieth time in the last fifteen minutes.

Matt turned to Kristin and said, "It's not your fault. They could've broken in even if the door was locked."

"Didn't you have a backup?" Alex asked.

"Yeah, my thumb drive. It's in my computer bag—also stolen."

"Shit. Sorry, dude."

Harvey stood with a groan. "Burglar did you a favor. First novels should be thrown away. They're always shit."

"I can't listen to this idiot," Matt said.

"Relax, guys," Alex said.

"You're the idiot," Harvey said to Matt. "I've forgotten more about writing and publishing than you'll ever know."

Matt stomped outside, slamming the door behind him.

"Was that necessary?" Alex asked Harvey.

"I'm doing him a favor," Harvey replied. "These self-published authors will never make a dime. Better he moves on now, before wasting his life writing shitty novels."

It took the police two hours to arrive, not that it mattered. The cop wrote a report of the missing items for their insurance companies. He told them that there had been a rash of burglaries over the past year. On his way out, the cop told them to make sure they locked their doors.

CHAPTER 22

Alex and the Kayak

Alex loaded dishes into the dishwasher. The house was finally quiet after the lunch crowd. He didn't mind doing the dishes. It was a simple job with easily measured progress leading to success—success he could see. It wasn't like his job. Being an HR manager for a large corporation was filled with fires to put out—a constant stream of dysfunctional people and problems to fix, but they were never really fixed. He simply did what was the best for the company, what protected the company from lawsuits. The sad thing was, he hated his job, but he wished like hell he still had it.

This vacation had blown by. It was supposed to be a respite, a vacation from the financial nightmare brewing. It was almost over, and the fantasy would end with it. The day after tomorrow he'd have to tell Emma.

Matt stepped into the kitchen, his brown hair disheveled.

Alex turned from the dishwasher. "Hey, bro. You're up late."

"Yeah, I was writing late last night," Matt replied, glancing at the clock on the stove. "I got on a roll. I didn't mean to sleep in until noon."

"You redoing your novel?"

Matt shook his head. "No, I'm working on something new."

"That's cool. What's it about?"

"A serial killer."

"I'm sure it'll be good."

"We'll see. I'm sure Harvey'll say it's crap."

"Dad feels threatened. You know how competitive he is. Let it go, man. Life's too short."

"Normally I do. It's a little more difficult with him here."

"Have you decided about leaving tomorrow?" Alex asked. "I know this vacation's been a disaster, but I think we finally used up all our bad luck. I'd love for you to stay the extra day."

"I need to get back to work," Matt replied. "You know there's rain in the forecast?"

"It's a 50 percent chance, last I checked. We could always stay in and play board games. I saw some in the basement. Harvey and Jeff'll be gone tomorrow. Rachel and Seth too. If we could just get rid of Brett, we'd have a perfect day."

"Sorry, I can't. I need the hours. I'm saving up for an editor."

"Well, if you change your mind …"

"Thanks, Alex." Matt took a deep breath. "There's something I need to talk to you about."

Alex shut the dishwasher and moved closer to his brother.

"Is anyone here?" Matt asked.

"I think everyone's down at the dock."

A toilet flushed in the basement.

"Why don't we step outside?" Alex said.

Alex and Matt exited the back door. They moved past the concrete patio to the grassy backyard. The family floated and played and relaxed at the dock—at least one hundred yards away, safely out of hearing distance. It was cooler than yesterday but still warm, the sun playing peekaboo with the clouds. A breeze blew through the trees, the leaves rustling in response. The air felt charged. The hair stood up on Alex's arms.

"What's up?" Alex asked.

Matt replied, "Last night, when I was working, I heard Brett and Kristin arguing. I feel bad eavesdropping, but I see why you're concerned about Brett. He's really rough with Buster."

"I know. Emma told him to leave the dog alone yesterday. It takes a lot for her to get mad."

"I think Kristin's pissed about Brett flirting with Rachel."

"That's no surprise," Alex replied. "It's a good thing. Hopefully she'll break up with him."

"I also think Brett has a problem with Buster. I didn't hear exactly what he said, because he said it low, but Kristin said something like, 'You're jealous of a dog?' It made me remember about how you thought he might've killed Kristin's dog. And if he'll kill a dog …"

"What or who else will he kill?"

The back door opened, and Jeff hobbled outside.

"What's goin' on?" Jeff asked as he approached.

There was an awkward silence. Jeff cocked his head as if trying to assess the situation. He had a deep scar at his hairline. Thirty years ago, when Jeff had only been three or four, he'd jumped off the couch to impress his big brothers. Split his head open on the coffee table. There was so much blood. Cathy was furious with Alex and Matt. Harvey had bragged about Jeff's hard head.

"Nothing," Matt said, barely looking at Jeff.

"I see how it is," Jeff replied, running his hand through his wavy brown hair.

"We're talking about Brett … and Kristin's dog," Alex said.

"That kid's a piece of shit," Jeff said to Alex. "I've been watching him like you asked, but he hasn't done anything in front of me."

"I appreciate it, bro."

Matt stared at Jeff, one side of his mouth raised in contempt, no doubt bothered by his big brother's cozy relationship with Jeff.

Alex could almost hear the wheels turning in Matt's head. Matt probably thought he was the only one Alex had asked to watch out for Brett. Alex was good at making people feel special, but his inclusive nature often diluted the exclusivity.

"If he killed her dog, he should be in jail or juvie or something," Jeff said.

"I wish," Alex replied. "I can't prove it, and Emma doesn't believe it."

"I could beat it out of him."

"The last thing we need is you going to jail because of that little creep."

As if on cue, a police boat nosed around their inlet.

"Check it out," Matt said, pointing. "You think they're looking for Danny?"

"Probably," Alex replied. "But I bet Danny's long gone by now."

"If I committed a double homicide, no way I'd stick around," Jeff said.

The police boat stopped near their dock. The cops pointed at one of Alex's yellow kayaks.

"What's happening?" Matt asked.

"I don't know," Alex replied. "We should check it out."

The three brothers walked down the hill toward the dock. Jeff hobbled a little, but he kept pace. The police boat docked, kitty-cornered from the pontoon rental. The police boat had big vinyl lettering that read Norris Lake Sheriff's Department. Two deputies boarded their dock. One young and pumped up with tatted arms and massive biceps; the other older and soft around the middle. Both had the obligatory copstache. The family had stopped what they were doing. The swimmers and floaters had come in and stood with towels wrapped around them. The others had risen from their camping chairs. Brett paddled on the lake somewhere in one of the kayaks.

"What's this about?" Harvey asked, his beefy arms crossed over his chest.

"Who's the owner of this kayak?" the older deputy asked, pointing to the kayak on the dock.

The younger deputy moved closer to the kayak and looked it over.

"It's mine," Alex said.

"Are you the only one who has access to this kayak?" the older deputy asked.

"No, anyone can use it."

"Call Sheriff Franklin," the older deputy said to the younger one.

Brett paddled toward the dock in Alex's identical yellow kayak with the Miami Dolphins' sticker on the side. The older deputy scowled at Brett and the kayak, then turned to Alex. "How many of these kayaks you got?"

"Just these two," Alex replied.

They were herded up the hill to the house. Sheriff Franklin and three more deputies arrived in cruisers. Everyone was in the living room, the family asked to sit on the couches. Sheriff Franklin stood front and center. He was a hulking man with a ruddy complexion. The sheriff was flanked by five deputies, the three new guys and the two guys from the boat. The deputies watched the family with blank faces.

"We'd like to search the house and your kayaks, with your permission of course," Sheriff Franklin said.

"What's this about?" Harvey asked.

"I can't say. It's part of an ongoin' investigation."

"Then you'll need to get a warrant."

The sheriff scowled at Harvey.

"If you tell us what this is about, maybe we can work something out," Alex said.

"This was Danny Stafford's house," Sheriff Franklin said, "and we have reason to believe he burglarized this house yesterday. There may be evidence here that might help us with another investigation. It also might help us recover your stolen merchandise."

"This is about that double homicide," Harvey said.

"Like I said, I can't talk about an ongoing investigation," the sheriff replied.

"Why do you need to search the kayaks?" Alex asked.

"Again, I can't say."

"They'll tear this house apart," Harvey said. "You can forget about your security deposit, Alex. They'll do thousands of dollars of damage."

Phil M. Williams

"We'll be careful and respectful of the property," Sheriff Franklin said.

Harvey narrowed his eyes at the sheriff. "That's bullshit, and you know it."

"We'll get a warrant."

"Until that time comes, I don't consent to a search," Harvey said.

Alex said to the sheriff, "I can't make my family consent to a search. Maybe you guys can search the common areas, but I'd have to take a vote. If you wanna search bedrooms, my family would have to consent for their particular room."

"Take a vote then," Sheriff Franklin said.

"Okay, who wants to let them search the common areas?" Alex asked.

Alex and Emma and Matt raised their hands. Kristin and Seth also raised their hands. Rachel frowned at Seth's disagreement. The vote was 6-5 in favor of no search. Harvey had always been protective of his civil rights and those of his family. Sixteen years ago, Jeff had been suspected of vandalizing his private high school. The police had wanted to search Jeff's bedroom for the spray paint cans. Harvey had told them to get a warrant, which never materialized. For a conservative Republican, Harvey could be awfully liberal at times.

"Sorry, Sheriff, no search," Alex said.

"What about the bedrooms?" Sheriff Franklin asked.

The same five raised their hands, consenting to the search.

Sheriff Franklin rubbed his temples. "Now I know who has somethin' to hide and who doesn't. I ain't gonna waste my time searchin' them rooms, but I will get that warrant, lickety-split."

"Until then," Harvey said, his jaw set tight.

"Y'all know how this looks, don't you?"

The room went quiet.

The sheriff cleared his throat. "How 'bout them kayaks?"

"You're welcome to look at them," Alex said, "but I don't want you taking them from the dock."

Sheriff Franklin nodded at the two deputies from the police boat. They exited the house for the dock and the kayaks.

"I'd also like to interview y'all down at my offices," Sheriff Franklin said.

"Are we under arrest?" Emma asked, her face and chest blotchy red from stress.

"No, ma'am. Nobody's under arrest. I think some of you might have information beneficial to our investigation. It'd be nice if y'all were more cooperative."

"I've already told you everything I know, and so did my son Jeff," Harvey said. "If you want to talk to me or my wife or Jeff or Rachel, you'll have to do it through my lawyer. Same goes for Seth and my daughter-in-law Gwen." Harvey stood and handed his lawyer's business card to Sheriff Franklin. Harvey took his seat and folded his muscular arms over his chest as if the matter was settled.

Sheriff Franklin frowned at the business card, then looked back at the family, scanning from left to right. "I know who Jeff is, but who's Gwen?"

Gwen raised her thin arm.

"Would you be willing to come to my offices to be interviewed?"

"No, she wouldn't," Jeff answered for his wife.

"Gwen?" the sheriff asked.

Gwen shook her head, not making eye contact with the sheriff.

Sheriff Franklin glared at Jeff. "You were helpful on Thursday, and now you're not. Why the change?"

"Look, Sheriff. I told you everything I know," Jeff said. "My wife doesn't know anything."

"I think that's somethin' I should decide."

"Not gonna happen," Jeff said, his eyes like lasers.

Sheriff Franklin approached Cathy. "May I ask who you are, ma'am?"

Cathy sat, wearing capris and a blousy shirt. Her thick thighs and hips sprawled on the couch next to Harvey. She pointed to Harvey. "I'm his wife."

Harvey shook his head at the sheriff as if to say, *Don't bother. She's not talking.*

"And Rachel and Seth, where are you two?" Sheriff Franklin asked.

Rachel and Seth raised their hands.

"Will you two come down to be interviewed? It's really important."

"Forget it, Sheriff," Harvey said. "Call my lawyer if you want to talk to Rachel."

"I'll talk to you," Seth said.

"Seth, no," Rachel said. "My dad said not to."

"I wanna help."

Sheriff Franklin nodded. "Good man. I appreciate your assistance." The sheriff addressed everyone. "Is there anyone else who doesn't wanna be interviewed?" The room remained silent. "Good, I'd like to interview you cooperative folks at my offices in an hour. If you need transportation, my deputies can give you a ride to and from."

"We can drive," Alex said.

"Suit yourself.

Brett raised his hand tentatively.

"Yes, young man," the sheriff replied.

"I, uh, don't wanna be interviewed."

Sheriff Franklin took a step toward Brett. "What's your name?"

"Brett, uh Brett Taylor."

"You don't wanna help us?"

"Leave the kid alone," Harvey said.

"I just think I should talk to my mom first," Brett said.

"That's fair," Sheriff Franklin replied. "Why don't you call her?"

"Cell phones don't work here."

Alex stood and grabbed the cordless phone from the end table and handed it to Brett. "The landline works fine."

With a shaky finger, Brett dialed his mother. Shortly thereafter he hung up. "She's not answering."

"Well, keep tryin," the sheriff said.

The interviewees changed from their swimsuits and caravanned to the sheriff's office.

Brett never did reach his mother.

CHAPTER 23

Alex and the Sheriff

Sheriff Franklin separated the adults. Matt was interviewed first by a deputy, while Seth waited for his turn. Kristin was interviewed by the sheriff with her parents present. Alex and Emma and Kristin sat across from Sheriff Franklin, his microphone between them on the desk. After fifteen minutes' worth of questions, he ended the interview with his most important query.

"Do you remember who used the kayaks last Wednesday in the afternoon?" Sheriff Franklin asked.

"I have no idea," Kristin replied.

"Well, hold on. Think about it for a minute."

"Everyone uses them, but I have no idea who used them on that day. I don't even remember if I used one that day."

Sheriff Franklin sighed. "Okay, that's all for now. Thank you, Kristin."

"May I go?" Kristin asked.

"Wait for us in the waiting room," Alex said.

Kristin stood. "Can I go home with Uncle Matt?"

"Yes, but I want you to stay inside until we get home."

"Why?"

"Because I said so."

Kristin slumped her shoulders. "Fine." She started for the door.

"Kristin," Alex said.

She turned, her hand on the doorknob. "What?" Her voice was impatient.

Alex glared, his jaw set tight. "I'm serious. Stay inside."

"I heard you the first time." With that she was gone.

Alex turned to Sheriff Franklin. "You gonna tell me why you're so interested in my kayaks?"

"I'd like to talk to you two separately," the sheriff said, looking from Alex to Emma. "Mrs. Palmer, would you mind stepping outside?"

"Of course not," Emma said, standing. She smiled toward Alex and left the room.

Sheriff Franklin leaned forward, his elbows on his desk. "Do you remember who used the kayaks last Wednesday in the afternoon?"

"I'm not sure. The only thing I can tell you is that Kristin, Jeff, Brett, and I use them the most. Rachel and Gwen and Matt and Harvey used them a few times. But I couldn't tell you who used them in the afternoon three days ago."

The sheriff stroked his mustache, the silence palpable.

Alex finally broke the silence. "I'm assuming this is about Danny Stafford and the murders."

"What makes you think that?" the sheriff asked.

"All I know is you're real interested in my kayaks and who was using them on Wednesday, the day those girls were murdered. I'm not a detective, but I think someone saw my kayak on that island on Wednesday."

"*Was* your kayak on that island on Wednesday?"

"I don't know. It's certainly possible."

"Jeff Palmer's your younger brother, right?"

"Yes."

"He said he hurt his ankle jumping off a rope swing. Did you see the accident?"

"I did. He was lucky it was just a sprained ankle."

The sheriff stroked his mustache for a moment. "You think anybody in your house is capable of murder?"

Alex sat up straight, his eyes wide. "No, … I don't think so."

"But it's possible?"

"Anything's possible, Sheriff." Alex thought of Brett and Kristin's dead dog.

"You got someone in mind?"

Alex nodded, almost imperceptibly. "My daughter's boyfriend, Brett. I don't think he's a murderer, but I think he killed my daughter's dog."

"What makes you think that?"

"He was watching the dog, and, when Kristin got the dog back from him, it was listless. The next day it died. The vet said the dog died from a head trauma. I think Brett kicked it in the head."

"Do you have any proof?"

"No."

"Did you confront Brett?"

"Yeah. He said the dog fell down the stairs. He said he didn't say or do anything because the dog seemed fine."

"You don't buy his story?"

"No. The dog was a puppy, and puppies can be clumsy, but something about his story didn't ring true. It wasn't what he said as much as how he said it."

"Was he remorseful?"

"Yeah, but it didn't seem genuine."

"What does your wife think?"

"She thinks it was an accident."

"What about Kristin?"

"Kristin only sees the good in people. She already thinks I don't like Brett. And rightly so. If she knew what I thought about him and the dog, she'd flip her lid. She'd say I was only saying that because I don't like Brett. It would push her toward him further. If I forbid her from seeing him, she'd just do it in secret. Besides, Emma and I aren't in agreement, so I'm outnumbered." Alex shook his head.

"I understand. It's a sticky situation. I got two girls at home. Eighteen and twenty-one." He pointed to his white hair. "I went white when my oldest daughter became a teenager."

"Do you think my daughter's dating a murderer?"

"I doubt it, but, if I were you, I'd keep an eye on him 'til we can rule him out. I'd like to interview Brett. Maybe you can persuade him into cooperatin'?"

CHAPTER 24

Kristin and WWJD

Matt drove his Hyundai Elantra on the twisty mountain road. His hands gripped the steering wheel—tight. The shade of the trees created moving shadows across his face. Kristin was in the passenger seat.

"Are you okay?" Kristin asked, staring at Matt's white knuckles and clenched jaw.

Matt glanced at his niece. "I'm fine. Why?"

"You seem upset."

"I'm fine."

Kristin nodded. "What did the police ask you?"

He loosened his grip on the steering wheel, looked at Kristin for a moment, then focused back on the road. "Your dad probably wouldn't want me talking about it."

"I'm not a little kid anymore."

"I know. You remember when I used to hold out my arm, and you'd hang on it and swing, like I was a jungle gym?"

Kristin laughed. "I remember that. And I remember when you and Angela took me to see *WALL-E*. It was my first movie at the movie theater. I loved that little robot." Kristin smiled at her uncle, but he stared at the road, his face expressionless. Her smile receded. "Do you miss her?"

He nodded.

"I miss her too."

They drove in silence for a few minutes.

Kristin broke the silence. "Did the police ask you who was using the kayaks on Wednesday?"

"Yeah."

"Wednesday's the day those girls were murdered on that island. I think one of the kayaks was on that island when the murders happened."

Matt swallowed. "Maybe."

"Come on, Uncle Matt. Why else would they ask about them? The police were looking at them a lot at the dock, and, when Brett paddled up, they were all upset and wanted to know how many kayaks my dad had."

"Maybe one of the kayaks *was* on that island on the same day, but that doesn't mean …"

"That someone in our family's a murderer."

Matt frowned. "Right."

"But it's possible."

"Anything's possible."

"Is that what you're upset about? The kayak?"

Matt shook his head.

"Is it because of Papaw and why you left the army?"

Matt didn't respond.

"I think you did the right thing. I don't think Jesus would fight in any war."

Matt looked at his niece with glassy eyes. "Thanks."

"You know, Jesus was persecuted for his beliefs. I think if you stand up for what's right, the people who are sinning are gonna get mad."

He nodded.

"I think they get mad because, if they don't get mad, they might have to recognize their own sins."

CHAPTER 25

Alex and the Exam

Alex stood. Sheriff Franklin stood.

"I appreciate your honesty," Sheriff Franklin said, holding his hand out over his desk.

"You're welcome, Sheriff," Alex said, shaking his hand.

Sheriff Franklin escorted Alex to the waiting room and called Emma back to be interviewed. The waiting room had a line of metal chairs along one wall, and the entrances to the bathrooms were on the opposite side. Alex had to pee, his bladder prodded by the tense situation.

The men's room had two urinals—sinks opposite and stalls along the far wall. Feet were visible under one stall. Grunts came from the man in the stall. Alex stepped up to the urinal, did his business, and went to the sink.

As Alex washed his hands, Seth exited the stall. "Hey, Seth."

"Hi, Alex." Seth washed his hands. His face was blank.

Alex dried his hands with a paper towel. "Are you all right?"

"I'm still not feeling very good." Seth dried his hands.

"I was a medic in the army, and an EMT for a while after I got out. I might be able to help. What are your symptoms?"

"I was nauseous, but thankfully I'm not anymore. I do still feel achy, and it hurts to pee. I think maybe I have a bladder infection. I also have a rash, but I think that must be from the heat. I'm gonna go to the doctor as soon as we get back."

Alex nodded. "Where's the rash?"

Seth's blush was visible, even with his sunburn. "It's, uh, kind of, like, in this area." He made a circular gesture to his crotch.

"What does the rash look like?"

"Just like little blisters."

Alex cleared his throat. "What you're describing sounds like herpes."

"I must be describing it wrong."

"Maybe."

Seth frowned and pursed his lips. "You got me really freaked out now. If I showed you, would you be able to tell what it is?"

"Probably. I saw a lot of guys in the army with herpes."

Seth hung his head. "This is so embarrassing."

"You're not feeling well, and you need help. That's nothing to be ashamed of."

"Can you keep this between us?"

"Yeah."

They went into the handicapped stall. Seth unbuckled his belt and pulled down his shorts and underwear far enough that Alex could see some sores. Alex leaned forward and looked at the clusters of tiny white blisters.

Alex stood upright. "You can pull up your shorts."

Seth pulled up his shorts and underwear and buckled his belt. "What do you think?"

"I'm sorry, dude. Looks like herpes to me."

Seth's voice was higher, his speech rapid. "How could I get herpes? I've only been with Rachel."

"A lot of people carry herpes for a long time without any noticeable symptoms. Maybe it's from a previous encounter?"

"I don't have *encounters*. When I said, 'I've only been with Rachel,' I mean ever, like my whole life."

Alex winced. "Oh …"

"Then how did this happen?" Seth held out his hands.

Alex was quiet, waiting for Seth to put two and two together.

Seth's eyes grew wide. "I'm gonna kill her." He stomped from the stall and the bathroom.

Alex watched from the window of the waiting area as Seth gunned his lifted Jeep from the parking lot.

CHAPTER 26

Man's Best Friend

He crept up the hill and entered the shed. He grabbed the shovel. It was right where he thought it would be. He moved across the backyard to the lake house and the concrete patio. The dog barked at the back door. *Yappy little mongrel.* He leaned the shovel against the picnic table, set down his backpack, and opened the back door. The dog bounded onto the patio, his tail wagging. He bent over and pet the terrier's head. The dog's tail wagged faster with the attention. He wrapped his gloved hands around the dog's neck, not tight. His hands easily encapsulated the dog's neck. He stood, holding the terrier by the neck. The dog squirmed and whimpered, his little paws swimming through the air. He looked into the dog's dark eyes and squeezed with the force of a python.

Gravel crunched. A car engine grew louder by the second.

Shit. Someone's home. He moved to the corner of the house, still strangling the little terrier. He listened to the crunching gravel. It stopped. Then the engine stopped. Car doors opened and shut. Voices. The front door opened and slammed shut. The dog jerked and seized violently as he went through the death throes. He shoved the carcass into a plastic bag, then inside his backpack.

He slung his pack over his shoulders, grabbed the shovel, and hurried to the neighbor's backyard. He hid behind a thick oak, listening. Nothing.

CHAPTER 27

Kristin and Curiosity

Kristin stepped out of the car and looked up. The cloudiness was a nice respite from the summer sun.

"It might rain," Matt said.

"I think there's a 50 percent chance," Kristin said. "At least that's what my dad said."

Matt glanced back at the imposing cliff that masqueraded as a driveway. "Let's hope it doesn't. We might be stuck here."

Once inside, Matt yawned and stretched his arms over his head. "I didn't sleep much last night. I think I'm gonna take a nap," he said to Kristin.

"Okay, see you later," Kristin replied.

Matt trudged up the steps toward his room.

The house was quiet. No barking. No click-clack of Buster's nails on the hardwood. *Where's Buster? Where's Brett? He better not be with Rachel.* Kristin exited the back door in search of Brett and Buster. She stepped into the backyard and peered down to the dock. It was deserted. She saw a flash of movement to her left, coming from the neighbor's property. She moved that way to get a better look. *Why is he over there? Where's he going? And why does he have a shovel?*

CHAPTER 28

The Mistake

He trekked uphill, away from the water. In the neighbor's front yard, he looked left and right down Lakeshore Drive. No cars or people. He hurried across the street and into the woods. He hiked farther uphill, moving away from civilization. A twig snapped. He stopped, listened, and scanned the forest. Squirrels scurried on leaves but nothing else. He continued hiking. He was at least a mile from the lake house.

He stopped again, and slammed the shovel into the earth so it stood upright. He set down his backpack and retrieved shoe covers and a swim cap. He knew the swim cap was overkill. Nobody would find hairs out here. With obscured tread, he walked in a circle, his feet searching for soft ground. He found a patch of relatively soft earth. He went to his backpack and opened it again. With gloved hands, he grabbed the plastic bag containing the dog carcass and then the shovel. He dumped the plastic-encased carcass next to the dig site.

The shovel was rusty and dull and short-handled. Not the best for large holes. Luckily it was a small dog. He cleared away the leaves with the shovel, then dug. He found a rhythm and, before long, had a deep-enough hole that the wildlife wouldn't dig up the dead dog. He dumped the carcass out of the plastic bag and into the hole. No reason to preserve the evidence in plastic. He left the plastic bag in the hole next to the dead dog. He removed the dog collar and ID tag, and shoved them into his backpack. He backfilled the hole and kicked leaves over the bare ground. When finished, he slung his backpack over his shoulders and turned around.

Leaves rustled. Not a light rustle that moved quickly, like a squirrel or a chipmunk. No, a heavy rustle that came from one place and didn't move.

Fuck. He looked around, listening, trying to pinpoint exactly where it came from. This area had big animals, like deer, but they were light-footed, and they would run. *What animal stays?*

He walked away from the gravesite, back the way he came. Every twenty feet or so, he stopped, scanned 360 degrees, and listened. The second time he did this, he heard the rustle again. This time he pinpointed the location. He approached an old tree with a trunk about as wide as him. He peeked around the tree. She sat with her knees pulled to her chest as if she were trying to hide inside herself.

"Hi," he said.

She screamed and put her hand to her chest.

"I'm sorry. I didn't mean to scare you."

Her chest heaved as she sucked in air. "That's okay." She stood.

He rounded the tree and faced her. "What are you doing out here?"

"Oh, I, uh, just wanted some alone time." Her voice quivered. She wrung her hands.

"What are the chances that I'd run into you *all* the way out here?"

"Must be God's plan."

He smiled. "Or the devil's."

She forced a laugh. "I should get going. My dad's expecting me back." She started past him, but he stepped in front of her.

"What did you see?" he asked, his eyes narrowed.

"Nothing." She swallowed.

"It's a sin to lie."

She paused, not sure how to respond.

In a blaze of fury, he coldcocked her in the face. She fell to the ground and shrieked, her jaw off-kilter. He straddled her, wrapped his gloved hands around her neck, and squeezed. Her blue eyes were wide, and her eyebrows arched in a stone-set face of fright. She pawed at his arms and twisted her body, but he was too strong and too heavy.

He was aroused. He thought about her lithe body in her bikini. The way her bottoms rode up her crack. That little bit of camel toe.

There's a condom in my backpack.

No, be a fucking professional. This is a mistake that has to be cleaned up. Quickly. Someone may know she's out here.

She bucked and flailed to no avail, her strength dissolving with each oxygen-free second. Tears slipped from the corners of her eyes past her temples and into her dirty-blond hair. She stopped struggling, resigned to her fate. She touched the earth. Minutes later, her eyes were empty, and her body spasmed involuntarily. Finally, she was limp, the life squeezed out of her.

He let go and leaned back on his haunches. "Motherfucker." He was breathing hard. "Stupid bitch couldn't mind her own fucking business."

He dragged her body to the gravesite. He moved the leaves again and dug. He moved soil frantically. His lower back ached because he had to bend over with the short handle. To make matters worse, the hole had to be much larger. This wasn't a nine-pound dog. As he dug deeper, rocks were more and more of a problem. His T-shirt was drenched with sweat. Soil stuck to his sweaty skin. His shoe covers offered little traction.

Hurry up, motherfucker. You're gonna get caught because you were sloppy.

He dragged her into the hole. The dog ended up between her feet. He snatched the gold crucifix from her neck and put it in his backpack. The hole was only two feet deep, but he was exhausted. He backfilled the hole and covered her up the best he could. *Something's gonna dig her up.* He kicked leaves over the site, but it was futile. He couldn't adequately cover it. If someone saw the site, they'd know something was buried there.

CHAPTER 29

Alex and Missing

Alex drove his pickup back from the sheriff's office. Emma was in the passenger seat.

"He asked about the kayaks and who was using them on Wednesday," Emma said.

"What did you tell him?" Alex asked.

"The truth. I don't remember." Emma took a deep breath. "I'm worried. Something must've changed. Sheriff Franklin was interested in Danny, but now I think he's interested in us."

"I think he's still interested in Danny," Alex replied.

"All this questioning about the kayak leads me to believe that someone saw one of our kayaks on that island the same day those girls were murdered."

"I came to the same conclusion."

"Do you think it's possible?" Emma asked.

"What?" Alex replied. "That the kayak was there, or that one of us actually committed double murder?"

She bit the bottom corner of her lip. "The double murder."

Alex glanced at Emma. "I don't know. I doubt it. But, if it *was* anyone, my money's on Brett."

"That's crazy."

"Is it? What if he did kill Kristin's dog? That's what psychopaths do. They kill animals for fun, and they eventually graduate to killing people."

"That's a big *what if*, Alex. And, even if he did kill Kristin's dog, maybe it was an accident. It doesn't make him a killer."

Alex drove the truck down the steep driveway, the tires kicking gravel as they half-slid, half-rolled. Every trip up and down that driveway created grooves, ensuring a tiny bit less traction for the next vehicle. Alex parked the truck, and they went inside.

"Kristin," Emma called out.

"Anybody home?" Alex called out.

Alex and Emma walked to the living room. There was water on the floor. Jeff limped into the living room from the basement, holding a beach towel, and wearing board shorts and a T-shirt. His hair was damp. His limp was only a slight hitch now. He tossed the towel on the floor, moving the towel along the water trail with his foot.

Jeff looked at Alex and Emma. "Sorry about the water. I went for a swim and forgot to bring a towel down to the dock."

"It's just water," Emma said.

"How did it go with the sheriff?" Jeff asked, picking up his towel.

"We might have a problem," Alex replied. "We think one of the kayaks was spotted on that island where they found the bodies."

Jeff winced. "I thought about that when they were asking about the kayaks. This is bad."

"Do *you* think they saw one of the kayaks on that island?" Alex asked.

"That's certainly possible," Jeff replied. "I personally don't remember ever going to *that* island, but I did stop at quite a few islands."

Alex nodded. "Have you seen Kristin?"

Jeff furrowed his brow. "Not since you went to the sheriff's station. She didn't come back with you guys?"

"Have you seen Matt?"

"I just got back from swimming. I haven't seen anyone except Gwen. She's in our room. And I think Seth's in his room. This is gonna sound strange, but Gwen told me that she heard Seth crying. Did something happen to him at the sheriff's station?"

"I don't think so," Alex said, yet thinking about his diagnosis.

"Maybe Kristin took a kayak out," Emma said.

"Both kayaks are gone," Jeff said.

"Maybe she went kayaking with Brett."

"I don't think so," Jeff replied. "When I went swimming, one kayak was still docked. When I came back, the other one was gone. Whoever took the kayaks went separately."

"How long were you out swimming?" Alex asked.

"I'm not sure, but it was a long swim, and I stopped on an island to do some core work, so I'd say at least an hour and a half."

Alex shook his head. "This isn't good. There's a storm coming, and we don't know where everyone is." Alex addressed Jeff. "Can you check the upstairs bedrooms? We need to figure out where everyone is."

Jeff nodded. "I'll double check who's downstairs too."

"We'll check the dock," Alex said.

"Where's Buster?" Emma asked.

Alex rubbed his hand over his face. "He must be with Matt or Kristin." *Or with Brett.*

Alex and Emma hiked down to the dock, calling for Buster the dog along the way. The dock was deserted; the kayaks were gone. Alex scanned the lake for signs of life. The water was a bit choppy, the wind occasionally gusting. Dark clouds loomed to the east. *A storm's coming. That's for sure.*

CHAPTER 30

Alex and from Bad to Worse

Alex and Emma scanned the lake for yellow kayaks. Alex turned from the water, his hands on his hips. Matt and Jeff trekked toward the dock from the house. Matt was a few steps behind, no doubt uninterested in talking to Jeff.

The two groups met at the shoreline.

"Where's Kristin?" Emma asked Matt.

"I don't know," Matt replied.

Alex clenched his jaw. "She was supposed to stay inside until we got back."

"She didn't say anything about that to me."

"From bad to worse," Alex said, rubbing his temples.

Emma turned to her husband. "We'll find her."

"Did she say where she was going?" Alex asked Matt.

"No. I was upstairs taking a nap." Matt pointed at the dock. "The kayaks are gone. Maybe she went out with Brett."

Alex rubbed his eyes with his thumb and index finger. "I don't know."

Matt looked around the dock, his eyes focusing on the dog bowl. "Where's Buster?"

"He's missing too," Emma said, the word "missing" hanging in the air, like a stench you can't get rid of.

Everyone was quiet for a moment.

Alex broke the silence and addressed Jeff. "Where's Dad and Cathy and everyone else?"

"My parents went shopping," Jeff replied. "Gwen and Seth are the only ones downstairs. I don't know where Rachel is."

Normally Alex bristled at these divisive comments: *my* parents. Never bad enough to say anything but Alex felt that Jeff and Rachel created an us-versus-them mentality. Jeff and Rachel were part of the *real* family. Alex and Matt were the bastard children from the crazy woman. At this point he didn't give a shit. He simply wanted to find Kristin.

"Maybe Kristin and Rachel went with Harvey and Cathy to the store," Emma said.

"I don't think so," Jeff said. "Gwen said my parents went alone."

Emma exhaled. "So we're missing Kristin, Rachel, and Brett."

Alex glanced up at the sky, his brow furrowed. "I'm gonna take the pontoon out to look for them."

"I'll help," Jeff replied.

CHAPTER 31

Alex and the Confession

Jeff came along on the boat. Emma took Alex's pickup around the neighborhood, searching the roadside along Lakeshore Drive. Matt promised to keep watch at the dock, and Gwen stayed in the house in case someone called or returned. All the bases were covered. Nothing like an emergency to bring a family together.

Alex sped from the dock, the pontoon at full throttle. *Fuck the no-wake zone.* Dark clouds rolled in, and the temperature had dropped. Alex turned right from the inlet into the vast openness of the lake. The wind had picked up, creating small swells, which the pontoon crested, the front end rising into the air and crashing back down in a steady rhythm. Rise, fall, splash. Rise, fall, splash. Rise, fall, splash. Jeff scanned the shorelines and islands in search of the yellow kayaks. He hobbled from the bow toward Alex.

Jeff leaned in and spoke loud enough to overcome the engine noise. "You think Brett might've done something to Kristin and Rachel?"

Alex shrugged. "I don't know. We just need to find them."

"Can you keep something between us?"

Alex nodded. "Yeah, what's up?"

"I'm worried that Rachel's hooking up with Brett."

"Did you see something?" Alex asked.

"No, but I've seen her flirting with him, and we all know she has a problem with men. She finally found a good one with Seth, and I'm worried that she's throwing it all away."

"Let's hope not."

"If we find her, let me talk to her first. Maybe I can talk some sense into her. She won't listen to me with you around. She'll be too embarrassed."

"That's fine with me. You know her better than me."

"Thanks, bro." Jeff patted Alex on the back and hobbled back to the bow and his job as lookout.

After a few minutes, Alex turned the pontoon around. "They must've gone the other way," he shouted, barely audible over the outboard motor.

They passed their inlet and kept going. Shortly thereafter Jeff turned to Alex, pointed, and shouted, "Up ahead!"

Alex guided the pontoon toward a large island, about the size of a soccer field. As they moved closer, Alex saw the two yellow kayaks. They were only a quarter mile from their dock. The kayaks were pulled far up onto the beach and were mostly concealed by trees. Jeff checked for boulders as Alex guided the pontoon toward the beach. Jeff opened the front gate of the pontoon and waited at the very front of the bow, ready to pounce.

The pontoon scraped the sand and came to an abrupt halt. Jeff hopped off the pontoon to the sand, using his good leg to brace most of his fall. He jogged with a little limp to the kayaks. From there, Jeff followed an informal pathway and disappeared into the wooded interior.

Alex exited the pontoon and hustled to the kayaks. He looked in the kayak storage compartments for any sign of Kristin's belongings. Empty. He followed Jeff's tracks toward a narrow trail. Brett appeared from the trail and walked onto the beach.

Alex moved into Brett's personal space.

Brett stepped back.

"Where's Kristin?" Alex asked.

Brett shrugged. "I haven't seen her since she left with you."

"Who's with you?" Alex motioned to the two kayaks.

Brett's face flashed red. "Rachel. We were just checking out the island."

"Bullshit. You're hooking up with her."

"I wasn't. I swear."

Alex stepped closer to Brett. "Did she tell you that she has herpes? You know there's no cure for that."

Brett's eyes were as wide as saucers. "I, uh, I didn't—"

"Cut the bullshit, Brett. How stupid do you think I am? Someone saw you two," Alex lied.

"It's Rachel's fault, not mine. She came on to me."

Alex grabbed Brett by the throat.

Brett's eyes bulged.

"Have you had sex with my daughter?"

"No," Brett choked out.

"If you gave her that shit, I will kill you."

Jeff and Rachel spilled onto the beach. Alex let go of Brett's throat. Brett gasped for air. Rachel's face was puffy, her eyes red.

"You okay?" Alex asked Rachel.

She nodded but didn't make eye contact.

"Have you seen Kristin?"

She looked up at Alex and shook her head.

Alex clenched his jaw. *Where is she?* He narrowed his eyes at Rachel, the wheels turning in his mind. Alex lifted his chin toward Brett. "Did he do something to you?"

"Not really," she replied.

"He did *something* then?"

"Tell Alex what you told me," Jeff said.

Rachel looked at Jeff then Alex. "I was out kayaking, and I saw Brett. He wanted to explore the island. We came on the island, and he was acting, like, really strange."

"Strange, how?" Alex asked.

"Like, jumpy. And he was looking around, like someone was coming to get him. I told him to, like, relax, and that's when he grabbed me."

"That's not true!" Brett said.

Alex glared at Brett. "You put your hands on her?"

Brett showed his palms. "I didn't do anything. I don't know what she's talking about."

Alex turned back to Rachel. "Did he hurt you?"

"No, I'm okay."

"How long were you kayaking?" Alex asked.

"A long time, like two hours."

"When did you see Brett?"

"Like fifteen or twenty minutes ago."

Brett cocked his head.

Big fat raindrops fell sporadically.

Alex stalked to Brett and poked two fingers to his thin chest. "Where's Kristin?"

"I don't know," Brett replied, backing away from Alex.

The rain increased. Cool drops pelted the trees and the lake, creating a splashing static that they had to speak over.

"Kristin's probably back at the house by now," Jeff shouted. "We should go check."

CHAPTER 32

Alex and Torture

Thirty seconds after the sporadic drops turned to heavy rain, they were all soaked from head to toe. The late afternoon sun was nearly blocked by the dark clouds.

They threw the kayaks into the pontoon and shoved off from the island. Jeff sat next to Brett, as a guard, not a friend. Rachel huddled under the canopy, shivering in her bikini.

"I don't know what's going on, but I didn't do anything," Brett said.

"Shut up," Jeff said.

The lake swelled like the sea. Trees on the shoreline and islands swayed in the wind. Even with the boat's headlights, visibility was only two hundred feet or so in front of them. Luckily, they weren't going far.

Alex guided the pontoon to their inlet. Their floating dock and the pontoon rocked from side to side in the choppy water. Matt was waiting for them. He had cleared their chairs from the dock. Jeff and Matt wrestled and tied the pontoon to the dock.

They all hustled up the slope to the house. Brett slipped on the hill. Matt and Jeff yanked him to his feet, and they kept moving. The house was dark and so were the neighbors' houses.

"The power's out," Matt said.

Emma opened the back door for them, and they spilled inside. A few candles flickered in the kitchen and the living room, augmenting what little sunlight was left. Cathy and Gwen handed out towels. Harvey and Seth stood back from the scene. Matt was the last person inside. He shut the door behind them.

"Where is she?" Emma asked, her eyes like saucers.

"She's not here?" Alex asked.

"Oh, my God." Emma put her hand over her mouth.

Alex attacked Brett, punching him in the face. Jeff and Harvey restrained Alex. Brett shrank back, his hand on his split lip.

"Relax, Alex," Harvey said, holding his son.

"What did you do that for?" Brett asked, his eyes wide.

"Where is she?" Alex said to Brett over Harvey's shoulder.

"I don't know. I swear, I don't know."

"Maybe she took Buster for a walk and got caught in the rain," Cathy said. "Maybe she's waiting out the storm at someone's house?"

"That makes sense," Matt said.

Alex walked away from Brett.

"Why else would they both be gone?" Gwen asked.

"One of the neighbors will bring her home," Harvey said.

"We have to find her," Emma said, her voice quivering.

"I need to talk to you, *now*," Seth said to Rachel. They disappeared into the basement, taking a burning candle with them.

The phone rang. Everyone turned to it, dead silent.

Alex rushed to the cordless and picked up. "Hello?" He was surprised the phone worked without power. *Must be a battery in the base.*

"This is Sheriff Franklin. I'm lookin' for Alex Palmer."

"This is Alex."

"Are you alone?"

Alex looked around at the crowd. "No."

"Can you go someplace private?"

"Yeah, is it okay if Emma's in the room?"

"That's fine."

"Hold on." Alex removed the phone from his ear and addressed his family. "The sheriff wants to talk to Emma and me alone." Alex moved into his bedroom and shut the door behind them. "I'm alone with Emma."

"We have a lead," Sheriff Franklin said, "but we can't follow up on it until this storm passes. There's already floodin', so we're gonna have to wait until mornin'."

"Sheriff, we have a—"

"Let me finish. What I'm fixin' to tell you is for your ears only. Got me? I'm only doin' this because I think you oughtta know what I know. This way you can take the necessary precautions to keep everyone safe through the night."

"Okay."

"One of the girls we found on that island was decapitated."

Alex gasped.

Emma mouthed, *Tell him about Kristin.*

Alex nodded to Emma.

The sheriff said, "In all my years in law enforcement, I've never seen nothin' like it. The headless girl had a gold chain and a crucifix around what was left of her neck. We've been investigatin' y'all, as you know. One of my deputies found a picture of what looked like that same crucifix and chain around Brett Taylor's neck. It was on your daughter, Kristin's, Facebook page. From the context and the picture, it looked like a birthday present for Brett—"

"Sheriff, I'm sorry to interrupt, but we have a serious problem—" The phone line died. "Sheriff? Sheriff?" Alex said into the phone, but no answer came.

Alex burst from the room and stalked to Brett who stood near the back door, shirtless with a towel draped over him. Alex pushed him against the door and jacked him up by the throat with both hands. Candlelight flickered across their faces.

"Where is she?" Alex said, spittle flying from his mouth.

"I don't … know," Brett said, barely able to choke out the words.

"What did you do? What did you do to my daughter?" Alex's eyes were glassy.

Alex let go, and Brett dropped like a sack of potatoes, his hands covering his face in anticipation of punches or kicks. Jeff stepped between Brett and Alex.

Brett stood, rubbing his neck. "I didn't do anything. Somebody call the police. He's gonna kill me."

"Where's the gold chain and cross that Kristin gave you?" Alex asked.

Brett cocked his head. "What does that have to do with anything?"

"Answer the fucking question."

"I don't know. I lost it."

"Where?"

"I don't know. I lost it right when we got here."

"Bullshit."

Harvey moved in front of Alex. "You can't keep beating on the boy. You'll end up in prison."

"He did something to Kristin," Alex replied. "I know it."

"How do you know?" Harvey asked.

Alex clenched his jaw. "Sheriff Franklin told me that they found his gold chain and cross on one of the dead bodies on that island."

There was a collective gasp.

"What do we do?" Emma's face was blotchy and tear-streaked.

"We go find her." Alex grabbed his wife by her upper arms. "We're gonna find her." He turned to the group. "The police won't be here until morning. We need to lock Brett up until then."

Brett's eyebrows arched; his face was taut. "What do you mean, *lock me up?*"

"We can put him in my room," Jeff said, ignoring Brett's question. "It doesn't have any windows. Gwen and I just need to clear out our stuff."

Alex nodded. "That's good. Why don't you guys get your stuff. You guys can take Brett's room upstairs."

Jeff stroked his chin. "We should search his room first."

"You're right. You and Dad hold him here. Matt and I will search his room."

Brett raised both hands, palms up. "Now you're going through my stuff?"

Alex pointed at Brett. "Shut up."

Jeff looked at his wife. "Gwen, can you move our stuff into the hall upstairs?"

"Yes," Gwen replied.

"I'll help her," Cathy said.

Alex looked around at the group. "If you wanna help find Kristin, get your rain gear on." Alex glared at Brett. "If we don't find her, you're gonna talk. If I have to cut off every one of your fucking fingers, I'll do it."

Brett balled his fingers into fists, unconsciously protecting his digits.

Alex and Matt went upstairs to Brett's room, armed with flashlights. Matt searched drawers, under the bed, between the mattress and box spring, in the closet. Nothing. Alex went through Brett's backpack and suitcase. The backpack was mostly empty, just a few pens and a damp beach towel. Alex took everything out of Brett's suitcase. He checked pockets of jeans and shorts and of the suitcase itself. Nothing out of the ordinary.

Matt had moved on to Brett's phone. "I should go down and get the password from him."

"Good idea." Alex shoved Brett's clothes back in the suitcase, zipped it, and turned it upright. There was a little metallic jangle. "Did you hear that?"

"Sounded like metal," Matt replied.

Alex shook the suitcase, recreating the jangle. His eyes widened. He opened the suitcase and dumped out the contents. He shook the suitcase again. The jangle was louder without the clothes buffering the noise. Alex set the suitcase down, the lid open. "Gimme a light."

Matt shone his flashlight inside the suitcase.

Alex ran his hand over the liner. "There's something in here." He felt the edges, finding a slit in the liner. He grabbed the slit and ripped it open. Kristin's gold chain with the crucifix and Buster's tag glistened in the flashlight. "Motherfucker." Alex ran downstairs. Brett sat on the floor in the living room, a towel draped over his shoulders. Jeff and Harvey stood over him.

"Get that piece of shit up," Alex said to Jeff and Harvey.

They hoisted him by his armpits. Matt joined the party. Emma emerged from her bedroom.

"He has Kristin's cross and Buster's collar hidden in his suitcase," Alex said to the group.

Like a lynch mob, everyone moved closer to Brett with furrowed brows and narrowed eyes.

"Why would I have that stuff?" Brett asked, holding out his hands, looking around for a friendly face.

Alex glared at Brett. "Where is she?"

"I *don't* know."

Emma stepped forward and smacked him across the face. Alex restrained his wife, who sobbed in his arms.

Matt grabbed Brett by the back of his neck. "You're gonna talk."

"Emma, go back in the room," Alex said while glaring at Brett. "Go."

Emma went back in the bedroom and shut the door.

Alex went to the kitchen and grabbed the knife set from the counter. He set down the wooden block filled with knives on the kitchen table and pulled out a chair. "Put him here."

Matt gave Alex a look as if to say, *Are you really gonna do this?*

"I said, 'Put him here.'"

Jeff forced Brett into the chair, while Harvey and Matt looked on. Brett's eyes were wide and bloodshot.

"I'm done fucking around with you," Alex said. "You're gonna tell me what I wanna know." Alex looked at Jeff. "Put his hand on the table and hold it there."

Brett struggled, but Jeff controlled him, using strength, weight, and leverage to hold Brett's butt in that chair and his arm in place. Matt stood at the edge of the kitchen, neither in nor out.

"Alex, don't do it," Harvey said. "We'll find her."

"Stay out of it, Dad," Alex replied.

Alex removed a steak knife from the wooden block and set it on the table. "Much too small." Alex removed a long skinny serrated blade. "This is like one of those blades that'll cut through a soda can."

Brett shook, trying to retract his hand, but he was held under control by a larger, stronger man.

Alex removed the chef's knife. "This is bigger." Alex held up the knife, then chopped down on the wooden table, denting the surface. "Almost but not quite." Alex removed the massive square meat cleaver. "Now we're talking. This'll take his hand off at the wrist." Alex held the knife up to Brett's face. "You got something to say now?"

"P-p-please, please don't," Brett said, stammering. "I-I swear to God, if I knew anything, I'd tell you. She's probably lost in the woods or something."

"Alex, let the police handle it," Harvey said.

"The police are busy at the moment," Alex replied, returning his attention to Brett. "Is she in the woods?"

"I don't know," Brett replied. "I was just saying."

"Not good enough." Alex looked at Jeff. "Hold that arm still."

Jeff clamped down on Brett's arm, his eyes dancing in the candle-light. He used his weight to hold Brett's body still.

Alex raised the cleaver and dropped it with the force of a guillotine.

Brett screamed and wet his shorts, urine streaming down his leg. The cleaver stuck in the table half an inch away from Brett's fingertips, his parts still intact.

Alex stepped back from the table, his fists clenched. He turned to Jeff. "Put him in your room. Can you and Dad keep an eye on him?"

"Of course," Jeff replied, yanking Brett to his feet.

"Should we check his phone?" Matt asked Alex, holding it up.

Alex turned to Brett who was shaking like a leaf. "What's your password?"

Brett lifted his gaze, his face tear-streaked. "UT soccer."

Matt thumb-typed the password into Brett's phone. "I'm in."

Jeff and Harvey escorted Brett to his old basement bedroom.

Matt searched Brett's phone. "Nothing's on here since we've been at the lake."

Alex frowned. "I guess that makes sense. No cell service here." Alex looked at Matt. "Let's go find her."

Seth appeared from the basement steps. He hurried toward the front door, rolling his suitcase.

"Seth, where are you going?" Alex asked.

"Home," Seth called out, without turning.

"There's flooding."

Seth responded by slamming the front door behind him.

CHAPTER 33

Alex and Chaos

Alex and Matt chased after Seth. They stood on the covered front porch as Seth started his lifted Jeep.

Alex waved his arms at Seth but was ignored.

Seth turned the Jeep around so he faced the steep rain-soaked driveway. The water cut minirivers in the gravel driveway, exposing the orange clay underneath. Seth paused at the base of the drive-way, no doubt considering the slippery ascent, his getaway, and his philandering fiancée. Yet his Jeep was made for these conditions. With four-wheel drive, a wide base, large knobby tires, and a snorkel snaking upward from the exhaust pipe, the vehicle could handle the mud and the flood.

Seth gunned the engine, the lifted Jeep spitting gravel and digging muddy ruts all the way up the driveway. The only four-by-four vehicle was gone in a cuckolded fit of anger.

"He just fucked up the driveway," Matt said, shaking his head. "I don't know if we can get a car up that hill now."

Alex ran his hand over his face. "We gotta find her—now."

They returned to the kitchen. Emma was already in her raincoat, raring to go.

"We need flashlights," Matt said.

Emma, Matt, and Alex searched drawers, rooms, and vehicles for flashlights. They placed the five flashlights upright on the kitchen table. Gwen entered the kitchen, wearing her raincoat. Cathy was right behind her in shorts and a T-shirt.

"Brett's locked up in our old room," Gwen said. "Jeff and Harvey are keeping watch."

Alex nodded. "Where's Rachel?"

"She's locked in her room. I asked her if she was going to help." Gwen winced. "But she didn't answer me."

"What's the plan?" Matt asked Alex.

"You and I will search on the lake with the pontoon," Alex said. "Emma, you and Gwen can take my truck through the neighborhood and talk to the neighbors."

Emma nodded, her face blotchy.

"Maybe she's at one of the neighbors' houses, like Cathy said."

"What do you need me to do?" Cathy asked.

"Do you have rain gear?"

"No, but I can wear a trash bag."

"Can you stay here and wait for Kristin, and answer the phone whenever it rings?" Alex asked.

Cathy nodded. "I'll do that."

"Let's get going. The longer we wait …"

Nobody wanted Alex to finish that sentence.

"You should probably drive your truck up the driveway for Emma and Gwen," Matt said. "You know that vehicle better than anyone."

"You're right," Alex replied.

Alex, Matt, Emma, and Gwen climbed into the rain-beaten pickup. Water gushed down the ruts created by Seth's Jeep. Matt and Gwen sat on the bench seat of the extended cab.

"What happened to the driveway?" Emma asked from the front passenger seat.

"Seth did that when he left," Matt replied.

Alex turned around his Ford F-150. He glanced at Emma, then punched the accelerator. The truck fishtailed and lurched forward.

The rear-wheel-drive vehicle stalled halfway up the hill, the rear wheels spitting mud on the rear quarter panels. Alex took his foot off the accelerator and put his foot on the brake. He rode the brake as he guided the truck backward down the hill.

"I'm gonna try again," Alex said.

The second try was slightly worse than the first. Alex parked his truck and slammed his palms against the steering wheel. "Shit!"

"We can walk," Emma said, stepping from the truck.

Alex exited the truck, running to his wife, Emma already hiking up the driveway, her flashlight on. Alex grabbed her by the wrist, and she whirled toward him. Her face was wet from the rain. If not for her puffy eyes, he wouldn't have known she was crying.

"Be careful," Alex said and hugged Emma. "We'll find her."

Emma nodded. Gwen and Emma trekked up the driveway, sticking to the edges and away from the ruts.

Alex and Matt hustled down to the dock and the pontoon, wearing raincoats, board shorts, and water shoes. They both slipped on the way down but were uninjured.

The dock and the pontoon rocked and pitched in the rough waters. Matt untied the pontoon and jumped on the boat. Alex started the engine, turned on the headlights, and steered the craft from their inlet. It was futile, visibility down to one hundred feet or so. Alex stood behind the helm, driving the pontoon into the oblivion. Matt searched from the bow, his eyes straining against the blackness. Rain and lake water came from every angle. Alex couldn't distinguish between the two.

CHAPTER 34

Alex and the Getaway

Alex glanced at the fuel gauge. It was near E. *Maybe Emma and Gwen found her at one of the neighbors' houses.* Alex checked his watch—*12:36.* They'd been out nearly three hours. He turned the pontoon around.

Twenty minutes later they found their inlet, which was no small feat. Matt struggled to tie the pontoon to the rocking dock, wrenching his shoulder in the process. With the pontoon secure, they hustled up the slope to the lake house, hopeful that Kristin was home. Inside, the house was dead silent.

"Where the hell is everybody?" Alex asked.

"I don't know," Matt replied.

Alex and Matt clomped down the basement steps, dripping rain-water on the floor. Jeff leaned back in his chair, sleeping, the cordless phone in his lap. Brett's door was wide open.

"Where is he?" Alex shouted.

Jeff jerked awake. He shot out of his chair, the cordless phone falling to the carpet. He looked at the open door in front of him. "Shit. Shit. I must've dozed off. I'm sorry, man." Jeff picked up the phone.

They searched the room with flashlights—checked the closet and under the bed to be certain.

"He's gone," Matt said.

"Where's Dad and Cathy?"

Jeff winced. "I told them to go to sleep. Shit, man, I didn't think I was tired. I'm really sorry. I think the phone's still out." Jeff held up the phone.

"I'll take that," Alex said, grabbing the cordless. He turned on the phone but heard no dial tone. Alex hung his head and rubbed his temples. "Shit."

They went back upstairs, and Alex reset the phone on the charger. A faint motor sound came from the driveway. It was barely audible amid the rain. Alex looked at Matt.

"Is that a car?" Matt asked.

The three men sprinted out the front door. Jeff lagged a little, still with a limp. Brett was in Kristin's Ford Fiesta. He spun the front drive wheel, stuck one-third of the way up the hill. The rain was heavy, the driveway a messy mixture of muddy ruts and gravel. The compact car slid, the single still-spinning front wheel moving the car sideways.

"He's not going anywhere," Jeff shouted over the rain.

Brett gunned the engine in desperation, only making the situation worse. The car had now turned around 180 degrees, the nose facing toward the house. The three men approached the car cautiously, Alex and Matt shining their flashlights. Brett exited the car and ran up the hill. Simultaneously, the compact car rolled toward them in Neutral. The brothers dove to the side to avoid the 2,500 pounds of unmanned metal.

The car zipped past them, headed for the line of cars parked in front of the house. Alex, still on the ground, watched as the little Ford-turned-runaway-projectile plowed into Harvey's BMW M5, smashing the front ends of both cars. The air bags deployed in the Ford. Harvey always backed into his parking spots, like readying to make a quick exit. Maybe he thought he was better than all those lazy front-first parkers. Unfortunately, the expensive stuff was in the front end of the M5.

Alex turned from the wreckage to see Brett disappear at the crest of the driveway. Jeff, closest to the crash site, approached the mangled cars—apparently handling that crisis—so Alex sprinted up the hill after Brett. Matt was right behind Alex. They slipped and clawed up the driveway, spilling onto Lakeshore Drive. They scanned the woods across the street. In the distance was a flash of white. Brett wasn't dressed for the occasion in his white T-shirt and board shorts.

Alex and Matt hustled after him. As they moved deeper into the woods, they lost sight of him. He was too fast. They abandoned their search and returned to the house.

Jeff surveyed the damage of the driverless car collision. He had turned off the Ford. As they approached Jeff, the crash, and the lake house, they heard another motor. This one was louder and coming from the lake.

"It sounds like a Jet Ski," Alex said.

"He must've doubled back," Matt replied.

Alex and Matt ran to the backyard and down the slope to the dock. Jeff galloped after them, still with a hitch in his gait. The Jet Ski engine noise quieted and silenced completely as the watercraft moved farther away.

Alex pointed across the inlet at an empty dock. "That Jet Ski's gone. The one that always had the keys in the ignition."

"I think he went to the right," Matt said.

"Let's get this piece of shit," Alex replied and boarded the pontoon.

CHAPTER 35

Alex and the Arrest

The dock and the pontoon rocked in the rough water. Jeff boarded, his legs kept wide to maintain his balance. Matt untied the boat and hopped aboard. Alex flicked on the headlights and gunned the engine, steering to the right once they cleared the inlet. Alex glanced at the controls, frowning.

Jeff approached. "What's wrong?"

Alex tapped on the fuel gauge. "We're running low on fuel."

Jeff moved toward the bow to look for Brett along with Matt. The sky was black, not a single star evident. The storm still raged, rain pelting their faces as they plowed through the rough water. Alex wondered if they'd even be able to see Brett. Even with the headlights, they couldn't see more than one hundred feet in front of them.

They sped along for the next ten minutes or so.

Matt pointed and shouted something inaudible. He turned back to Alex and pushed his open hands down, signaling Alex to slow his speed. Alex throttled down the pontoon. Something white floated up ahead. The Jet Ski.

As they approached the abandoned Jet Ski, Alex thought, *Out of gas? Maybe the engine's flooded.*

They scanned the lake and the shoreline for Brett.

Matt pointed to his right at a bobbing bit of white in the water about eighty feet away. "He's swimming for shore!"

Brett's head bobbed in the whitecaps, as he struggled to swim to safety. Alex gunned the pontoon toward Brett. As they closed in, Matt dove off the side and swam after Brett.

"I'll get a life preserver," Jeff said.

Matt grasped the teen around the neck. Brett took a massive gulp of lake water. He coughed and hacked, the will to fight—or rather the will to flight—gone. Jeff threw a life preserver. Matt put it on Brett and hauled him back to the boat.

Matt and Jeff shoved Brett on the bench seat at the bow of the pontoon. Brett coughed and shivered. Jeff and Alex and Matt stood over him.

Brett looked up at the angry men, his eyes red. "I didn't do anything. I swear to God. I swear to God." Brett hung his head and began to sob.

Alex grabbed him by the hair and forced his gaze upward. "You're gonna tell me where she is. If you don't, so help me God, I will kill you." Alex let go, and Brett's head hung again.

Alex turned the pontoon around and headed back to the lake house. Jeff and Matt sat on either side of Brett, guarding their prize catch.

Matt stood and walked wide-legged to Alex and the helm. "How we doing on fuel?" Matt asked.

"Not good," Alex replied, glancing at the fuel gauge in the red.

"How are *you* doing?"

"Not good either."

Matt patted his brother on the back. "We'll find her."

At the bow, Brett held out his palms to Jeff.

"It looks like Brett's still pleading his case," Matt said. "I should get back over there."

Alex nodded.

Matt moved away from Alex toward the bow. They hit a large swell, the pontoon rocked and dipped and took on water. Matt fell to one knee. Brett punched Jeff in the face with a right cross. Jeff pitched to the side, away from their captive. Brett stood, hopped over the small front gate, and dove off the front of the pontoon.

A *thump-thump* and a hiccup came from the outboard motor, then the motor resumed its normal operation. Alex had a sinking feeling in his stomach as he cut the engine. Jeff and Matt joined him at the helm.

"I felt something. And the motor hesitated," Alex said with a pained expression.

Matt winced. "Shit, we might've hit him."

They gathered at the stern, shining flashlights into the water, looking for Brett.

"I don't see anything," Jeff said.

"I think I should turn the boat around and look," Alex said.

Matt nodded in agreement.

Alex started the pontoon and turned the boat 180 degrees. The pontoon crawled at low speed. It didn't take long to spot Brett's white shirt. He was facedown in the water, the rain pummeling him without mercy. Matt dove off the side, swam toward Brett, and turned him over. Matt recoiled, startled by the gashes and massive crevices where Brett's face should've been. Brett's mouth hung limp from one side of his jaw. He looked like a stroke patient with a gaping mouth hole the size of a softball. His nose was gone, replaced by a deep red gash. One eye was perfectly intact, staring back at them, the other pried out by the propeller. His forehead was gouged, and brain matter leaked into the water.

"Check his pulse," Alex called out from the boat.

Matt's eyes widened. He reached out with two shaky fingers and pressed against Brett's neck, over the carotid artery. Matt looked at Alex and shook his head.

CHAPTER 36

Alex and the Watcher

The ride back to the dock was a depressing affair. They were concerned that they'd run out of fuel before making it back. Nobody wanted to be trapped on the pontoon in a storm with a dead body. Thankfully they had enough juice to make the return trip.

Alex and Matt and Jeff trudged up the hill, soaked and shivering and somber. Brett and his hideous face were left in the bow of the pontoon, wrapped in a tarp. Alex glanced at his watch. It was after 2:00 a.m. Candlelight flickered in an upstairs window of the house next door—the peeping old man. *I hope you're enjoying the show, you piece of shit.* They entered the back door. The living room and kitchen were still illuminated by candlelight.

The guys removed their raincoats. Matt was soaked to the bone, his teeth chattering. Alex went to the laundry and grabbed three dry towels. He returned and handed two of them to his brothers. The front door opened and closed.

"Alex?" Emma called out.

"We're in the kitchen."

Emma and Gwen trudged into the kitchen, rainwater dripping from their coats. They both looked worn out and cried out—especially Emma. Her fair skin showed her emotions like a mood ring.

"Kristin's car is crashed into Harvey's," Gwen said.

"We know," Jeff said. "Brett tried to get away in Kristin's car. He couldn't get up the driveway, so, when he bailed from the car, it came back down the hill and smashed into Dad's car."

"Jesus."

"Y'all didn't find her, did you?" Emma asked.

Matt went to the laundry room.

Alex shook his head. "No. Did you see *any* sign of her?"

"No." A tear slipped from Emma's red-rimmed eyelids.

Matt returned from the laundry with two towels for Emma and Gwen.

"Thank you," Gwen said to Matt as she took the towel.

Emma dabbed her eyes with her beach towel.

"We thought maybe Kristin was in the accident," Gwen said.

"Just Brett," Jeff replied.

"Where is he now?" Emma asked.

Matt dipped his head as if embarrassed.

"Dead," Alex said.

Gwen gasped.

Emma put her hand to her chest. "Alex?"

"I didn't kill him," Alex replied. "He jumped off the boat and got caught up in the propeller."

"My God."

Alex walked over to the cordless phone. He tried the phone, but there was no dial tone. He slammed the phone back on the receiver. "Damn it. We need to get the police out here to help us search."

"I don't think they can get here with the flooding," Gwen said. "Lakeshore's closed off less than a mile from here."

"Did any of the neighbors have a working phone?" Alex asked.

"No."

"Maybe we should talk to the old guy next door," Matt said, a towel around his shoulders like a cape. "He's always watching. Maybe he saw something."

Alex looked at Emma and Gwen. "Did you guys talk to him?"

"He didn't answer the door," Gwen said.

"I saw a candle flickering in his window," Alex said. "He must be home."

"We have to go back out," Emma said, her voice quivering. "We can't leave her out there."

"We will," Alex replied, moving to Emma and wrapping her up in his arms. "We'll find her. I promise." Alex absorbed her trembling and muted sobs.

Emma pushed Alex away and wiped her face with her towel. "We have to go, *now*."

"We should talk to the guy next door first," Matt said. "Maybe he can point us in the right direction."

Emma glared at Matt. "I'm not just gonna sit here and do nothing."

Matt didn't respond.

"Matt's right," Alex said to Emma. "We won't be long. In the meantime, get everyone organized. Raincoats, flashlights, batteries, and anything else you can think of."

Emma nodded. "Hurry."

"We should take some food and water with us," Jeff said. "Especially if we're gonna be out for a long time."

"We're on it," Gwen said.

Alex and Matt ran next door. They stood under the front porch, and Alex pounded on the door. After a few moments with no response, Alex pounded louder. The door opened, and a shadowy figure shone a flashlight in their faces. Alex and Matt used their hands to shield their eyes.

"What the hell's all the racket about?" the figure said.

"We're sorry to bother you at this hour, but it's an emergency," Matt said.

The figure lowered the flashlight, his face now visible—an old man with narrowed eyes, a puckered face, and a white mustache stretched across his lip.

"My daughter's missing," Alex said. "I need to ask you a few questions."

"I don't know nothin' about your daughter," the old man replied.

"I've seen you watching us. Maybe you know something. Please, sir. My daughter's out in this storm all by herself."

The old man exhaled and stepped aside. "All right, come in."

Alex and Matt followed the old man into the living room. A candle sputtered on the coffee table. The old man set his flashlight, beam up, next to the candle. The room looked like a cheap lodge and smelled like a smoker's lounge. The walls were 1970s' wood paneling, the carpet a brownish shag. A massive rear-projection television faced a dingy couch and a recliner. Twenty years ago, the TV must've been cutting edge. Now it probably cost more to dispose of than the old man could sell it for.

"I'm Matt, by the way, and this is my brother Alex." Matt motioned to Alex.

"Name's Hank Marshall."

They shook hands.

"You said your daughter was missin'?" Hank wore stained burgundy sweats.

"Yes." Alex removed his cell phone from his jacket pocket and pressed the button on the side, waking up the screen. His phone still had battery life despite not being charged for nearly two days. Without cell service, it had been mostly used as a camera. "I have a picture." Alex showed a snapshot of Kristin on his phone to Hank.

Hank squinted at Kristin's smiling face. "I saw her yesterday at your dock."

"What do you mean by *yesterday*?" Alex asked. "Technically it's Sunday now, so did you see her on Friday or Saturday?"

Hank frowned. "I know what dang day it is. I saw her on Saturday before all them cops came."

"What was she doing?"

"Swimmin' and floatin' by your dock. Your kin was there. An old man with big muscles. A middle-aged lady. A few more people."

"Did you see her after that?"

"I saw all of you when the cops showed up at your dock. At least I think it was all of you."

"Did you see her after the cops left?"

"Nope."

Alex fiddled with his phone and pulled up a picture of Kristin with Brett. Alex showed the photo to Hank. "Have you seen this guy?"

"I saw him on Saturday too."

"Before or after the cops showed up?" Alex asked.

"Both," Hank replied.

"What was he doing?"

"Which time?"

"Either, both," Alex replied.

"I saw him go off in a kayak before the cops showed up."

"Who was he with?"

"He was by himself," Hank replied. "He came back when the cops showed up. Y'all were there."

"Did you see him after that?"

Hank clenched his jaw. "Yeah. I saw him after the cops left."

"What was he doing?"

Hank grunted. "I saw him fornicatin' in the water."

Alex and Matt looked at each other.

"Who was he with?" Alex asked.

"Not your girl. Some woman. Looked young but older than that boy."

Alex showed Hank a picture of Rachel. "Her?"

"Yeah, that looks like her."

"What did they do after they were done … messing around?"

"They went on them kayaks."

Alex and Matt glanced at each other again.

"So, they went out on the kayaks together?" Alex asked.

"That's what I said," Hank replied.

"Did you see anything after they left?" Matt asked.

"Nope," Hank replied.

"Why have you been watching us?" Alex asked, his hands on his hips.

"I been watchin' because y'all need watchin'. You people come here and make my life a livin' hell. I got dogs shittin' on my property. I've had people drinkin' and fornicatin' on my property. I used to have a canoe, but it got too damn heavy for me, so I gotta kayak, and then some fool stole it. You people ain't got no respect."

Alex glowered at the man. "Did you do something to my dog?"

The old man raised one side of his mouth in contempt. "Why the hell would I bother? I got rentals on both sides of me and across the street. Two days from now some other yappy mutt'll be shittin' in my yard."

Alex ran his hand over his face and turned to Matt. "We need to get going."

"If you see anything, let us know," Matt said to Hank.

"I'm goin' to bed, so I ain't gonna see nothin'."

Matt frowned. "When you wake up, whatever."

"Let's go," Alex said.

Hank slammed the door behind them.

Standing on Hank's covered porch, Matt said, "I need to talk to you in private before we go back to the house."

"Let's talk in my truck," Alex said.

Alex and Matt ran back toward the lake house, the rain pelting their coats as they dashed for Alex's truck.

Inside the truck, Matt said, "You heard what the old guy said. Brett and Rachel were together when they went kayaking. If that's true, Rachel and Jeff lied."

"But Jeff didn't say that Brett and Rachel went out together, only that one kayak was there when he went swimming, and it was gone when he came back."

"Which would be a lie if Brett and Rachel went kayaking together. Nobody else took the kayaks. And Rachel did say that she went out by herself and saw Brett later."

"You really think that old man can make a positive ID from his window?" Alex asked. "Rachel and Kristin don't look that different."

"I don't know, but he can tell if someone's alone or not. Jeff and Rachel said that Rachel went kayaking by herself. But, if Brett was with Rachel the whole time, he would've never even seen Kristin."

"Unless he and Rachel did see her. Let's think this through. The second time we went to the police station for questioning, Brett, Rachel, Jeff, Harvey, Gwen, and Cathy stayed here."

"While we were at the police station, Rachel and Brett hooked up?" Matt asked.

"I think so," Alex said. "Then Sheriff Franklin interviewed Kristin first, and she wanted to go home."

"She came home with me, and I took a nap. She didn't tell me what she was gonna do, but I think she'd probably go find Brett."

"Kristin *would* go find Brett. I agree." Alex rubbed his throbbing temples for a moment. "I should've known she wouldn't stay inside. I should've known. So *stupid*."

"Don't do that. Don't start blaming yourself. We have to focus."

"You're right." Alex nodded. "Maybe she came home and saw Brett and Rachel together?"

"Or maybe Seth came home and saw them together? Didn't he leave the sheriff's station right after Kristin and me?"

"Yeah." Alex hung his head and smacked the steering wheel. "Maybe things got out of hand."

"Maybe."

Alex looked up, his eyes glassy. "I think Brett may have killed Kristin."

"We don't know that."

Alex stared into the rain, into the blackness surrounding them.

"But how do Rachel and Jeff fit into the lie?" Matt asked.

"Maybe the old man's mistaken on the details. Eyewitnesses are notoriously unreliable."

"Maybe Jeff and Rachel know more than they're letting on," Matt said. "Don't you think it's odd that both times Brett escaped, it was Jeff's fault? Maybe he let him escape on purpose."

"First of all, Brett punched him in the face—"

"It was a pretty weak punch."

"What possible reason could Jeff have to let Brett go?" Alex asked.

"The same reason he'd lie," Matt replied, serious as a heart attack.

"You think he had something to do with …"

"Yes."

Alex shook his head. "I need you to be objective. All evidence points to Brett. I can't have you projecting because you hate Jeff."

Matt's face was darkened by his damp beard. "Jeff and Rachel said one thing, and the old guy said something different. We should at least ask them about it."

Alex nodded.

CHAPTER 37

Alex and the Accusation

Alex and Matt entered the front door and marched to the kitchen. The wind whistled against the house and blew the rain sideways, pelting the windows. Emma, Jeff, and Gwen were already in their rain gear, loitering in the kitchen. Cathy and Harvey were awake but still in their pajamas. The flashlights were lined up on the kitchen table, along with granola bars and bottles of water.

Alex and Matt made a beeline for Jeff.

"It's just a car, Dad," Jeff said to Harvey.

"That's easy for you to say," Harvey replied. "That little bastard didn't wreck your car."

"Where's Rachel?" Alex asked, interjecting himself into their conversation.

"I think she's sleeping," Jeff replied, stuffing his raincoat pocket with granola bars.

"Wake her up. We need to talk to her," Matt said.

Jeff glared at Matt and ignored his command.

"We need to talk to you two, *now*," Alex said.

"About what?" Jeff asked.

"About something the neighbor told us."

"What did he say?" Emma asked, joining the conversation.

"I'll tell you later," Alex replied over his shoulder.

156

"We're wasting time," Jeff said.

"Jeff's right. We're wasting time," Harvey said, moving between Alex and Jeff.

"We need to go," Emma said, her hand clenched around Alex's wrist.

"Just give me a minute, Jesus. This is important," Alex said.

Emma let go of his wrist.

"All right," Jeff replied. "I'll talk to you, but not Matt."

Matt glared at Jeff.

Alex and Jeff went to the basement and woke up Rachel. They went into Brett's former jail cell and shut the door. Alex set a candle on the dresser. The room was trashed—clothes everywhere and drawers open. Rachel tiptoed around the mess, her brow furrowed.

"What's this about?" Jeff said, crossing his arms over his chest.

Alex took a deep breath and looked at Rachel. "The guy next door said he saw you and Brett leave together in the kayaks yesterday."

"So?" Rachel replied, shrugging.

"So, you said you went kayaking alone, and Jeff said that he saw one kayak gone when he went swimming, then both gone when he came back."

"So what?" Rachel had her hands on her hips. "Maybe the old man's, like, senile."

Jeff narrowed his eyes at Rachel for a split second. She was dry as a bone in her pink pajama pants and tight T-shirt. She was petite, her face girlish in the dim light.

"Maybe he has the day mixed up," Jeff said.

"Or you two are mixed up," Alex replied.

Rachel glowered at Alex.

Jeff exhaled and shook his head. "This is bullshit, Alex. If you have something to say, say it."

Alex rubbed the back of his neck. "If the old man's telling the truth, then Brett probably didn't even see Kristin, much less do something to her."

"That's certainly possible," Jeff said.

"I agree. But why did y'all lie?"

"We didn't lie," Rachel said, her voice shrill.

"Just tell the fucking truth," Alex said, pointing at Rachel. "Kristin's out there, right now."

"You need to, like, get your finger outta my face."

Jeff hung his head and pinched the bridge of his nose. After a moment, he looked at Alex, his eyes glassy. "I've been holding this in, because we need to focus on finding Kristin, but now this is getting in the way, so I'm gonna be straight with you. I don't appreciate you calling me and Rachel liars, and I don't appreciate being treated like an outsider. I've always looked up to you and Matt as older brothers. I've never once thought of us as half brothers, but you trust Matt implicitly, and you think we're liars. Matt was the last person to see Kristin, but nobody's questioning him."

"That's right. Matt saw her last," Rachel said.

Alex said, "Look. I'm not—"

"Let me finish," Jeff said. "I don't know why that old man said what he said. He's either lying or he's mistaken. I don't really care which one, and neither should you. I don't know if Brett did something to Kristin or not. Maybe Danny Stafford did something, or maybe the old man did. I think it's more likely that she's alive but lost somewhere, and we need to get our asses outside and find her. Can we do that?"

Alex nodded. "I'm sorry, bro. Sorry, Rachel."

"Let's go get her."

Alex opened the door, and Gwen stood, blushing, caught in the act of eavesdropping.

"I came down to tell you that the phone's working," Gwen said to Alex.

CHAPTER 38

Alex and the Search

"Unfortunately, the first boat probably won't arrive for at least two hours," the 9-1-1 operator said.

"Please hurry," Alex said into the cordless phone. "Every minute she's out there ..."

"I understand, sir. We're inundated with emergencies. We'll be there as soon as we can."

"The sooner, the better."

"Of course."

Alex slammed the cordless back on the receiver. "Jesus Christ."

His family stared at him from the kitchen, waiting for an ETA on the police.

"They won't be here for at least two hours," Alex said.

"I'm not waiting that long," Emma said.

"Me neither." Alex marched from the living room to the kitchen.

Emma, Matt, Jeff, and Gwen were dressed in rain gear and ready to go. Jeff shoved a bottled water into his pocket. Matt checked his flashlight. Rachel, Cathy, and Harvey were still in pajamas.

"I can stay here and wait for the police," Rachel said.

"That's fine. We need at least one person to stay here," Alex replied.

"I don't have a raincoat," Cathy said.

"You can wear mine," Alex said.

"I couldn't do that. What are you gonna wear?"

"I'll be fine."

Cathy winced. "I'm worried that my old knees might slow you down. I think I need surgery."

"Why don't you stay with Rachel?" Alex said.

"Oh, I couldn't," Cathy said. "You need all the help you can get. I just don't wanna hold you up."

Emma pursed her lips, her eyes narrowed at Cathy.

"I'm just not gonna worry about the pain. Kristin's more important," Cathy said.

"If you're coming, get dressed, because we're leaving now," Alex said.

Cathy's eyes widened. "I need some time to get ready. Maybe it's better if I stay. I really don't wanna hold you up."

"Dad?" Alex turned to Harvey.

"I'll search down by the dock," Harvey replied.

Alex, Emma, Jeff, Gwen, and Matt grabbed their supplies. They decided to concentrate their efforts on the woods, mainly because Brett had mentioned the woods during his interrogation. When pressed, Brett had said, it was just a suggestion, but maybe there was more to it. Either way it was all they had to go on. Besides, searching the lake was no longer an option with the pontoon on *E*.

"We need a strategy for the search," Matt said, holding a compass in his hand. "Just running around the woods isn't efficient."

"What do you have in mind?" Alex asked.

"If we spread out in a line—like maybe twenty yards between each of us—we could cover a hundred yards in width." Matt held up his compass. "If we follow a compass bearing out, then, when we turn around and come back, we just have to move over a hundred yards, so we're not covering the same ground twice. Basically, we're searching by grid."

"How far should we go?" Emma asked.

Matt shrugged. "I don't know."

"I think chances are higher that she's not that far from here," Alex said. "Let's take a course for thirty minutes, then come back, and do it again."

"We can probably walk a mile and a half in thirty minutes," Matt said, "so, in two hours, we can cover an area 400 yards wide by a mile and a half long. That's a big area."

They trudged up the muddy driveway, across Lakeshore Drive, and into the woods. The wind whistled through the trees near the edge, but, deeper in the forest, the wind was nonexistent. The rain continued, but the forest canopy sheltered them somewhat. Matt and Jeff humped extra supplies in their backpacks. The five of them walked through the forest, evenly spaced, calling out for Kristin, flashlights searching the blackness. Matt was in the middle position, keeping the line on the right compass bearing.

After thirty minutes of fruitless searching, Alex turned them around. They covered a different hundred-yard swath of ground on the way back. They took turns shouting for Kristin, their voices hoarse. They made it back to Lakeshore Drive and still no sign of Kristin. They trekked back into the black, covering another hundred-yard swath of forest. Still nothing.

On the way back, only a mile or so from the lake house, Matt stopped and shouted, "I think I found something."

Alex and Emma hustled toward Matt, and so did everyone else. Matt shone his flashlight on the ground. Leaves lightly covered a mound the size of a grave. The rain peppered the leaves and branches overhead.

"No," Emma said, her hand over her mouth.

"It can't be," Alex said to Emma.

Matt removed his backpack and set it on the ground. A wooden handle stuck out of the top of his bag. He opened it and removed a short-handled shovel. Alex and Emma looked at the rusty shovel with wide eyes.

Why would he pack a shovel?

"It's probably nothing," Matt said. "I can check to make sure."

Alex nodded to his brother.

Matt made quick work of the loose soil, despite his careful digging. He pressed the shovel into the earth tentatively with his foot, then tossed the loose soil to the side. After around thirty shovelfuls of soil, a flash of white was unearthed. A single hand reached from the grave, small and bluish white, no nail polish.

Emma knew that hand instantly by the faded scar across the top where her daughter's hand had been slammed in her friend's hatchback. Emma collapsed, curling into herself and weeping. "No, no, no."

Matt stepped back in a daze, shocked at what he'd uncovered.

Alex rushed to one end of the grave, fell to his knees, and dug like a dog, both of his hands removing the loose mud. Gwen knelt in the mud next to Emma. She held on to Gwen like a port in the storm. Jeff stood with his head bowed.

Alex struggled with the mud, but nobody suggested the shovel. It was too sharp, too cold, too impersonal. Alex finally unearthed his daughter's face. He brushed bits of dirt and mud from her as if she were a priceless piece of an archaeological dig.

The rain continued, unabated, indifferent to their suffering. Raindrops hit Kristin's face and slipped off like tears. Her eyes were open, bloodshot, and vacant. Fat purple bruises clustered around her neck. Alex pressed two fingers to her neck, over her carotid artery, checking for a pulse he knew wasn't there. He squeezed his eyes shut, hoping it was all a nightmare that'd be over when he opened them again. He opened his eyes, his vision blurry with tears, and his only child, his sweet sixteen-year-old daughter, was still gone. He shook, his body convulsing with sobs.

CHAPTER 39

Alex and the Aftermath

Sheriff Franklin and his deputies came by boat. The road was still flooded, and the power was still out. The sheriff had obtained his warrant. Apparently one of the judges lived on the lake. Everyone was forced to wait in the living room under the watchful eye of a young deputy. Once the cars were searched, the family members were forced outside into their vehicles while the deputies searched the house. Emma was with Gwen and Jeff in their car, nearly comatose with grief.

Sheriff Franklin worked on interviews while his deputies searched the house. Alex sat in the front seat of his truck next to the sheriff. A portable MP3 recorder was on the center console.

"I'm sorry to do this to you again, but I don't wanna miss any details," Sheriff Franklin said. "Let's pick up where you searched Brett's room."

Alex nodded. "I searched Brett's room, and I found Buster's dog collar and tags and Kristin's gold necklace and cross." Alex gripped the steering wheel and hung his head. "She never took off her necklace. She did take it off once, … when we were at the beach. She almost drowned that day."

"Where exactly was the necklace and the dog collar?" Sheriff Franklin asked.

Alex raised his head. "In Brett's suitcase. He'd cut a compartment between the liner and the outer shell of the suitcase."

"Did you see him cut the compartment and place the items inside?"

"No."

"Where did you put the necklace and collar?"

"In my room, in the top dresser drawer. I touched the stuff." Alex shook his head. "I wasn't thinking."

"What happened after that?" Sheriff Franklin stroked his salt-and-pepper mustache.

"Jeff and Gwen moved out of their basement room, and we put Brett and his stuff down there."

"Why did you do that?"

"Jeff offered, and that room doesn't have any windows."

The sheriff nodded. "What did you do after Brett was confined to the basement room?"

"I went to search for Kristin. Matt and I searched on the lake with the pontoon boat I rented."

"How long did you and Matt search the lake?"

"Two or three hours. We were running low on fuel, so Matt and I came back to the house. I thought she'd be home."

"What happened when you and Matt returned?"

"It was really quiet. Emma and Gwen had gone door-to-door in the neighborhood. We thought maybe Kristin was waiting out the storm with a neighbor. They weren't back yet, so we went down to check on Brett, and he was gone. Jeff was supposed to watch him, but he'd fallen asleep."

"Where did Jeff fall asleep? Was he outside Brett's room? Inside? In a chair? On the floor?"

"He was sitting in a chair outside Brett's room," Alex replied.

"What did you do when you realized Brett was gone?" Sheriff Franklin asked.

"I woke up Jeff, and that's when we heard Kristin's car outside. Matt and Jeff and I went outside. Brett was in Kristin's car, trying to drive up the hill, but it was too muddy. The car spun around, so it was facing the house. Brett got out and ran up the hill. He must've put the car in Neutral because it rolled toward us. We had to dive out of the way. The car crashed into Harvey's BMW." Alex glanced out his truck window at the wreckage.

"Did you chase after Brett?"

"Yes. Matt and I chased Brett up the hill and into the woods across the street. We lost him in the woods. He was too fast. So we came back to the house. Then we heard a Jet Ski, and we ran to the dock. It was gone, but we heard which way it went."

"How did you know it was Brett?"

"We didn't, but we had all seen this Jet Ski near us that had keys hanging from the ignition. That Jet Ski wasn't there. It had been a joke that we'd take it for a joyride, so it made sense to me that Brett took it to try to get away."

"Why do you think he wanted to get away?"

Alex rubbed the back of his neck. "He was guilty and afraid."

"What would Brett be afraid of?" Sheriff Franklin asked.

"Getting caught." Alex paused. "And me."

"Why was he afraid of you?"

"I threatened him."

The sheriff winced, almost imperceptibly. "How did you threaten Brett?"

"I told him that I'd cut off his fingers if he didn't tell me where Kristin was."

Sheriff Franklin furrowed his brow.

"Don't worry. He has all his fingers," Alex said.

"Did you threaten to kill Brett?"

Alex cleared his throat. "Yes."

"And now he's dead."

"It was an accident."

The sheriff frowned. "Did Brett tell you where Kristin was?"

"He said she might be in the woods."

"Let's go back to the Jet Ski. What did you do after you went to the dock and heard the Jet Ski?"

"I followed him in the pontoon boat."

"Were you by yourself?"

"No, Matt and Jeff were with me."

"What happened next?" Sheriff Franklin asked.

"We found the Jet Ski," Alex replied. "It was abandoned. Brett was swimming for shore, so we drove closer, and Matt jumped into the water and grabbed him."

"Did Matt hurt Brett?"

"No, he just brought Brett back to the boat. Then we were driving back, and we hit a large swell, and the boat rocked, and Jeff was off balance. Brett punched Jeff and dove off the front of the boat. The rest happened so fast. Brett was sucked into the outboard motor, and he was killed."

"Was Brett pushed into that motor?"

Alex turned to the sheriff, glaring. "No, but I would've killed him if he hadn't jumped."

"Lucky for you, fate intervened."

Alex smacked the steering wheel. "You think I'm lucky?"

Sheriff Franklin blanched. "I'm sorry. Poor choice of words."

They sat in silence for a moment.

"Who pulled Brett out of the water?" the sheriff asked.

"Matt."

"What did you do when you got back to your dock?"

"We rolled up Brett in a tarp and left him in the pontoon. When we were walking up the hill, we noticed that the neighbor was awake, or at least he had a candle burning in the window."

"What time was it?"

"I don't remember exactly, maybe 2:00 a.m."

The sheriff nodded.

"We decided to go back out and search for Kristin, but Matt and I wanted to talk to the neighbor first. We'd seen him watching us a lot.

We thought maybe he saw something that might help with the search. So we went over there."

"This neighbor is Henry Marshall? Hank? The next-door neighbor to your right?"

"Yes."

"What did Mr. Marshall tell you?"

"Not much, only that he saw Brett and Rachel together in the water by the dock."

"What were they doin'?"

"Hank said, *fornicating.*" Alex wagged his head. "To be honest, I don't know what the hell that means to Hank. Maybe they were kissing. Maybe they were having sex. I don't know. You'd have to ask him."

"Do you think Brett and Rachel were havin' sex?"

"Yes. Rachel's always had some issues with … promiscuity. And Brett was pressuring Kristin to have sex." Alex gripped the steering wheel, his knuckles white. "I think Kristin said no, and it pushed Brett over the edge."

"How do you know Brett was pressurin' Kristin?"

"Matt overheard them arguing about it."

"Did Mr. Marshall tell you when he saw Rachel and Brett at the dock?"

"It was on Saturday. He said he saw them after you guys left, so I'm guessing in the afternoon sometime."

"Anything else that was notable?" Sheriff Franklin asked.

"There was a discrepancy," Alex replied. "Hank said that, after they were … done in the water, Rachel and Brett left together on the kayaks."

"How's that a discrepancy?"

"Jeff went for a swim on Saturday afternoon at about the same time. He said, when he went for his swim, only one kayak was at the dock, and, when he came back, they were both gone. Rachel said she took the first kayak by herself and saw Brett kayaking almost two hours later. Rachel also said that Brett was acting strange when she saw him, and he grabbed her."

"Grabbed her how?"

"She didn't say."

"Did Brett hurt Rachel?"

"I don't think so."

"How was Brett actin' strange? Did Rachel give any details?"

"I think she said he was fidgety and looking around, like he was worried that someone was coming for him."

"Jeff swimmin' and Rachel kayakin' and Brett actin' strange, did this all happen after we interviewed Kristin at my offices?"

"Yes. Kristin left your offices with Matt. He took a nap, and I think Kristin went to find Brett. Maybe she found Brett and Rachel together. It was a small window of time—only a couple of hours when Kristin was alone."

"Do you think Rachel had somethin' to do with this?"

"I don't know. … I doubt it, but she may know something."

"What about Jeff?"

"I don't think so, but he could be covering for Rachel, not wanting her to be embarrassed further."

"Embarrassed about havin' sex with Brett?"

"Yes."

"What happened after you talked to Mr. Marshall?" Sheriff Franklin asked.

"We went to the woods to search," Alex replied.

"Everyone?"

"My dad, Cathy, and Rachel stayed behind to wait for you guys."

Sheriff Franklin nodded. "Why search the woods?"

"Because Brett mentioned it when I was questioning him, and the pontoon was out of fuel."

"Who found Kristin?"

Alex took a deep breath. "Matt found the grave. It was shallow. He offered to dig. We all hoped it wasn't her, but …" Alex shook his head again.

"Did Matt have a shovel?" Sheriff Franklin asked with raised eyebrows.

"He had one in his backpack. It was from the shed out back."

"Did you ask Matt to bring that shovel?"

Alex pursed his lips. "No."

"What happened next?"

"Matt dug, and he unearthed one of her hands." Alex's voice wavered. Tears slipped down his face. He wiped his face with his sweatshirt sleeve. "I dug by hand because I didn't want the shovel to hit her."

CHAPTER 40

Alex and Going Home

Alex drove his truck on US 40 West, the headlights carving a path through the night. Emma leaned against the passenger door, staring into the darkness. They'd barely spoken since they'd left Norris Lake.

Alex's phone buzzed. He picked it up from the cup holder and glanced at the text message.

Blanche Taylor: U think im stupid. I know you killed my son.

Alex clenched his jaw and put his phone back in the cup holder. Seconds later the phone buzzed again. He checked it again.

Blanche Taylor: U will pay.

Alex turned off his phone and dropped it in the cup holder.
Emma turned to Alex. "Who is it?"
"Brett's mom."
Emma sat up straight. "What did she say?"
"She thinks I killed her son."
Emma deadpanned, "Did you?"
Alex furrowed his brow. "Are you *fucking* serious?"

"I don't know what happened on that boat."

"*Yes*, you do, because I told you what happened. If you don't believe me, you can ask Matt and Jeff."

"You nearly cut off his fingers."

"So what! That piece of shit killed Kristin."

"And killing him didn't bring her back."

"*I* didn't kill him."

Emma glared at Alex. "No, you scared him to death." Emma turned back to the passenger window.

"I was trying to find Kristin."

Emma didn't respond.

Alex glanced from the road to his wife and back. "You're gonna shut down now?"

Emma stayed silent.

"You finally say something, and you accuse me of murder, then you fucking shut down. This is *bullshit*."

The rest of their ride home was dead silent.

* * *

Alex turned his Ford F-150 into his neighborhood of McMansions on acre lots. The houses were mostly dark except for porch lights and landscape lighting. He stopped his truck short of their stone-and-stucco slice of the American dream. A Toyota Corolla was parked in the driveway, the front end facing out.

Emma sat up and spied the car as well. "Is that Blanche's car?"

"I think so." Alex ran his hand over his face. "She's got a lotta nerve showing up here."

"Sheriff Franklin said he wasn't certain about Brett."

"I'm certain."

"She lost a child too."

Alex gunned the V-8 into their driveway and parked next to Blanche's Toyota. Blanche exited her car and waited next to Alex's door as he stepped from his truck to the driveway. Her eyes were black-circled and puffy. She was skinny and tan and weathered with the puckered mouth of a smoker. She removed her hand from behind her back and pointed a silver .380 revolver in Alex's face.

Alex's mouth was an O as he raised his hands in the air.

She held the .380 in one shaky hand. "Admit what you did."

"It was an accident," Alex replied.

"Oh, bullshit. You done it. I know you did. Brett told me how you didn't like him."

Emma approached from the passenger side of the pickup. "This won't bring him back, Blanche."

"Stay back," Blanche said, pointing her gun at Emma, then back to Alex. "This ain't about you."

Emma stopped dead in her tracks. "If taking someone's life could bring Brett back, I'd give mine."

Blanche focused on Alex, her eyes narrowed. "I just want him to admit what he done."

"I didn't do anything," Alex replied.

"Liar!" Blanche cocked the hammer, her finger on the trigger.

"I scared him, okay? And he was scared enough to jump off the front of a boat. But his death wasn't intentional."

Her eyes were glassy, the gun twitchy in her hand.

Alex stared down the stubby barrel, his heart pounding in his chest.

She lowered the gun and began to cry. She sank to the concrete in a sobbing heap. Alex bent down and carefully took the gun from her hand. Emma sat next to the woman and pulled her into an embrace. Alex opened the cylinder.

No bullets.

CHAPTER 41

Alex and the Funeral

Alex stood behind the lectern, the massive crucifix hanging on the wall behind him, a packed audience and Kristin's coffin in front of him. The church was beautiful with its stained-glass windows, a pitched roof with exposed wooden beams, Jesus-inspired artwork, and rows of ornate pews.

Alex glanced at his eulogy resting on the lectern. It was what they wanted to hear, but it wasn't how he felt. He cleared his throat. "Kristin at sixteen was the best person I've ever met, and she was just getting started." He looked around at the audience. Gwen and Matt sat on opposite sides of Emma in the front row. Jeff and Harvey and Cathy were there too. So were Rachel and Seth. Matt's ex-wife, Angela, sat a few rows behind them. The bulk of the church was filled with parishioners and Kristin's friends.

"People keep telling me that God needed her. That she has a higher purpose in heaven." Alex was off script now. "I guess that's comforting to some. To think that God engineered this whole thing because He needed her to do important work in heaven." Alex ran his hand through his disheveled hair and shook his head. "No, I'm not buying that. You know why? Because it's not true." You could hear a pin drop. "Kristin died because someone murdered her. Pure and simple. This isn't about God. God didn't cause it, and God sure as hell isn't gonna fix it."

A few huffs came from the audience when Alex said *hell*.

"Kristin was generous and kind and loving and smart, and the best daughter I could ever hope for. Her beauty radiated from the inside out. As her father, my job was to protect her. I failed at the most important job I'll ever have. I have to carry that weight whether I want to or not.

"There are people in this world who prey on the goodness of others. They exploit the kindness and empathy of people like Kristin." He paused. "This church ..." Alex shook his head. "This church is partly to blame."

The audience gasped.

The pastor approached the lectern.

Alex glared and pointed at the young pastor. "Sit your ass down."

The pastor turned around and found his seat.

"Alex," Emma said from the front row, her eyes imploring better behavior.

"I'm fine," Alex said to Emma, then looked at the audience. "This church teaches us that we're all God's creatures, that we're all inherently good. That sounds great, right?" Alex nodded his head, scanning the audience. "But what if some people are evil? If we believe that we're all inherently good, we don't recognize evil when it's standing before us. Instead we get involved and help these people. The evil among us use our love and kindness to take advantage of us.

"That's what happened to Kristin. She tried to help by loving evil, but you can't. The truly evil have no remorse. They can't love. Therefore, they cannot be loved. The next time your intuition's warning you that someone's evil, make sure you heed that warning."

Alex took a deep breath. His eyes watered. "She was the best of us." A tear slipped down his cheek, then another. "I miss her." He took another deep breath. "I miss her." He turned and walked out the rear exit of the church.

The metal door shut behind him. Alex walked outside into the beautiful summer sun. He leaned over, his hands on his knees, the tears flowing. He stood and removed his handkerchief from the breast pocket of his suit jacket. He wiped his face.

The metal door opened and shut again. Matt approached, wearing a dark suit, his beard trimmed and brushed. Matt patted Alex on the back.

"Emma sent me to check on you," Matt said.

"I'm surprised she gives a shit," Alex replied. "We've barely spoken since the lake."

"I'm sorry."

Alex nodded.

"That was one helluva eulogy."

"I probably shouldn't have said that about the church. I doubt Kristin would've approved. It wasn't on my written eulogy, but I didn't wanna say some bullshit just to make people feel better."

"I think Kristin would've been happy that you told the truth."

"Did you see Angela?" Alex asked, clearly changing the subject.

"Yeah, I talked to her for a few minutes. She's seven months' pregnant."

"You all right, seeing her?"

Matt frowned. "No, but this day's not about me. She loved Kristin too. She and I took Kristin to her first movie at the movie theater. *WALL-E*."

"She wanted a robot for years after that."

"Kristin and I talked about that time in the car on the way back from the sheriff's station."

Alex swallowed and looked away.

"I'm sorry. I don't know what I'm supposed to say or not say. Whatever you need."

Alex looked at his brother. "Can you give me a few minutes alone?"

Matt nodded and walked back inside the church.

Alex paced up and down the sidewalk, collecting his thoughts and emotions. His phone vibrated in his jacket pocket. He took it out and checked the screen. He had a new voice message. He checked the number, then dialed his voice mail. It was the call he'd been waiting for.

"Alex, this is Sheriff Franklin. I told you that I'd call if I had any updates on the case. I have some updates. Gimme a call anytime at 865-555-1477."

Alex disconnected from his voice mail and tapped the number.

"This is Sheriff Franklin."

"Sheriff, this is Alex Palmer. I was returning your voice mail."

"We have some new developments on the case."

"Okay?"

"We found Brett's hairs on Whitney's and Kate's bodies."

Alex clenched his jaw. "I knew there was something wrong with that kid."

"Don't go jumpin' the gun. We also found DNA and fingerprint evidence that Danny Stafford was in the lake house where you were stayin'. I think he burglarized the home. I also think it's possible he was in the home more than once. I interviewed his parents, and they seem to think he may have had a key to the house. His fingerprints were found on Brett's suitcase, so it's possible Danny planted Kristin's gold chain and Buster's dog collar. It's also possible that he stole Brett's gold chain at an earlier date and planted it on Whitney along with Brett's hairs. If Danny had access to the house, he certainly had access to hairbrushes. Danny's still in the wind, but I have most of my deputies trackin' him down. I'm sure he'll turn up. He doesn't have enough money to disappear forever."

"You think Danny Stafford might've murdered Kristin?"

"I don't know yet. Brett Taylor's still the main suspect, but he's not the only one. It's still very early in our investigation."

"Are there other suspects besides Brett and Danny?"

"We're lookin' at anyone with access and opportunity."

Alex furrowed his brow. "That could be anyone in my family."

"I'm not ready to confirm that at this time. However, I am keepin' an open mind."

CHAPTER 42

Alex and Obsession

A week after the funeral, Alex and Emma settled into their new roles—not as parents or as grandparents but as parents of a murdered child. It was the final role, a role that trumped every other one.

Alex stood in his office, wearing sweats and a five-o'clock shadow. White hairs had appeared nearly overnight, mixing with his original light brown. The window shades were drawn, but summer sunshine still slipped through the slats. He sipped lukewarm coffee and stared at the corkboard along the wall. It wasn't attached to the wall; it was free-standing and flippable, so you could tack up items on both sides. One side of the corkboard was completely empty—this was the side that was evident when he was out of his office, but now, with his door locked, Alex studied the other side. The one that housed his deepest and darkest thoughts—his suspicions.

There were pictures and news articles, handwritten and typewritten notes. There were lists and timelines. There were different colored strings making connections. It looked like the scattered thoughts of a crazy conspiracy theorist.

His cell phone buzzed on his desk. Alex ignored it, engrossed in the mystery—the who-done-it. He scanned the corkboard, thinking, trying to make sense of it all. *Could it have been more than one person?*

Maybe they were working together. His phone buzzed again, breaking his concentration. He gulped his last bit of coffee, stepped to his desk, and picked up the cell. It was Matt. Alex rejected the call and felt a pang of guilt as he scanned his suspect list. Matt was on the list.

Alex used a numbering system to assign guilt or innocence to each suspect. The higher the number, the more likely they were the murderer. He looked over the details of each suspect. *Matt was the last person to see Kristin +15. Matt found the body +3. Matt had that shovel +5. Matt can be quiet and weird at times +2. Matt pointed the finger at Brett and Jeff +2. Matt's always been good to Kristin -5. Matt's my brother -5. I trust Matt implicitly -20. He calls me every day, even though I don't take his calls -2. He calls me every day, even though I don't take his calls +4.* Alex glanced at the textbooks on psychopathy and sociopathy on his desk. *Wouldn't a psychopath enjoy injecting himself into the situation—a situation he ... or she ... created?*

The suspect ranking read from most likely to least likely to be the murderer:

+105 Brett Taylor
+73 Danny Stafford
+25 Jeff Palmer
+21 Rachel Palmer
+18 Henry Marshall
+17 Seth Roberson
+16 Dorothy Stafford
+14 George Stafford
-1 Matt Palmer
-2 Harvey Palmer
-4 Ed Dellinger and/or septic worker
-12 Cathy Palmer

Brett had the dog collar and Kristin's necklace and crucifix. Also, his necklace showed up around Whitney's neck stump. The police found his hairs on Whitney's and Kate's bodies. It's also possible that all those items were planted by Danny. Brett also ran away, had an affair with Rachel, refused to talk to the police, and probably killed Kristin's first dog.

Danny's still a strong suspect. His island home was the murder scene for Whitney and Kate. He likely burglarized the rental house, his childhood home, a home he was recently kicked out of. His fingerprints were found on Brett's suitcase. Danny also did odd jobs near the scene of the crimes and conveniently disappeared after the murders. Hopefully they'll find him soon.

Jeff's a weird one. He didn't go to the sheriff's station the second time, so he had the opportunity. He let Brett go twice. His story about seeing a single kayak when he went swimming, then both being gone when he came back, doesn't jive with Hank Marshall's story of Rachel and Brett kayaking together. If they left together, Brett probably didn't have time to kill and bury Kristin. What about Rachel and her affair with Brett? Maybe she helped Brett do it.

Maybe Henry Marshall should be higher on the list. It was strange the way he was always watching us. Maybe he was lying about Brett and Rachel leaving together. But how would he know that bit of information would be relevant? I think he's more interested in being left alone. Plus, not too many seventy-year-olds are active murderers.

Seth might've been involved somehow. Rachel was having an affair with Brett, but it wasn't Kristin's fault. Maybe Seth wanted to kill Brett or Rachel, and Kristin got in the way somehow. Seth was pretty upset when he left the sheriff's office. And he hightailed it out of the rental house in the middle of a serious storm. Maybe he was running from what he did?

Danny's parents are probably a shot in the dark. Again, there aren't too many seventy-year-old active murderers. But who knows? Maybe they helped their son. Maybe they taught him. George Stafford didn't seem to make excuses for his son like Dorothy did. She'd be more likely to help. She wears the pants in that relationship, so George would probably do whatever she says.

Harvey and Cathy and the septic guys? There's literally nothing to suggest they had anything to do with this.

Alex stared at his suspect list, the wheels turning in his mind. *There's always the possibility that whoever killed Kristin isn't the same person who killed Kate and Whitney.*

Alex pulled the corkboard away from the wall and flipped it around so the empty side showed. He pushed the board back against the wall. Alex left his office for the bathroom, the coffee running through him. He peed, washed his hands, and started down the hall back to his office. The whimpering stopped him in his tracks. It sounded like Kristin when she was young, when she watched a scary movie and then had nightmares.

His bedroom door was shut. He approached, the whimpering getting louder. Maybe it was all a bad dream. She'd be sleeping in their bed like she did when she was little. *I told her not to watch* Insidious. *I told her that she'd have nightmares, but she said she was a big girl.*

Alex entered his bedroom. The thick curtains were drawn, almost eliminating the sunlight. A bright skinny ray slipped between the thin line where the curtains were supposed to connect.

Emma whimpered. She was having a nightmare or whatever you call a bad dream in the middle of the day.

Alex circled the bed, knelt, and put his hand on her shoulder. "Emma, wake up." He shook her lightly. "Emma, wake up."

Emma's eyes flickered and registered recognition of Alex.

"You were having a bad dream," Alex said.

Emma wiped her red eyes. Her face was pale and washed-out. "What time is it?"

"After eleven."

"Aren't you supposed to be at work?"

Alex winced. He had lied and said that he was given bereavement leave until, well, today. He wanted to wait until after the funeral to tell Emma the bad news about his job, but it had never been a good time;

then he had forgotten about it. It wasn't important to him. Nothing mattered anymore.

"Why aren't you at work?" Emma asked, sitting up in bed.

Alex took a deep breath. "I was let go."

Emma sat up straight. "They can't do that. You're on bereavement—"

"I was let go before—"

"Before what?"

"Before the lake."

"All this time?"

"I didn't wanna ruin ..."

Emma's face was beet-red. "Ruin what? Our wonderful vacation?"

Alex dipped his head.

"You lied to me."

"I just wanted everyone to be together. To have a good time."

"But you lied to me." Emma pointed a shaky finger at Alex. "If you would've told me the truth, I would've said no to the vacation, and Kristin would still be alive." Emma shook her head. "For the life of me, I couldn't figure it out. Why would God allow this to happen to Kristin of all people? She was always a good Christian—always. Now I understand. God's punishing us for *your* lie."

Alex stood, his fists clenched. "I failed to protect her. That's true." He glared at his wife. "But *I* didn't cause this. And goddamn you for blaming this on me." Alex stalked from the room, slamming the door behind him.

He stomped to his office and slammed that door as well. He sat behind his desk, his heart racing. Alex hung his head, rubbing his throbbing temples. *Maybe she's right. If we'd faced my job loss like a family, we never would've gone to the lake, and Kristin would still ...*

His phone buzzed. It was a number he recognized, and the only one he answered these days. "Sheriff?" Alex asked.

"Yeah. How you holdin' up?" Sheriff Franklin asked.

"About like you'd expect."

"I'm sorry, Alex."

Alex didn't respond.

"I have some news. It might end up in the press at some point, but I thought you should know before it does. Do me a favor and keep it between us in the meantime."

"Okay."

"First, we caught Danny Stafford."

"That's good."

"He was holed up in some meth house, high as a kite. He had the knife that was used to kill Whitney and Kate on that island. There was a tiny droplet of blood on the handle that matched one of the victims. Danny swears up and down that he didn't have anything to do with the murders. He denied plantin' the gold chains or the dog collar or Brett's hairs on Whitney and Kate. Danny's DNA and fingerprints weren't found on the chains or the collar or even Brett's hairbrush."

"But they were found on Brett's suitcase."

"Danny's prints were on the *outside* of the suitcase, like he had opened it, but not inside where that compartment was cut."

"He could've used gloves."

"You're right, he could've, but we have his fingerprints throughout the house. I guess he coulda put on gloves only for those items, but it doesn't make sense. I think he either wears gloves or he doesn't, and Danny clearly didn't. He did admit to burglarizin' the house. He still had one of your iPads, but he said he sold the rest of your stuff and refused to snitch on the fence. Once we're done with his case, we'll send you the iPad."

"You don't think Danny killed those girls?"

"I don't, but I'm not certain. Apart from the knife, no physical evidence ties him to the bodies. I've known Danny for a long time. He's a piece of shit and a thief, but I don't think he's a murderer."

"Then it's still Brett?"

"Possibly. We're not sure."

Alex gasped. "You found Brett's hairs on Whitney and Kate. We found Kristin's gold chain and Buster's collar hidden in his bag. He probably killed Kristin's first dog."

"I didn't say he *wasn't* our guy. I still think he is, but we're explorin' every possibility. It's possible Brett killed Kristin but not Whitney and Kate. Or maybe it was the other way around. Or maybe he didn't kill anyone."

"This doesn't make any sense. You have physical evidence tying Brett to Whitney and Kate *and* Kristin."

"A lot of people had access and opportunity to plant that evidence. Maybe Danny did plant the evidence. It's also possible that someone else might've planted the evidence. Now this is a big *might* and just a theory at this point. The issue is, we have a lot of hairs at a scene that appears to be planned, and yet no hairs at the scene that appears rushed. We think it's possible that someone took hairs from Brett's hairbrush and placed them on Whitney and Kate but didn't have the same opportunity to implicate Brett at Kristin's murder, because it wasn't planned."

"Jesus." Alex thought about his suspect list. "If it's not Brett or Danny, then it had to be someone else who had access to Brett's room. It had to be someone in my family."

"Don't go jumpin' the gun. This is a theory. Hell, Brett might still be our guy, but maybe he was bein' controlled by someone else. Bottom line is, we gotta lot of theories and leads, but we don't know yet. We'll see where the evidence takes us. There's a lot of movin' parts in this case. I'll keep you updated, but you gotta promise me that you'll stay out of it."

Alex was quiet, looking at his handiwork on the corkboard.

"You understand me?" the sheriff asked.

"I hear you."

CHAPTER 43

Alex and the Invitation

Alex trudged outside, wearing shorts, a T-shirt, and slippers. He squinted into the sun. It still felt like summer, even though by the calendar it was fall. His neighborhood was like a ghost town. Apparently, he was the only one not at work at 11:00 a.m. on a Tuesday. People spent more time at work to pay for their overpriced and over-size houses. If they were lucky enough to have a job. The unemployed didn't live in his neighborhood. Not for long anyway. His mailbox was stuffed to the gills. It had been a week since he had checked it. He grabbed the stack of mail and went back inside.

On the way to his home office, he passed the living room. The couch cushions were depressed, his comforter half on the floor, half on the couch. As he walked upstairs, the steps creaked in the silence. He meandered past his office to Kristin's bedroom. Alex opened the door and stood at the threshold. Her canopy bed was made, with a frilly white comforter and lace hanging from above. She had a pine dresser with a mirror attached.

Alex stepped across the threshold, his slippers sinking into the thick white carpeting. He looked at himself in the mirror. He appeared to have aged ten years in ten weeks. He had a beard that was more Ted Kaczynski than manicured hip. He had bags under his bloodshot eyes.

The mirror was framed with snapshots of Kristin and her friends.

There were missing squares in that collage of good times. Alex had taken the Brett pictures. They were part of his investigation now.

He glanced around the room. Dust motes hung in the air where sunshine slipped between the slats of her blinds. Alex shut Kristin's door and walked to the master bedroom. He stepped through the open door and surveyed the room. The comforter was swirled. A corner of the fitted sheet had come off, exposing the mattress. Emma was a fitful sleeper now. She had taken a job as an administrative assistant at a hospital—thirteen dollars an hour. She worked as many hours as they'd give her. Anything to get out of the house and away from him.

Alex returned to his office and locked the door behind him. He now had six freestanding double-sided corkboards, one side for each of the twelve suspects. He kept his office door locked because Emma wouldn't approve of his investigation. In fact, she'd be appalled, especially with his suspect list. Thankfully Emma didn't seem to notice or care what he was doing. She was a zombie, going through the motions of work and sleep.

He sat behind his desk, the stack of mail in hand, and pulled the trash can close. He tossed most of the letters without opening them. Alex stared at a past due notice from Chase Bank. *How long will it be before they come for us?* He'd read online that it often takes a bank over a year to foreclose. With the economy and the real estate market in shambles, it had to be at least that long, maybe longer. *Should we move out? Should we live in the house rent- and mortgage-free for as long as possible?* The latter was happening by inaction. *I should talk to a bankruptcy attorney.* Alex tossed the past due notice into the trash.

Maybe foreclosure will be a relief. Maybe it'll force us to move on. He sighed. *I doubt it. What's that saying? Wherever you go, there you are.*

At the bottom of the stack of mail was a white envelope, addressed to Alex and Emma Palmer, and handwritten in loopy cursive. The return address was preprinted from Harvey and Cathy Palmer. Inside the envelope was a handwritten letter in the same loopy cursive and an invitation on heavy cardstock. A sprig of dried lilac was pressed on the card and held with a plastic covering. In fancy printed cursive, the invitation read:

Mr. and Mrs. Harvey Palmer request the pleasure of your company at the marriage of their daughter,

Miss Rachel Palmer
to
Mr. Seth Roberson

Sunday, the 14th of October, 2018, at 4:00 p.m.

The Sanderling
1461 Duck Road
Duck, North Carolina 27949

Reception immediately following

Alex opened the handwritten letter. It read:

Alex & Emma,

I'm sorry for the late invitation. I wasn't sure if you wanted to be included, and I didn't want to add any stress to your lives. I know things have been terribly hard for you two. Everyone would love for you both to come to the wedding, but we don't want you to feel obligated. I know that you need time to heal.

I also wanted you to know that you are welcome and loved by everyone. Our hearts and prayers go out to you both.

If you'd like to come to the wedding, please send me a text. My number is (615) 555-9824. But, again, please don't feel obligated. Also, there's a rehearsal dinner at 7:00 p.m. on Saturday, October 13. You are welcome to attend that as well.

Love,
Cathy Palmer

Less than two weeks away. They don't actually want us to come. Nobody wants the parents of a recently murdered child at their festive occasion. Not to mention I know about the herpes. I doubt Seth wants to see my face at his wedding. The letter should say, we don't want you to come, but we feel bad, so we're sending this invitation late so you can't come, but our conscience is clean because we sent an invitation. We wanna feel good about ourselves, and we wanna have a fun time without you and Emma killing our buzz. What a bunch of bullshit.

Alex tossed the invitation on his desktop. He took a deep breath and gazed at his investigation corkboards. Brett and Danny had the most developed and cluttered boards, followed by Jeff, Rachel, and Seth. Alex added every thought, every intuition, and every detail to the corkboards—no matter how innocuous. Much of it was speculation and inconsequential details. Every time he added a bit of information, he recalibrated the suspect list that sat before him on a single sheet of paper. Alex picked up the list and scanned the names from top to bottom—from most likely to least likely to be the murderer.

+79 Brett Taylor
+68 Danny Stafford
+36 Jeff Palmer
+34 Rachel Palmer
+31 Seth Roberson
+24 Henry Marshall

+22 Matt Palmer

+15 Harvey Palmer

+14 Dorothy Stafford

+10 George Stafford

-4 Ed Dellinger and/or septic worker

-12 Cathy Palmer

Brett was still the most likely culprit, but he lost points after Sheriff Franklin raised the possibility that the gold chains, dog collar, and Brett's hairs were planted. Danny Stafford lost points because, apart from the knife, nothing physically tied him to the murders. Danny was being held without bond on burglary and larceny charges while the Sheriff's Department worked to unearth enough evidence to charge him with murder.

Jeff, Rachel, Seth, Harvey, and Matt gained points for having the access and the opportunity to commit the murders and to plant evidence. Matt gained additional points because Alex remembered when Matt was being bullied in middle school and had snapped one day and beat the kid to a pulp. He had been suspended for a week and forced to see the school counselor for the rest of the school year.

At the time Alex had been proud of his little brother. Now it spoke to Matt's penchant for violence and moved him up a few spots on the suspect list. Henry Marshall and Dorothy and George Stafford dropped mostly for being old and decrepit.

Sheriff Franklin still worked the case, but there hadn't been any new developments in quite some time. *It all comes down to the planting of evidence. Was it done or not? If not, Brett's the guy. If so, it's probably Danny, but it could be someone else. It could be anyone with access and opportunity.* Alex thought of his family. When he'd mentioned his family as suspects, the sheriff had told him not to jump the gun. Alex didn't have the resources to investigate Danny and Brett as thoroughly as the Sheriff's Department, but his family members were a different story.

Alex looked down at the letter and the invitation. He grabbed his phone from the desktop and sent Cathy a text.

Alex: RSVP 1. It'll just be me. Thank you for the invitation.

Alex just jumped the gun.

CHAPTER 44

Alex and the Destination Wedding

Alex sat in the middle of the long table. He ate, even though he wasn't hungry—swordfish caught locally in the Outer Banks and responsibly on a line. He thought about what Emma had said before she left.

"It's sick. She slept with Kristin's boyfriend and *murderer* for heaven's sake. It's disrespectful to Kristin *and* God."

"I feel like I should go," Alex had said. The truth would've made her angrier.

"I don't want anything to do with her," Emma had replied.

"I'm not asking you to. I'm just telling you why I won't be here for two days."

"You know what? I don't care what you do. I'm gonna stay with my parents for a while."

The rented dining room had high ceilings and exposed wooden beams repurposed from an old ship. Clear string lights hung from the ceiling, giving the room a warm yellow glow. Fall flower arrangements adorned the table, dominated by red and yellow chrysanthemums. Despite the soothing ambiance, the crowd was raucous. Alex was quiet while the wedding party gossiped and joked and laughed—the room enveloped in a constant cacophony of chatter. Much to Rachel's and Cathy's chagrin, Harvey was the center of attention, regaling bridesmaids with the intricacies of his latest novel–sure to be another best seller and maybe a feature film.

Toward the end of the rehearsal dinner, Jeff tapped a spoon on his wineglass to quiet the crowd. He stood at the foot of the table, wearing a traditional southern suit. Rachel was wide-eyed, unaware that he'd be speaking. Gwen looked up at Jeff with big green eyes.

Jeff held his half-full wineglass. "I wanted to make a quick announcement because I didn't want this to come out tomorrow at the wedding. Tomorrow's about Rachel and Seth."

"So is tonight," Rachel called out from the head of the table.

The crowd laughed, thinking she was joking.

Jeff smiled at his sister. "You're right, sis. Please indulge my selfishness—just this once."

Rachel raised one side of her mouth in contempt. "Don't I always?"

The crowd laughed again, loving the sibling banter.

"Gwen and I are pregnant," Jeff said, grinning.

The crowd hooted and hollered. Alex remained quiet.

Cathy clasped her hands together, her eyes moist. "That's wonderful, honey."

Gwen smiled, her hand instinctively touching her still-flat belly.

"We're only three months along," Jeff said after the crowd quieted. "Anyway, I figured you guys would wonder why Gwen wasn't drinking." Jeff looked at the bridesmaids, wagging his finger in their direction. "And I didn't want you wild women over there tempting Gwen with apple martinis. The last time I had to be her nurse for three days."

The bridesmaids laughed along with the rest of the wedding party.

Jeff held up his glass. "I'd like to make a toast to Gwen and my unborn child." He looked down at Gwen. "I love you, baby. And I love our baby."

"Hear, hear," the crowd said, rejoicing the baby-to-be.

Alex thought of Kristin.

Rachel stood from the table, her face taut.

"Where are you going?" Seth asked.

Rachel scowled at her husband-to-be. "To the bathroom. Is that not okay?"

"It's fine." Seth showed his palms as she stalked from the table.

The happy couple-to-be. Alex stood from the table and followed Rachel into the hall. He waited outside the ladies' room. A few minutes later she appeared, nearly bumping into Alex.

She furrowed her brow. "Oh, hey, Alex."

"Congratulations," Alex said.

"Thanks."

"I need to ask you something in private."

"I should probably get back." She glanced over his shoulder, biting her lower lip.

"It's important. It won't take long."

Alex led her farther down the hall and into the business office—which was a narrow room with a fax and three desktop computers for guests to use. He shut the door behind them, blocking the exit.

Rachel crossed her arms over her chest.

"The sheriff thinks Brett might not've killed Kristin," Alex said.

Her eyes widened.

"What do you think about that?"

"What about that other guy?" Rachel asked. "The one that, like, stole our stuff?"

"Danny Stafford?"

"Yeah, that guy."

"They're not sure it's him either."

"Why are you, like, telling me this? I mean, I feel bad and all, but it's, like, my wedding."

"Because I think you lied."

She scowled and pursed her lips. "I don't know what you're talking about."

"I think you and Brett left that dock together. And, if you two left that dock together, then Brett didn't kill Kristin, which means someone else did."

"I don't even, like, remember anymore."

"Why did you lie?"

"I didn't." She tried to brush past Alex, but he stood firm. "Move."

"Not until you tell me the truth."

She glared at Alex. "You can't, like, keep me in here."

"Rachel, please help me."

She raised both hands in frustration. "I don't know what you want from me."

"The truth. Look, I don't care about you hooking up with Brett."

"Fuck you, Alex. I can't believe you'd say that at my wedding." She pushed past Alex.

"Rachel, please. I need to know."

She slammed the door behind her.

He rubbed his temples. *Shit.*

* * *

After dinner, Rachel and Seth went for a walk on the beach with a flashlight. Alex suspected Rachel wanted to get far away from him.

"So romantic. We should do that," Cathy had said to Harvey.

But Harvey was too enamored with his scotch, the bridesmaids, and his stories of greatness, so they settled around the fire pit with everyone else, sitting in comfortable outdoor furniture. The fire was natural gas fed, with fake wood. The flames warmed the sea air, and the firelight provided a perfect contrast to the starry night. As the night wore on, bridesmaids disappeared with the good-looking groomsmen. The less attractive meandered back to their rooms alone. Cathy and Gwen went to bed. Only Jeff and Harvey and Alex remained, sipping their scotch.

"It's a shame Grandpa Palmer can't be here," Jeff said.

Harvey nodded. "Make sure you call him and tell him the good news."

"I will." Jeff turned to Alex. "You sure you don't wanna crash in our room?"

"I'm fine." Alex stood, his head swimming from the alcohol. "I'm just down the road at the Comfort Inn. I should get going."

"We'll see you tomorrow," Harvey said.

"Yeah, see you tomorrow," Alex replied.

"It's good to see you, bro," Jeff said.

Alex patted his brother on the shoulder. "Congratulations."

"Thanks."

Alex left the fire pit. He walked on the compacted sand pathway to the massive deck attached to the back of the hotel. The resort and hotel were nearly vacant at this hour during the off-season. He entered the back door to the lobby and the hotel bar. He returned his empty glass to the bartender. A young girl with dirty-blond hair walked by, headed for the deck. Something was familiar about the back of her head, her gait, and that cardigan. He had a powerful sense of déjà vu.

"Are you okay?" the bartender asked.

Alex blinked. "Yeah, I'm fine. ... Thanks."

He followed the girl outside. She walked down the deck steps, toward the fire pit. Alex followed, but, instead of taking the same path, he hid behind a juniper tree near the corner of the building, about fifty feet away. The young woman approached the fire pit. The wind whipped her hair around her face and her dress around her legs.

She said something to Jeff.

He smiled, replied, and gestured with his open hand.

The crash of waves in the background made it virtually impossible to hear what they were saying.

She moved to a seat across the fire from Harvey and Jeff. She stared into her cell phone, swiping and tapping. The young woman was very young, maybe sixteen. Her face was round and radiant without makeup. Jeff stared at her. With the look of a predator.

Harvey said something to Jeff.

Jeff turned from the girl and said something to Harvey.

Alex wanted to get closer, so he could hear, but he'd be spotted as he had no cover between the juniper tree and the fire pit.

Harvey spoke again.

Jeff smirked and replied.

Harvey clenched his jaw, the firelight dancing across his face. He spoke to Jeff, his face taut.

Jeff glanced at the girl, then back to his father. He raised one side of his mouth in contempt.

Alex watched and waited.

The conversation appeared more amiable now. Eventually, Harvey and Jeff left the fire pit. The girl remained, still glued to her phone. Harvey and Jeff approached the juniper and the deck steps.

Alex crouched as they ambled past and entered through the back door of the hotel. Alex continued to watch the girl. Shortly thereafter, the flame disappeared. The girl looked around, as if searching for the person who had turned off the fire. Alex glanced at his watch—11:00 p.m. *It's probably on a timer.*

She stood from the fire pit, walked around the massive deck, toward the ocean. Alex followed from a safe distance. She passed a small shed where the resort rented surf and aquatic gear. She climbed the wooden steps up a sand dune and stood on a small deck at the crest of the dune. A post light illuminated the area. She sat on a wooden bench and gazed out at the ocean.

It was a clear night, the stars bright, but Alex doubted she could see much of the ocean. He hid in the darkness behind the shed.

Jeff passed the shed, startling, but not seeing, Alex. *Where did he come from?* Alex's heart pounded as Jeff climbed the steps to the top of the dune. He stood with his hands on his hips, looking at the ocean and the starry night. He still wore his southern suit from dinner. The girl sat on the bench with her knees pulled to her chest. Jeff turned and spoke to her.

From Alex's vantage point, he couldn't see Jeff's expression, and the waves muffled their words. She looked up at Jeff. *Was that a smile?* They talked, Jeff doing most of the talking and making hand gestures.

After a while, the girl talked more animatedly, with hand gestures, big smiles, and hair flips.

The conversation then fizzled. Jeff said something, waved to the girl, turned around, and walked back to the hotel. Shortly thereafter, the girl rose from the bench and headed toward the hotel. Instead of climbing the deck steps to the rear of the hotel, the girl followed the sand pathway to the left. Landscape lights provided dull yellow circles of light along the path. She trudged past the lap pool. Alex was behind her, but in the open now. She turned right onto a narrow path that led to a ground-floor room. She stopped and pivoted, her eyes narrowed at Alex.

"Are you following me?" she asked.

Alex stopped in his tracks. The girl no longer looked familiar. "No, I, uh, … I was just walking. I'm sorry."

She rolled her eyes, turned, and continued to her room—or more likely her parents' room.

Alex pinched the bridge of his nose. *I'm losing my mind. Jesus. He's your brother.* Alex walked to his truck and drove to the nearest rest stop. He didn't have a room. He stretched out across the bench seat in his extended cab and closed his eyes. *I need to go home, … while I still have one. I doubt I'll be missed at the wedding. I have no business being here. I just need a few hours' sleep, then I'm outta here.*

CHAPTER 45

Alex and the Puzzle

Alex sat at his desk, looking at wedding pictures on Jeff's Facebook page. *Was their happiness proof that they didn't care about Kristin? Proof that they were somehow involved?* His phone chimed. Alex picked up his phone and swiped right.

"Sheriff," Alex said, his heart pounding in anticipation of new information.

"Good morning, Alex. I'm sorry it's been so long since I've called. I haven't had anything new."

"I understand."

"Danny Stafford pled guilty to burglary and larceny, so he's goin' to prison."

"For how long?"

Sheriff Franklin cleared his throat. "A year. I'm sorry—"

"I don't give a shit about the burglary."

"I know." The sheriff paused. "We're closin' Kristin's case, pendin' further evidence."

"What does that mean?"

"It means, based on the evidence, we think Brett's our guy. If he were alive, we would've arrested him. Unless new evidence surfaces that changes that fact, we're closin' the case."

Alex rubbed the back of his neck. "What about the hairs? It doesn't make sense that the rushed scene didn't have hair evidence, but the other did."

"That was just a theory. I should've kept it to myself. I'm sorry."

"How is it that new evidence is supposed to surface if you're not looking for it?"

Sheriff Franklin took a ragged breath. "It prob'ly won't. I'm sorry, Alex."

Alex disconnected the call and tossed his phone on his desk. The phone chimed, as if the impact caused it to ring. Alex picked it up and swiped right, thinking it was Sheriff Franklin.

"Yeah," Alex said.

"Is this Alex Palmer?" a young woman asked.

"Yeah. Who's this?"

"My name's Clara Harris, and I'm a producer for *48 Hours Mystery*. We're airing a piece on the Norris Lake Murders next Friday—"

"I'm gonna stop you right there. I already told the other producer no. Please don't call me again."

"Many families of victims have told us that appearing on our show offered them closure and comfort."

"Don't call me again." Alex disconnected the call and tossed his phone back on his desk.

He hung his head and rubbed his temples. He took a deep breath, raised his head, and stood from his desk. He approached the six cork-boards cluttering his office. They were nearly filled, front and back, one side for each of the twelve suspects. Every day his investigation got a little more complicated. Another picture, a handwritten note, a thought, a theory.

No more worries about Emma seeing his crazy conspiracy theories. She'd been staying with her parents since Alex left for the wedding four days ago. She was pissed that Alex had gone, even though he hadn't attended the ceremony. She had said that she needed some time away from him. *Of course, even when she was here, she wasn't here.*

Alex stared at the corkboards. It was like a puzzle, missing a crucial piece—a piece that could create the lightbulb moment that would make sense of the jumbled mess. He thought about Sheriff Franklin closing the case. Alex thought about his own "investigation." *Why continue?* It was bullshit really. A way to deal with the pain of losing Kristin. A way to feel useful, even though he knew he was useless. Whatever he did would never bring her back. Still, he couldn't let go. He still had too many unanswered questions. *I won't give up on you, Kristin.*

CHAPTER 46

Alex and *48 Hours Mystery*

Alex sat on his couch, the house quiet and dim, a single lamp shining. He grabbed the remote from the coffee table and flipped on the television. He changed the channel to CBS and watched commercials until the main event.

Finally, a male voice-over spoke while crime scene images flashed across the screen. "'The Norris Lake Murders,' tonight's *48 Hours Mystery*." A high school soccer picture of Brett appeared on the screen. "He was a scholarship athlete with a bright future. Underneath his all-American exterior, did he have a sinister compulsion he couldn't control?"

Pensive intro music played over graphics of chalk lines, bullets firing in slow motion, and police lights turning.

A balding man appeared, identified by a caption as Richard Schlesinger. "Welcome to *48 Hours Mystery*. Imagine it's summer, and you and your family travel to picturesque Norris Lake, Tennessee, for a week of fun in the sun." They cut to images of Norris Lake. Beautiful blue waters, tree-lined cliffs, water-skiers, and a family fishing from a pontoon boat. "Now imagine your perfect family vacation takes a horrifying turn." They cut back to Richard Schlesinger. "Tonight, we'll take you through the case of 'The Norris Lake Murders.'"

A dramatization began with Alex telling Jeff about Brett and his suspicions regarding the recent death of Kristin's dog. The Alex actor said, "Help me keep an eye on him this week."

The *48 Hours Mystery* program cut to Facebook pictures of the Palmer family, and Richard Schlesinger gave brief descriptions of each member. They showed the Palmer family fishing off the dock, jumping from the rope swing, and kayaking—likely pictures supplied by Rachel. "The week started like any other family vacation," Richard said in voice-over. "The weather was beautiful. The Palmer family rented a pontoon boat, went fishing, jumped from rope swings, and went kayaking."

Rachel appeared wearing a designer black dress, perfect makeup, and her blond hair in an updo. A caption appeared that read Rachel Palmer-Roberson. "We were all having a great time until Thursday. After that, it was like we were cursed. My husband and I should've gone home when the bathrooms stopped working."

A Facebook picture of Alex appeared. He held up a beer and stood with the septic guy, while the wiry man sucked shit from the septic tank.

Richard spoke in voice-over. "The rental house's septic system overflowed, causing a backup of waste into the toilets and showers and sinks."

They cut back to Rachel. "It was totally disgusting. We couldn't even, like, use the bathroom. We had to go out in the woods until it was fixed."

Richard appeared on the screen. "The septic backup was fixed the following day. It should've been one of those inside family jokes, but it was a harbinger of far more serious hardships to come." Then *48 Hours Mystery* showed footage of Bubba's Brews. "The Palmer family traveled by boat to the popular sports bar and restaurant, Bubba's Brews." The footage showed a dramatization of a family parking their pontoon boat dockside, in front of the restaurant. "It was here that Rachel Palmer played cornhole with Brett Taylor." The footage showed a couple tossing little bean bags onto wooden platforms, and jumping up and down when one slid into the hole.

They cut to Rachel and Richard Schlesinger sitting across from each other. Rachel said, "Brett asked if anybody wanted to play cornhole, but nobody did, so I, like, played with him. I was just being nice." They showed Rachel in close-up. "Then, while we were playing, he came on to me. I told him no, and his mood went, like, real dark. I figured he was young, and he, like, made a mistake, so I didn't tell anyone. I didn't wanna make things worse."

They cut to Richard. "But things did get worse."

They showed Rachel again. She nodded, her eyes wet. "They did."

The program went to a commercial break. Alex sat on the edge of his couch, his fists clenched. The show returned with a dramatization of the Palmer family joking and laughing on their pontoon. They docked the pontoon and walked up the hill to the house. Shortly thereafter was a bloodcurdling scream. The Alex character in the dramatization ran inside and asked the Kristin character what was wrong. Her room was ransacked.

"Someone was in here," Kristin said.

Richard Schlesinger appeared. "While the Palmers enjoyed their dinner at Bubba's Brews, the rental house was burglarized. The burglar or burglars took electronic devices, jewelry, and women's underwear."

They cut to Rachel. "I felt, like, violated. Someone had been through my stuff."

Then *48 Hours* showed a dramatization of a tattooed man pressure-washing a deck and watching a fake Palmer family playing at the dock across the inlet. Richard spoke over the video. "The Palmers were largely unaware that Danny Stafford had been casing his childhood home—the very same home they were renting. The convicted felon had been evicted from the home by his parents because of his drug and alcohol abuse."

A woman wearing a dress two sizes too small appeared. A caption appeared that read Gina Parker, Danny Stafford's Ex-Wife. "We had it good for a while, but Danny couldn't stay sober. When Danny's parents kicked us out, we didn't have no place to go. We was homeless. I couldn't take Danny's drinkin' and druggin' no more, so I told 'im I was leavin', and I was takin' our little girl with me. I got a job, and I take care of my girl now. I ain't seen Danny since."

The *48 Hours Mystery* program showed Richard Schlesinger and Gina, sitting across from each other. "Was Danny ever violent with you?" Richard asked.

"Sometimes, when he was high," Gina replied.

"Do you think Danny's capable of murder?"

"I sure hope not, but I don't know."

Richard spoke over images of a Norris Lake island. "Danny Stafford, homeless and without his family, settled on this island, where he lived in a tent and took odd jobs. On this island the unthinkable occurred. Was Danny simply living in the wrong place at the wrong time?"

Next, *48 Hours* showed news footage of the island surrounded by Sheriff's Department boats. Two corpses were carried from the woods to the shore in body bags. Richard Schlesinger spoke over the footage. "On Thursday, July 19, University of Tennessee college students, Whitney Lane and Kate Franks were found dead on the very same island that Danny Stafford called home." They cut to Richard in a close-up. "But Danny was nowhere to be found."

Rachel appeared on the screen. "We had been to that island, like, two days before. My brother Jeff found Danny's camp. The guy was wasted, and he had this knife that I guess he, like, used for gutting fish. We got out of there before he woke up. Then, when I saw the island on the news and heard those girls had been killed, I was, like, really scared."

Footage of the island and the body bags appeared again. Richard said, "According to a source in the Norris Lake Sheriff's Department, Whitney Lane was stabbed with a gutting knife, a knife identical to the one Jeff Palmer saw in Danny Stafford's camp. Kate Franks was brutally raped, and her throat was cut. Whitney Lane was decapitated postmortem, and her head was posed in a sexually suggestive position."

They cut to Rachel. "My brother Jeff went to the police to tell them what he'd seen, with, like, the camp and all."

Richard appeared on the screen. "The day after talking to the police about Danny Stafford, every parents' worst nightmare occurred. Kristin Palmer went missing along with her dog, Buster." They showed pictures of Kristin with Brett and Kristin with Buster. "Kristin was last seen with her uncle, Matt Palmer."

Richard spoke over pitch-black skies replacing blue ones. "When *48 Hours* returns, a massive storm approaches, and the Palmer family desperately searches for Kristin and Buster."

The show returned with the dramatization. The Emma Palmer character called for Buster, but he didn't come. Everyone searched, but Kristin and Buster were nowhere to be found. The search expanded from the house to the dock outside. The kayaks were missing, so Alex and Jeff took the search to the water with the pontoon boat. They found Rachel and Brett on an island. Alex interrogated Brett, but Brett claimed he hadn't seen Kristin.

Rachel appeared on the screen. "I was on my way back from kayaking, when I saw Brett. He wanted me to check out this island with him, so I went." Rachel took a deep breath, her blue-tinted contacts moist. "I'm, like, lucky to be alive. I don't know what would've happened if my family didn't, like, … find me."

The adaptation continued with the rain falling in earnest and the search party bringing Brett and Rachel back to the house. The power was out, the house dimly lit with what little remained of the sun. The phone rang, and the Alex actor picked up. The Sheriff Franklin actor dropped the bombshell about Brett's gold chain and crucifix being found on Whitney Lane's dead body. The sheriff said they couldn't come until morning because of the storm and the flooding. Alex tried to tell the sheriff that Kristin was missing, but the phone line died.

Alex grabbed Brett by the collar, shoved him against the wall, and demanded to know where Kristin was. Alex threatened to kill Brett and had to be held back by the Jeff and Harvey actors. Brett was shoved into his basement "jail cell." Alex and Matt searched Brett's room, and they discovered the hidden compartment in Brett's suitcase. With dramatic flair, Alex removed Buster's dog collar and Kristin's gold chain and crucifix.

The *48 Hours Mystery* program cut to a young woman—fresh faced, thin—wearing a long peasant dress. The caption on the screen read Wendy Wilkerson, Friend of Kristin Palmer. Wendy said, "Kristin never took off her cross. Never. This one time, she took it off to go swimming at the beach, and she almost drowned. She never took it off again, not until ..."

The adaptation showed the Palmer family searching in the driving rain, on foot, with flashlights cutting through the dark neighborhood, and on the lake, the pontoon being rocked by rough water.

They showed the Jeff actor, nodding off, while sitting in a chair outside Brett's "jail cell." Brett crept from the basement room and slipped past the sleeping guard. Richard spoke over the dramatization. "Brett Taylor was desperate to get away. Maybe he was afraid of the police. Maybe he was afraid Alex Palmer would make good on his threats."

The adaptation showed Brett stealing Kristin's keys and Alex and Matt entering the house through the back door. Brett hurried out the front door as Alex and Matt went to the basement to check on their captive. Alex and Matt were stunned at the open door and empty room. Alex yelled at Jeff to wake up. A car engine whirred from outside. The three brothers raced outside to see Brett stuck one-third of the way up the steep driveway. The car spun 180 degrees, and Brett jumped from the car, leaving it unmanned to race on a collision course toward the brothers. Alex and Matt and Jeff dove out of the way, the car narrowly missing them, crashing into Harvey's BMW.

They showed Rachel. "My brothers chased after Brett, but they lost him. Then when they came back to the house they heard the Jet Ski. There was this Jet Ski near our dock that the people always left the keys in the starter thingy. Brett, like, took it."

The dramatization continued with Brett zipping through the dark, stormy lake on a Jet Ski and the brothers chasing in a pontoon boat. The brothers found the marooned Jet Ski and Brett swimming for shore. Matt swam after Brett, subdued the teen, and pulled him back to the boat. As they motored home with their captive, the pontoon pitched on the rough waters; Brett punched Jeff and dove off the front of the pontoon. There was a thud; the motor sputtered, and a cloud of dark red blood came from their wake. Alex turned the pontoon around. Matt dove in the water again and swam to Brett's floating form. He turned over Brett and reeled back.

They cut to Richard Schlesinger. "Brett Taylor was sucked into the propeller face-first and killed. His death left many unanswered questions. When *48 Hours Mystery* returns, the search for Kristin comes to a dramatic conclusion."

CHAPTER 47

Alex and MO

Alex still sat on the edge of his couch, the remote in hand. He had planned on turning it off, but it was like a bad accident—he couldn't look away.

The *48 Hours'* dramatization portrayed the somber ride back to the dock, the boat on *E*, and Brett wrapped in a tarp. What *48 Hours* didn't know or simply didn't include was Alex's and Matt's tangent with Henry "Hank" Marshall and his assertion that Rachel and Brett left the dock *together* on their kayaks.

The search continued through the woods, the Palmer family spread out, their flashlights cutting through the darkness. Matt found the grave and alerted the search party. The *48 Hours'* rendition omitted Matt's shovel. Kristin's hand was already reaching from the grave. Alex and Emma dug frantically. Kristin's face was pale, her lips blue, with bruising around her neck. The Kristin double was close enough that Alex had to turn away from the television. The Alex and Emma doubles sobbed in the driving rain, their dead daughter's muddy face exposed.

Alex turned back to the television. The dramatization cut to the lake house, with police boats at the dock. Sheriff Franklin interviewed Alex. He talked about the evidence they'd found in Brett's suitcase. He talked about Kristin's other dead dog, Charlie, and his suspicions that Brett was responsible.

The *48 Hours Mystery* program cut to an overweight teen. The caption underneath him read Rusty Laffer, Former Classmate of Brett Taylor. Rusty said, "He was nice to the girls and the popular boys, like the athletes and stuff, but he was a bully to everyone else. When we were in middle school, he took all my clothes in gym class and threw them in the trash can."

Kristin's friend Wendy reappeared. "Kristin knew Brett had a dark side, but she thought, deep down, he was a good person. Kristin was like that. She always saw the good in everyone."

Another teen boy was shown, this one pimply and gangly. "Brett was a bully. He used to push me in the hall and throw firecrackers at my cat. Then he'd act all innocent and nice when a teacher or an adult was around."

They cut to a thin woman with deep crease lines and the puckering mouth wrinkles of a smoker. The caption read Blanche Taylor, Brett's Mother. She said, "My son wasn't perfect. I never said he was. He got into his fair share of trouble, but he sure as hell ain't no murderer. That Danny Stafford set him up."

They cut to Richard and Blanche sitting across from each other. "What makes you think Danny Stafford set up Brett?" Richard Schlesinger asked.

"Danny Stafford admitted to breakin' into their house," Blanche replied. "He could've taken hairs from Brett's hairbrush. He could've planted the hairs on the bodies. It don't make no sense that they found Brett's hairs on two girls he didn't even know, but no hairs on his girlfriend."

A rusty trailer home appeared on the screen. The caption underneath read One Week Later. The dramatization portrayed Sheriff Franklin and his deputies forcefully entering the trailer. Inside, drug addicts lay on soiled mattresses. In reality, Danny was high as a kite and nearly comatose when they found him. During the dramatization, Danny was spry as he ran through the back door, directly into a handful of deputies. They found the gutting knife with a droplet of Kate's blood on the handle.

The program presented real-life footage of Sheriff Franklin interrogating Danny Stafford in a small room with a one-way mirror.

"I didn't have nothin' to do with them girls," Danny said, sitting handcuffed.

"They were killed in your camp, with your knife," Sheriff Franklin said, sitting across from Danny, his hat on the table.

"I came back from work and found 'em like that."

"Where were you workin'?"

"I was on Lakeshore at the Wilson place. Mrs. Wilson had me hand weedin' their riprap. Crappy job. She don't like usin' Roundup."

"What time?"

"All day. Got there around eight. Didn't leave until at least five."

"Can Mrs. Wilson vouch for that?"

"She wasn't watchin' me all day, but she saw me in the mornin' when I started and *agin* in the afternoon to pay me."

"I'll check it out." Sheriff Franklin paused for a moment and narrowed his eyes. "If you're innocent, why'd you run?"

"I'm not stupid. I knew you'd think I did it." Danny took a deep breath. "I was scared too. What happened to them girls"—Danny shook his head—"was just plain wrong. I never wanna see somethin' like that *agin*."

"Why'd you take the knife, Danny?"

"'Cause I was worried you'd use it to pin a double murder on me."

The *48 Hours Mystery* program cut to Richard Schlesinger. "Danny Stafford pled guilty to burglarizing the Palmers while they were renting his childhood home. Danny remains steadfast in his innocence of the murders of Kate Franks, Whitney Lane, and Kristin Palmer. Danny Stafford's alibi checked out. Mrs. Wilson did see Danny in the morning and the afternoon but not during the day, so it is possible Danny left the jobsite, committed the murders, and returned to work.

"The Norris Lake Sheriff's Department recently closed the case, citing a lack of physical evidence to prosecute Danny Stafford. Apart from the murder weapon, no physical evidence ties Danny Stafford to any of the murders. Did Brett Taylor use Danny's knife? Brett had been to the island before and knew the knife was there. Or did Danny commit the murders and plant Brett's hairs on the body? What about Kristin? Did Brett Taylor kill his girlfriend, and, in a grisly bit of serendipity, Danny framed Brett for the double murder of Kate Franks and Whitney Lane? Or were they working together—Brett the young apprentice and Danny Stafford the modern-day Charles Manson?

"The case of the Norris Lake murders continues to provoke questions without answers. Danny Stafford will be free in eleven months. Did he get away with murder?"

Alex turned off the television, the house now silent. He was startled by the chime of his cell phone on the coffee table. He leaned forward, picked up his phone, checked the Caller ID, and swiped left, sending the call to voice mail. Almost immediately, his phone chimed again. The same caller. Alex sent the call to voice mail again. His phone chimed for a third time.

Alex blew out a breath and answered the call. "Hey, Matt," Alex said.

"I know you don't wanna talk to anyone right now, but I have something really important to tell you," Matt replied.

"Okay?"

"Did you watch *48 Hours*?"

"Yeah."

"I know you wanna put all this behind you, but I saw something tonight that I think you should know about."

"I'm listening."

Matt took a deep breath. "When I was in Afghanistan, there was this rumor—this rumor about this SF captain who was killing Afghani women and calling in airstrikes to cover up the evidence. Nobody believed that shit, but it was like a ghost story guys passed down."

"I don't understand."

"It's the details of the story that you need to hear. According to what

I was told, there was this sergeant who was with this captain when he was interrogating this family in the Ghazni Province. The captain ordered the sergeant to leave the house. There were a few gun shots, and then, like half an hour later, the captain came out of the house, and he had blood on him. The captain then ordered an airstrike. The sergeant snuck into the house, even though an airstrike was coming. He found the parents shot dead. The daughter was naked. Her head was cut off and put between her legs—"

Alex lurched upright from the couch, his heart pounding. "Holy shit. It's the same MO."

"I know. And we both know an SF captain who was in the Ghazni Province."

Alex clenched his jaw, rage coursing through his veins.

"You still there?" Matt asked.

"Yeah. What happened next?"

"Supposedly, the captain saw the sergeant coming out of the house, and the captain went crazy, threatening to court martial the sergeant for disobeying an order. The sergeant never made it back to the FOB. He died in a friendly fire accident."

"If this story's true, the sergeant must've told someone on his team before he died."

"Yeah, but I couldn't tell you who. I was probably hearing this fifth-hand, so who knows how distorted the story is or if it's even true?"

"Do you think it's true?"

"When I was in Afghanistan, I thought it was bullshit. Now … I don't know. I mean, there were different versions of the story I told you. Not all of them said the guy was an SF captain, and not all of them even took place in Ghazni Province. The only common thread is that it took place in Afghanistan, and the girl was decapitated, and her head was staged in a sexual-type position." Matt paused. "I think we really need to call the sheriff about this."

"They didn't prosecute Danny Stafford, and he had the murder weapon. What do you think they'll do with a rumor?" Alex asked.

Matt blew out a breath. "Nothing."

"Could you do me a favor and keep this between us?"

"What are you gonna do?"

"I don't know yet."

CHAPTER 48

Alex and Justice

After Matt's revelation, Alex went to his office and typed and clicked at a frenetic pace, searching murder cases involving decapitations of young women, rape, and the staging of the bodies in sexually suggestive positions. By hour six, he was relatively numb to the sick stories of murder and rape and decapitation. Some offenders liked to rape postmortem, others while the woman was still alive. Some played with their dead victims, dressing them up, washing their hair, and doing their makeup. Some held their victims' captive for days before the murder, others for hours; and some murdered in a spontaneous spree.

Alex researched news articles and websites and a few books—immediately downloaded to his Kindle. After ten hours, the morning sun pierced his blinds, and he had four cases that stood out. These cases all had female victims in their teens to early twenties, all raped premortem, decapitated, and posed in sexually suggestive positions. They all died from exsanguination. They were all white, which didn't jive with Matt's story of the Afghani girl. Of course, there probably weren't many young white girls walking around Afghanistan.

The first case was in Perry Township, Pennsylvania, October 29, 2014. A twenty-two-year-old prostitute was found in the woods, naked, her head severed and placed between her legs. As far as Alex could find online, there were no suspects and no arrests.

The second case was in Key West, Florida, June 3, 2016. A twenty-year-old college student was found in a cove, her head severed and her body posed, also with her head between her legs. A twenty-one-year-old UCF senior was arrested for the crime. His semen was found inside the victim. His hairs and fingerprints were found on the victim's body. The murder weapon—a fixed blade—was found in the young man's hotel room. The young man was two years into a life sentence.

The third case was in Duck, North Carolina, August 23, 2017. A twenty-two-year-old woman was found in her parents' beach house, decapitated and posed like the others. She had recently broken up with a local landscaper. According to text messages between her best friend, the landscaper was desperate to get back together. He had shown up to her house unannounced on several occasions. One time he had grabbed her. The incident had shaken her up enough to get a restraining order. The woman's body was found with hairs that matched the landscaper. The fixed blade used to cut the woman's throat was found in the landscaper's shed.

The fourth case was in Jackson Hole, Wyoming, January 3, 2018. A seventeen-year-old high school senior was found in a hotel basement with her head severed and again the head posed between her legs. Two men were arrested for the crime—a thirty-two-year-old yoga teacher and a forty-five-year-old mentally challenged man. The yoga teacher's semen was found inside the victim, and his skin was found under her fingernails. Fresh scars were found on the yoga teacher's back. The mentally challenged man was a hotel employee who lived in a basement room. Hairs from the mentally challenged man were found on the victim. The murder weapon—a fixed blade combat knife—was found on his dresser with his fingerprints and blood from the victim.

The police believed that the yoga teacher had manipulated the mentally challenged man into killing the young woman after the yoga teacher had raped her. The yoga teacher was currently serving life in prison, and the mentally challenged man was in a mental institution for the criminally insane.

Alex checked his phone. It was nearly 8:00 a.m. He called Sheriff Franklin.

"It's Saturday, Alex," the sheriff said in lieu of a greeting.

For the next hour, Alex told the sheriff what he'd discovered. "I think Jeff committed these murders and framed these guys to take the fall, just like Brett and Danny."

"Two of your cases involve more than just hairs and murder weapons. How do you explain the semen?"

"The sex was consensual."

"The young girl at the hotel had the yoga teacher's skin under her fingernails."

"I think it was part of their thing. If he raped the girl, he probably would've restrained her, or, if she was trying to stop it, scratching his face or eyes would make much more sense than his back."

"Except for the Perry Township case, these cases have all been closed—by *professionals*," Sheriff Franklin replied. "And, even if you did have somethin', these departments aren't gonna be interested in reopenin' cases. Opens them up to lawsuits."

"What about justice? These guys are in prison for crimes they didn't commit. My daughter's murderer is still out there."

The sheriff sighed heavily. "First of all, you don't know that. You can't just go around puttin' pieces together because you want them to fit. Brett's our guy. Maybe Danny had somethin' to do with it, but we don't have enough on him. My gut says he didn't have anything to do with it. You're gonna have to let it go, Alex."

"All you have to do is check if Jeff was in these places during the murders, and you got him."

"It's not that simple," Sheriff Franklin said.

"Can't you check his credit card receipts and cell phone records? You should check Gwen's too."

"Even if it turns out he was in these places, that doesn't mean he did it or, more important, that I can *prove* he did it."

Alex frowned. "You can't be serious? I mean, what are the odds? Young women just turn up dead and decapitated every time this asshole goes on vacation? And some poor sap ends up with his hairs at the scene?"

"You were sure that Brett Taylor was the killer too."

Alex huffed. "Are you gonna look into it or not?"

"How's your family doin'?"

Alex was quiet for a moment. "It's been a struggle."

"I can't tell you that I understand what you're goin' through, because I don't. But I do know that, at some point, you have to let it go, or this piece of shit will take everything from you. You have a wife who needs you. If I check this out, and the dates don't match Jeff's or Gwen's activities, you have to promise me that you'll let it go."

"Okay."

"The warrant we did in July gave us access to the lake house, your cars, and everyone's phone records, bank statements, and credit card statements for the prior twelve months. I'd need another warrant for the first two cases, but I'll check the two recent cases. If you're right, I should see activity that matches from Duck, North Carolina, and Jackson Hole at the time of those murders."

CHAPTER 49

Alex and the Investigation

Alex dumped a bag of fun-size Snickers bars into a large bowl. He placed the bowl outside with a sign that read Trick or Treat, Take Two. He turned on the porch light. It was only four in the afternoon, but it would be dark in an hour or so. Alex glanced up and down the street, hoping to see a few kids in their costumes. His neighborhood of acre lots and McMansions was like a ghost town. He didn't expect many trick-or-treaters. The houses were too far apart. It was a long walk to each potential treat, and more than a handful of the wannabe-wealthy gave healthy snacks instead of candy.

When Kristin was seven, she had begged them to allow her to dress up as Jesus Christ for Halloween. Many parishioners of their church forbid Halloween. They considered it a satanic holiday. Kristin didn't mean any disrespect. If anything, she meant the opposite. She loved Jesus so much that she wanted to be just like him. Alex and Emma thought it might be on the side of blasphemy, so they had compromised, and Kristin went as Moses. They told their friends from church that she was Socrates.

Alex went back to his home office. The six freestanding corkboards were now solely dedicated to Jeff and his suspected murders. The Norris Lake corkboard was the most developed, but the others had taken shape over the past four days. Alex sat behind his desk and woke up his laptop. He went back through Jeff's real estate records. It was amazing what you could find out with an internet connection and a social security number.

As the backup executor to Harvey's will, Alex was privy to paperwork and social security numbers of the beneficiaries. Harvey's estate and future book royalties would go to Cathy first, then they would be passed down to Alex, Jeff, and Rachel—split evenly. Alex never told Matt that he was left out, although Alex didn't think Matt would be surprised. Harvey and Matt had never bonded as father and son. Matt was only two when Harvey left. Alex had never talked about his love for Harvey to Matt. They shared a strong bond as father and son. Well, as strong a bond as you could have with Harvey. Alex was four years older than Matt and consequently had spent more time with their father before the divorce.

According to the background check Alex bought, Jeff had his townhouse in Alexandria, but nothing else. Alex had expected to find a place in Pennsylvania or West Virginia, near the state line—close to the earliest murder on his corkboards. It was the only unsolved murder in the eyes of the authorities. *Maybe Jeff has learned to frame people as he's matured as a serial killer. Maybe he didn't like that, technically, as long as the case was open, someone was looking for him. Maybe he's learned to not shit where he eats, as Harvey would say.*

Alex's cell phone chimed. He swiped right and put the phone to his ear. "Sheriff," Alex said.

"Alex," Sheriff Franklin replied. "I checked those dates you gave me against Jeff's records. There's nothin', Alex. No credit card transactions, no cell phone records, nothin' from those places."

"What about Gwen's records?"

"I checked her phone and credit cards too."

Alex frowned. "Maybe he paid in cash. Don't you think it's strange that they have no records?"

"I said, 'nothin' from those places.' They both have phone records and credit card transactions in Northern Virginia durin' the Duck,

North Carolina, murder and records from Tennessee durin' the Jackson Hole murder. They were at home in Virginia and, I'd guess, visitin' Harvey in Tennessee when those murders occurred. In fact, they have no records from Duck or Jackson Hole at any time over the twelve months I searched."

Alex banged the side of his fist on the desk like a gavel. "Something's not right. He did it. I don't know how, but he did it. I can feel it in my bones."

"That's not evidence, Alex. I think you know that. You're too close to see clearly."

The men were silent for a moment.

Sheriff Franklin broke the silence. "When I was first elected sheriff, a young girl was raped. She was so ashamed about what happened that she washed every bit of evidence off her. After sittin' with the shame, she got angry and reported the rape. The young man who she accused was the son of a well-to-do lawyer with a mansion on the lake. It was a no-win case from the get-go. The girl's father was obsessed with the case. He wanted revenge. He tried to kill the young man with a tire iron, but the young man defended himself—beat the guy up pretty bad. The well-to-do lawyer wanted us to arrest the father, but I refused, citin' lack of evidence.

"Unfortunately, there was footage of the incident on a security camera outside the bar where it happened. I struck a deal with that piece-of-shit lawyer. I told him that I'd drop the rape case against his son if they dropped the assault case. From my perspective, it was a good deal because I knew we'd never win the rape case. The lawyer knew that too, but he didn't want his son dragged through the papers."

"What does this have to do with me?" Alex asked.

"The girl's father couldn't let it go. He was obsessed with the case. He started stalkin' the young man, tryin' to find more evidence, tryin' to make him pay for what he'd done. Meanwhile, his daughter didn't wanna be reminded of what happened. She wanted to move on, but he couldn't let it go. She ran away from home, and he committed suicide."

"What happened to the girl?"

"She died a few years ago of a meth overdose."

Alex hung his head. "My daughter's already dead."

"That's not the point," Sheriff Franklin said. "If you surround yourself with evil, it'll consume you piece by piece until you got nothin' left. Let it go."

Alex was quiet.

"You hear me?" the sheriff asked.

"I hear you."

"Take care of yourself, Alex."

Alex disconnected the call and stared into the tiny screen on his cell. He thought about what Sheriff Franklin had said about surrounding himself with evil. *I won't give up on Kristin. Is this really about her? Maybe I'm well on my way to losing everything.* He thought about Emma. They hadn't talked in weeks and hadn't seen each other in a month. He tapped Contacts and tapped the Emma icon.

"Alex?" Emma said.

"It's me." Alex swallowed the lump in his throat. "I'm sorry for everything."

"No, I'm—"

"You were right. I lied, and our daughter's gone. If I had told the truth about my job, we might never have gone to the lake, and Kristin would still be alive. I'm sorry. I know how little that means now. I don't know what else to say."

"No, I'm sorry. It's not your fault. I was angry, and I had no right to put this on you. I've been wanting to call you and tell you that, but I've just been … avoiding everything."

"I want you to come home. Maybe we can make a nice dinner and talk."

"I'm actually working right now. Well, technically, I'm on break."

"Oh."

"Nobody wanted to work on Halloween, so I'm working a double shift."

"Maybe tomorrow?"

"Are you ready to move on?" Emma asked.

"Did you watch *48 Hours*?" Alex replied.

"Oh, Alex."

"Just hear me out. Matt saw it, and the MO from the island murders matched murders that happened in Afghanistan by an SF captain. Jeff used to be an SF captain in the same place where the murders happened. Then more murders with the same MO happen at Norris Lake. What are the chances?"

Emma blew out a breath. "You're unbelievable. Now you're blaming Jeff? Brett killed our little girl. End of story. We can't go back and fix it. We can't get justice. It's over. Jeff and Gwen have been nothing but supportive. They'd be devastated if they heard you talking like this."

"Have you been talking to them?" Alex's eyes were wide.

"Did you know that Gwen's pregnant?"

"You've been talking to Gwen?"

"Yes, she's been my Facebook friend for a long time, and she wanted some baby advice, so we've been talking—"

"I don't want you going anywhere near Jeff."

"Would you stop. This is insane. Who are you gonna accuse next? Matt? Me? You know, Jeff actually calls me every week to see how you are. I think he's really hurt that you never call him back. You have to stop this. Everyone loves you. God loves you—"

"Fuck God."

"I'm hanging up if you're gonna talk like that."

Alex rubbed his temples. "I'm sorry." There was a moment of silence. "Please, Emma, don't go near Jeff. I'm begging you."

"I'm not going anywhere. I barely have time to think, much less travel to Virginia. Gwen did invite me to their house for a girls' weekend."

"I don't want you going."

"That's not your decision. Not that I can go anyway. *Someone* has to work."

Alex grit his teeth.

"Besides, it's just some of Gwen's friends from college. Jeff's not even gonna be there. He's going to some cabin for the weekend, and she didn't wanna be alone."

Alex sat up straight. "What cabin? Where?"

"I don't know."

"What weekend?"

"It's next Saturday, the tenth, I think."

"I have some trick-or-treaters at the door. Can I call you tomorrow?"

"Are you gonna bring up this craziness again?"

"No."

"I'll talk to you tomorrow."

"I love you, Emma."

She paused. "Me too."

She disconnected the call, and Alex tossed his phone on the desk. He went to his laptop and ordered a background check for Harvey. His Tennessee mansion was listed in his real estate records, along with his first starter house and the two houses in between.

Alex sat, tapping his finger to his lip. *What about Gwen's parents? Maybe they have a cabin. No way. They're city people. I can't imagine them anyplace that's not climate-controlled.* Alex smacked his palms on the desktop. *Grandpa Palmer.*

Alex searched for Roger Alan Palmer. He didn't have his grandfather's social, but, with Harvey's number, Alex was able to find the right Roger Alan Palmer. Alex searched his grandpa's real estate assets, and there it was. A cabin in Monongalia County, West Virginia. Alex checked Google Maps. It was a hop, skip, and a jump from the Pennsylvania line and Perry Township where Alex believed the first stateside murder had occurred.

There's still the problem of the phone records and credit card receipts. Maybe Jeff hired someone to use their credit cards and phones while they were away. It wouldn't be hard to find some dirtball on Craig's List to use your phone and spend your money.

Jeff's not stupid. If he were gonna go on vacation and commit serial murders, it would make sense to not have a record that he was there. It wouldn't be that hard, but how would he get Gwen to go along with it? Maybe he tells her that he wants it to be a romantic vacation without being bothered by their phones. Maybe he tells her that he doesn't wanna run up their credit cards. He doesn't wanna feel stressed about money when they're supposed to be on vacation. Maybe. If I'm gonna do this, I need verification. There can't be any doubt.

Alex navigated to Facebook on his laptop. He had already searched the murder locations on Jeff's Facebook page, but had found nothing. Alex logged out of his account and into Emma's. He knew her email, and her password was simple and no secret—Kristin4142001. First name and birth date.

He wasn't Facebook friends with Gwen, not because he didn't like her, but it just had never happened. She often showed up in his potential friend list with many friends in common, but he never made the request and neither did she. He couldn't do it now. It would be suspicious.

Alex, using Emma's account, searched Gwen's page for Key West, Florida; Jackson Hole, Wyoming; and Duck, North Carolina, plus alternately the Outer Banks, North Carolina.

There was nothing. Absolutely nothing. Alex shook his head. *I'm missing something. This is what Facebook's for, so people can brag about their stupid-ass vacations. Maybe I'm wrong. Maybe they were never there. But surely they've been on vacation together.* Alex searched Gwen Stanton-Palmer and vacation. He scrolled through the results. There was a public post from a Stacy Porter-Clark. Gwen was tagged on the post that posed the question, Where was your best vacation ever?

Gwen Stanton-Palmer: Sorry, the hubby and I keep our spots secret. He wants to have me and me alone, no distractions and nobody but us. It's a way for us to really reconnect. We don't even bring cell phones. I love it. ☺

Stacy Porter-Clark: Awwwww, aren't you lucky.

Alex smacked his palms on his desk. "I knew it." He opened Emma's Instant Messenger and found Gwen. There was a long string of messages back and forth with various baby tips and encouragement from Emma and gratitude and sympathy from Gwen. Gwen's sympathy revolved around Alex and Emma's crumbling marriage, not Kristin. The dead-daughter topic was too nuclear hot to broach. Gwen mostly typed platitudes like, *He'll come around*; *It'll get better*, and *My heart goes out to you*. Alex typed a message:

Emma Palmer: As you know, Alex and I have been struggling. ☹ I want to take some time off and go away with Alex. Maybe if we can get away from the memories, we can start over. I was wondering if you had any recommendations for vacation spots? I was interested in going to one or maybe a few of the following places, but I can't seem to make up my mind. Have you been to any of these places recently?
San Francisco, California
Jackson Hole, Wyoming
Bermuda
Duck, North Carolina
Niagara Falls, Canada
Key West, Florida
Acapulco, Mexico

Alex threw in a few other vacation spots so he didn't arouse any suspicion. *Who knows? Jeff might monitor Gwen's Facebook account.* Alex sent the message to Gwen. He waited, watching the screen with steepled fingers. A few minutes later, Messenger read **Gwen Stanton-Palmer**: *Typing*. Alex sat up straight in anticipation.

Gwen Stanton-Palmer: A vacation sounds like a great idea! ☺ I could use one myself. Jeff and I have been to a few of those places. Duck, Key West, and Mexico, but not Acapulco. We went to Cancun for our honeymoon. We had a blast, but I'm too old for that stuff now.
I would definitely go back to Duck and Key West. As you know, we were just in Duck for Rachel's wedding. It's much too chilly to get in the water now, but offseason in the Outer Banks is really relaxing. Key West is beautiful, but I don't know what it's like in the fall. We were there in the early summer, and it was gorgeous!
I hope this helps!

They've been to two of the hot spots. But not Jackson Hole? That's weird. The Key West murder took place June 3, 2016. Technically, that's not early summer, but it's close. Let's see if I can narrow it down.

Emma Palmer: Thank you, Gwen! I was reading about Key West, and a few reviews complained about construction this past summer. When you were there, was there lots of construction?

Gwen Stanton-Palmer: I don't remember any construction, but we were there in 2016.

Bingo.

Emma Palmer: I'd like to go to Duck next summer, but before it gets too hot. With my fair skin, I burn up in the heat. Did you guys ever go there in the summer? How hot was it?

Gwen Stanton-Palmer: We were there in August. It was HOT. Jeff and I do okay in the heat. We both tan pretty well. If you don't like the heat, I would go in the spring or maybe early summer.

The Duck murder took place August 23, 2017.

225

Emma Palmer: Thank you, Gwen! You've been so helpful. I think I'm leaning toward Jackson Hole. Have you ever been there? I thought Harvey mentioned something about you two going there.

Alex waited for a reply. Messenger showed that Gwen started to type, then stopped. Then typed again.

Gwen Stanton-Palmer: No, we've never been. I think Harvey and Cathy may have been there though. But I don't know for sure.

Alex frowned. *May have been, don't know for sure—she's withholding.*

Emma Palmer: Thank you so much, Gwen. ☺

Gwen Stanton-Palmer: Can you not mention this to anyone? Jeff's weird about me talking about our vacations. He wants to keep "our" spots a secret. As if Key West and Duck are secrets!

Emma Palmer: Of course. I understand. Thank you again. ☺

Alex printed the message string, then deleted it, and logged out of Emma's Facebook account. He logged into Emma's email account and deleted the Facebook notification emails relating to the messages with Gwen. He closed Emma's email and tapped his finger to his lip. *Why would she be fine with telling me details about Duck and Key West, but not Jackson Hole? Maybe they were never there. Maybe Jeff didn't do it. Harvey does have access to the cabin. Harvey could've killed Kristin, then went to the store with Cathy. He could've killed Whitney and Kate on that island. He wasn't in Afghanistan, but he was in Iraq. Maybe the story Matt told had followed guys to Afghanistan and gradually changed to fit the new location. Storytellers often personalize stories to the audience.*
Or maybe Gwen's lying about Jackson Hole. But why? What's different

about Jackson Hole? In Duck, the woman was found dead in her parents' beach house. In Key West, the woman was found outside in a cove. In Jackson Hole, the woman was found in the basement of a hotel. Maybe Gwen didn't wanna mention Jackson Hole because the murder happened in her hotel. Maybe she suspected Jeff but doesn't wanna believe it. Maybe they were gone before she heard about the Key West and Duck murders. Or maybe he keeps the news away from her when they're vacationing. They don't have their cell phones. He probably says no to watching the news or any television for that matter. But it would be hard not to know about a murder that occurs in your hotel.

Alex navigated to Google Maps. It would take him at least twenty-six hours to drive from his house in Mount Juliet, Tennessee, to Jackson Hole, Wyoming.

CHAPTER 50

Alex and Jackson Hole

Alex drove on NE 2 West through the Nebraska prairie. The two-lane highway was bordered by straw-colored grass and endless cattle fencing. The sun was low on the horizon. He flipped on his headlights. His phone chimed. It was Emma.

Shit.

He picked up his phone and swiped right. "Hey, Emma."

"Hey, honey," she replied. "How did it go last night?"

"How did what go?"

"With the trick-or-treaters? How many did you have? Any cute costumes? You did have candy, right?"

"We only had a few kids, and I had little Snickers' bars. I didn't want kids egging the house or putting a flaming pile of shit on the front porch."

Emma laughed. "Kids don't do that stuff."

"They don't? I did."

"Because you were a degenerate."

Alex laughed. It had been so long since they had laughed together.

"I thought you said you were gonna call me today," Emma said.

Alex sucked air between his teeth. "Yeah, I'm sorry. I totally forgot. I have this interview in Missouri tomorrow. HR manager for a freight company. I didn't tell you about it yesterday because I didn't think it was legit, but the owner called me this morning and told me that they'd pay for my miles and put me up in a room. I guess they're really interested in me. I'm in Missouri now. I'm sorry I didn't tell you. I guess I got excited and forgot my head."

There was a moment of silence. "I used to be the first person you'd talk to if you were excited about something."

"I know. It's been an adjustment with you not at home."

"Were you even gonna discuss moving to Missouri, or were you just gonna leave me?"

"No, I wouldn't take the job unless you agree to come with me. I've been on a ton of interviews, but I don't like telling you because I've been turned down every time. I'd rather tell you when I have something real." Alex hadn't been on a single interview, and he certainly wasn't traveling to one now.

"I should get back to work."

"Emma, don't be mad."

"I'm not. I gotta go." She hung up.

* * *

Alex made it to Jackson Hole the next afternoon. He had slept in his truck at a rest stop in southern Wyoming. He felt like shit after thirty-four straight hours in his truck. Alex drove through the town square past cowboy bars, restaurants, outfitters, boot shops, banks, realty companies, and rugged clothing stores. The town was full of foot traffic—white people in North Face and Patagonia gear, carrying their shopping bags. The car and truck traffic were brisk as well. Late model SUVs and 4x4s mingled with luxury cars. Jackson Hole was where rich people went to feel down-to-earth.

Beyond the quaint, yet high-end shops and restaurants stood the Teton Mountains. Even among the shopping and modern luxuries, it was hard not to feel insignificant in the shadow of those snow-covered peaks.

Alex found the Grand Teton Resort and Spa fifteen minutes outside of town. He parked in the lot marked Guests Only. Most of the vehicles had hotel parking passes, but a few didn't. *I doubt they tow very often. If a guest had their car towed, they'd be seriously pissed.*

He was surprised the resort was still open. *The girl's family must've sued. The yoga teacher and the mentally challenged man both worked for the hotel. What were their names?* He leaned over and grabbed the file folder from the passenger seat. *Jerry Tripp and Javier Vasquez.*

Alex glanced in the rearview mirror. *I look like shit.* And he did—stubbly face, bloodshot eyes, and disheveled hair. He grabbed his electric razor from his duffel bag and shaved his stubble. Then he combed his hair, grabbed his jacket, and walked toward the front entrance. The stone-and-wood resort was five stories tall with a massive entry framed with logs and guarded by a stuffed black bear. Alex entered, the large automatic doors opening for him.

The lobby was three stories of open air; at one end was a massive stone fireplace and a sitting area with cushy leather furniture. Opposite the sitting area, three receptionists checked weary travelers into their rooms. Alex walked past reception as if he were a guest. He found the elevators.

From his research, he knew that Javier had worked in the laundry room and was supervised by housekeeping. He also knew that the murder took place in the basement, and Javier had also lived down there. Inside the elevator he looked at the panel, but the lowest floor was *1.* He stepped out of the elevator and noticed a freight elevator, but it was only accessible by key. *I guess they learned their lesson. No guests in the basement.*

Alex found the stairwell and walked down a flight of stairs. He grabbed the door handle, but the door to the basement was locked. *They really did learn their lesson.* He gazed through the small window. There was a dingy hallway with weathered gray carpeting. *The employees definitely know they're not on vacation.* He put his hands on his hips. *Well, shit. What am I supposed to do now?*

The door opened, and a tiny Latina entered the stairwell, her face glued to her phone. She propped the door with a piece of wood, turned around, and looked up at Alex. She smiled. "Hello. Did you need something, sir?"

Alex smiled. "Yes, I have a meeting with the housekeeping supervisor."

She narrowed her eyes. "With Flora?"

"I assume. I wasn't told her name. I work for the company that makes all the little soaps and shampoos."

"Prob'ly you're supposed to meet with Flora." She opened the door and stepped into the dim hall. "It's the third door on the left."

"Thank you."

Alex walked down the hallway, past the laundry and the supply room. The placard next to the third door read Flora Jimenez. The door was open. A woman sat behind a metal desk, clicking on a laptop. Alex knocked on the open door. She looked up. She was pretty—straight dark hair in a ponytail—and had a young-looking face with symmetrical features, although Alex reckoned she was in her mid-thirties.

She stood with her brow furrowed. "May I help you?"

"Are you Flora Jimenez?"

"I am."

"I was hoping I could talk to you about Javier Vasquez."

Her jaw tightened. "I'm not allowed to comment. Who are you, and what is your business here?"

"I have some information that may prove his innocence—"

"Are you a police officer?"

"No."

"You need to leave before I call security."

"This is really important."

She picked up her phone, staring at Alex with her eyebrows raised.

"Please, just hear me out."

She dialed nine, then hit two digits for security.

"My daughter was murdered," Alex said.

She stared at Alex for a moment. "No, ... everything's fine. Sorry. I dialed the wrong extension." She hung up.

"I think the person who killed my daughter also killed the girl here."

"How do you know?"

"He's my brother."

Flora's eyes widened.

"May I sit down and talk to you, just for a few minutes?" Alex asked.

She nodded and sat behind her desk. "Leave the door open."

Alex nodded and sat in the metal chair in front of her desk. He cleared his throat and reached into his pocket. "It's just my phone," he said as he removed his cell. Alex woke up his phone and found a picture of Jeff. He pushed his cell across the desk to Flora. "Did you ever see this guy here when the murder occurred?"

She stared at the screen, her eyes and memory searching for a match. "He doesn't look familiar, but it was ten months ago, and I don't see all the guests." She pushed Alex's cell back across her desk.

Alex grabbed his phone and put it back in his pocket. "Did you know Javier and Jerry?"

"I knew Javier better than Jerry, but I knew them both."

"What were they like? Do you think either of them were capable of murder?"

"Jerry was a creep, so many people weren't surprised. He had numerous relationships with teenage girls who came here with their parents."

"And Javier?"

"I liked Javier very much. He did anything I asked, no matter how disgusting the job. And he was always smiling. He had worked here for like fifteen years. Never any problems. But Javier's a little slow, so maybe Jerry made him do it, like they said. I don't know. It's so sad." She wiped the corners of her eyes with her index finger.

"Did Javier say that someone gave the knife to him?"

"He told the police that he got the knife from a friend."

"Did he describe this friend?"

"He said he was white with big muscles."

Alex removed his phone again and showed Flora a picture of Jeff shirtless at Norris Lake. "Like this?"

Her eyes were like saucers. "How do you know your brother did this?"

"I know of a series of these murders, at least six, with the same MO—"

"MO?"

"MO is the way the crime was committed."

She nodded.

"I found six murders with the same MO, and my brother happened to be visiting these places at the same time of each murder. This is the only location I'm not certain of yet."

"The hotel would have a record if he stayed here."

"I think he pays cash and uses a fake name. That's why I asked if you saw him here. Do you think you could show his picture to some people who might've been more likely to see him here?"

"Yes." Flora picked up her cell phone and sent a text.

A minute later, the young woman from the stairwell appeared.

After a brief introduction, Alex showed her the picture on his phone. "Have you ever seen this man?"

The woman stared at the picture. "*Guapo*. Looks familiar, but I don't know. Sorry." She handed the phone back to Alex. "You don't sell soaps, do you?"

"No, sorry."

She smirked and loitered—curious. Two more women appeared—both middle-aged. Neither of them remembered Jeff either.

"Could you look at one more picture, please?" Alex asked the women and handed his phone back to them.

"*Bonita*," one of the middle-aged women said.

"She was here. I remember her," the young woman said, in reference to the picture of Gwen.

"Are you sure?" Alex asked.

"Yes, she was crying in her room. I didn't think anyone was in there.

She didn't have the Do Not Disturb sign out. I remember asking her if she was okay, if she needed anything. You know what she said?" The young woman paused for effect. "*A new husband.* I laughed because it was funny, but then I felt bad, but then she laughed too."

"Do you remember when that was?" Alex asked.

"I think right after New Year's. I remember because it was right before all that stuff happened with the murder. That was crazy."

Alex thanked Flora and the women, and left the resort. He hurried to his truck, the cold biting his nose. *I have enough evidence now. There's no going back. It has to be done.* He started his truck and cranked the heat. On his way out of town, he called Matt and told him everything.

"This is crazy. You need to go to the sheriff," Matt said.

"I've already tried that. He's not interested," Alex replied.

"What do you mean, *he's not interested?*"

"Sheriff Franklin still thinks it's Brett."

"Then go to someone else."

"They won't do anything. That's why I'm coming to you."

"For what?"

"I'm gonna kill Jeff next Saturday when he goes to that cabin."

"Jesus, Alex. Are you crazy? You can't just kill someone."

"He did."

"You'll go to jail," Matt said.

"Not if they don't catch me," Alex replied.

"I have no idea how you feel, but I know this is a terrible idea. If you do this, your life will never be the same."

"That's what I'm hoping. Will you help me?"

"Help you … kill him?"

"You don't have to do it. I just need you to watch my back."

"I can't. I'd be an accessory to murder. Alex, I'm begging you. Don't do this."

"He killed Kristin." Alex's voice wavered. "Choked her and dumped her in a shallow grave. Revenge is all I have left."

"What if you're wrong?"

CHAPTER 51

Alex and the Cabin

Alex crept along the log cabin, holding his Glock 17 handgun. Leaves crunched with each step, his heart beating a mile a minute. The lighting was dim, the morning sun still low. Oak and hickory trees dominated the surrounding forest. He checked the back door, his hands covered in latex. It was locked with two dead bolts. He peered around the corner. A narrow gravel driveway snaked from the cabin into the woods beyond. No car parked on the side. *No windows. That's strange.* Alex moved along the back of the cabin to the opposite side. No windows here either. He snuck along the side to the front and peered around the corner. There was a porch, a metal front door, two windows with bars over them, and an empty gravel parking area that could fit two or three vehicles.

He stepped onto the porch and peered into a window. Blinds obscured his view. He tried to open the metal door. It was locked with two dead bolts. Alex holstered his handgun at his hip and hid behind a large oak near the front corner of the cabin. Papery leaves rustled in the breeze. Dark clouds hung overhead. He'd thought about wearing his raincoat, but he didn't like the *whoosh* that the nylon made when he moved. He'd settled on a black hoodie, knit cap, and forest-green camo pants.

His readiness degraded over the next two hours. He went from standing and alert to sitting and nearly asleep. The crunch of gravel and a faint engine noise startled him. He stood and peered around the tree. An old pickup truck drove along the narrow drive and parked in front. *Whose truck is that? Do I have the wrong house?*

Jeff stepped from the driver's side and walked around the truck to the passenger's side. *Definitely the right house.* He grabbed the paper grocery bags from the passenger seat, shut the truck with his boot, and stepped to the front door of the cabin. Jeff set his groceries on the bench next to the door and fished his keys from his front pocket. Alex crept from the woods toward the corner of the house. Leaves rustled, and a twig snapped under his foot.

Jeff looked around. Alex crouched, obscured by brush. Jeff unlocked the two dead bolts and opened the door. Alex grabbed his handgun from his holster and sprinted toward his brother. Jeff turned as Alex stepped onto the porch. Jeff's eyes were wide, but he smiled. The smile vanished as Alex pointed that Glock in his face.

"Get inside," Alex said, his handgun steady.

"What the fuck, Alex?" Jeff said, raising his hands.

"You know what. Get inside."

"I don't know what," Jeff said, stepping inside.

Alex followed Jeff, shutting the door behind them. Inside was a fireplace, a bearskin rug, a couch, and a recliner. A hallway to the right probably led to the bedroom and bathroom, and, from an open doorway to the rear, kitchen counters were visible.

Jeff turned around in the middle of the room and faced Alex and his gun. Jeff dropped his hands. "You gonna tell me what this is about?"

Alex clenched his jaw. His finger was straight and off the trigger. "What do you think it's about?"

Jeff showed his palms. "I have no fucking clue. You come to my cabin uninvited and hold me at gunpoint. Have you lost your mind? I'm worried about you. You disappeared at the wedding. You haven't been returning my phone calls. I know things have been hard for you. Why don't you put that down so we can have a conversation like brothers?"

Alex narrowed his eyes. "Tell me what you did to Kristin."

"What are you talking about? You don't think—"

"I don't think. I *know*."

"Bullshit. Brett killed Kristin and probably those girls on that island. Unless Danny Stafford did it." Jeff frowned. "Jesus, I can't believe you'd think I'd do such a thing. I'm your brother, man."

"You've done it before. Ghazni Province. Perry Township, Pennsylvania. Key West. Duck, North Carolina. Jackson Hole." Alex glowered at Jeff. "And Norris Lake."

Jeff shook his head. "This is insane. I have no idea what you're talking about. Please, Alex, put down the gun. Don't do something you'll regret for the rest of your life."

"Put your hands on your head and get on your knees." Alex motioned with his Glock.

"Have you ever killed anyone before?" Jeff asked, as he sank to his knees.

"Shut up."

"Maybe I deserve this." Jeff was on his knees, his hands atop his head, his gaze on the wood floor. "I did kill someone in Ghazni Province. A civilian. I murdered him. I thought he had a rifle. It was a fucking shovel. I dream about him every night. I see his face in my nightmares. I tried to kill myself when I first came back from Afghanistan." Jeff looked up at his brother. "Did you know that?"

Alex's eyes were glassy, his latex finger on the trigger. He stepped closer, the gun pointed at Jeff's forehead.

Gravel crunched under rubber, and the rumble of a motor approached.

Alex glanced at the door over his shoulder. "Who's that?"

"Dad." Jeff shrugged. "What are you gonna do now, big brother? You gonna kill Dad too?"

"Shut up. When he finds out what you did, he'll do it himself."

A car door shut. Steps sounded on the wooden porch. Alex moved around Jeff, so he was facing Jeff and the front door. The door opened.

"You left groceries outside," Harvey called out as he stepped inside, carrying the grocery bags. Harvey's eyes widened at the sight of Alex with a gun pointed at Jeff.

CHAPTER 52

Alex and Loyalties

"Alex?" Harvey said, grocery bags in both arms.

"Put the groceries down," Alex said.

Harvey set the groceries on the floor and stepped toward Alex.

"Stop. Don't move any closer," Alex said.

Harvey stopped in his tracks and showed his palms. "Okay. What the hell's going on here?"

"Jeff killed Kristin."

Harvey dropped his hands. His face was hard, his voice authoritative. "No, he didn't. Brett did. Maybe Danny Stafford had something to do with it. I don't know about that, but I *do* know that Jeff had *nothing* to do with it. Now put that goddamn gun down."

Alex shook his head. "I have proof."

Harvey stepped closer, one slow deliberate step after another, his hand outstretched. "Give me the gun, Alex. I'd like to see the proof. If he had something to do with Kristin's death, then ..." Harvey shook his head. "I don't care what you do to him. But we have to do this right. If you're wrong, there's no going back."

A tear slipped down Alex's cheek. He pointed the handgun at Harvey. "Stay back."

Harvey stopped in his tracks and showed his palms again.

Alex pointed the Glock at Jeff again. "You did it, you piece of shit."

"Give the gun to Dad," Jeff said.

Harvey took another tentative step in Alex's direction. "Show me the proof, son. You don't have to do this."

Alex had a lump in his throat as tears dripped from his eyes. He lowered the gun, just a little, and Harvey lunged for Alex's arm. As Harvey grabbed Alex's wrist, Alex pulled the trigger. The shot reverberated through the tiny cabin. Jeff lay on the floor, gripping his armpit, blood leaking between his fingers.

Harvey pried the gun from Alex's hand. Alex didn't resist.

"What the hell's wrong with you?" Harvey asked.

Alex was shell-shocked—speechless.

Jeff looked up at Harvey holding the Glock. He stood, holding his bloody armpit.

"You okay?" Harvey asked.

"Fucking burns," Jeff replied. "I think it just nicked me. I'll be fine."

Alex woke from his stupor. "I have proof."

Harvey ignored Alex, glaring at Jeff. "This is why you don't shit where you eat. Get the tarp."

Alex looked at Harvey with a tilted head. "What are you talking about?"

Harvey was unresponsive, his face blank.

Jeff left the room.

"Where's he going?" Alex asked Harvey.

Harvey turned the handgun on Alex. "Put your hands up."

Alex furrowed his brow. "What are you doing?"

"I said, put your *fucking* hands up."

Alex showed his gloved hands, his heart racing.

Jeff returned to the room with a canvas tarp. He spread it out on the floor.

"What the hell is that for?" Alex asked.

"On the tarp. Move," Harvey said, motioning with the Glock.

"Jesus, Dad. What are you gonna do? Shoot me?"

Harvey glared at Alex. "I said, 'on the tarp.'"

Alex stepped on the tarp, his arms still held up. "I don't understand. You don't want me to kill Jeff, but now you're gonna shoot *me*?"

"In the middle."

Alex took a few more steps.

"Turn around and kneel," Harvey said.

Alex kneeled but didn't turn around. "If you're gonna kill me, *Dad*, at least look me in the eyes when you do it."

Harvey glanced at Jeff. "This is the last time."

"You fucking *knew*," Alex said, glaring at his father.

Harvey paused, speechless.

Jeff frowned at Harvey. "Gimme the gun if you don't wanna do it."

"No." Harvey clenched his jaw, the muscles in his jawline pulsing. "You've done enough." Harvey walked around Alex, so he was behind his son, the front door to his back.

Alex closed his eyes. He thought about Kristin and Emma. Harvey pressed the square barrel to the back of Alex's head. The front door opened, and someone crashed into Harvey as he fired the gun.

CHAPTER 53

Alex and Reap What You Sow

There was a deafening *pop*. Alex fell from his knees to his side. Matt was on top of Harvey, wrestling for the gun. Alex lay on the ground, in a fog, his right ear ringing. Jeff stepped over Alex's motionless body, reached behind his back, and removed a knife from the scabbard under his shirt. It was an eight-inch fixed blade with a razor-sharp edge. Jeff stalked toward the Matt and Harvey scrum. Alex stood behind Jeff.

Matt was on top of Harvey, his back a large and inviting target. Jeff raised his knife. Before he could become a literal backstabber, Alex yanked Jeff backward with enough force that he fell to the wood floor. Alex straddled Jeff like an MMA fighter and punched his brother in the nose. Blood gushed from Jeff's nose. Alex smashed Jeff's wrist on the floor, trying to dislodge the knife from his grip.

Jeff bucked Alex and rolled, moving from under to atop Alex. In the process, Alex let go of Jeff's wrist. With his knife-wielding hand free, Jeff plunged the blade downward. Alex grabbed Jeff's forearm and wrist again, holding the business end of the blade mere inches from his chest cavity.

Another gunshot echoed through the cabin. Jeff was too strong. He had the leverage, and gravity was with him. The knife moved downward, despite Alex's shaky arms and red-faced survival instincts. The tip pressed into Alex's hoodie.

Matt pistol-whipped Jeff on his forehead.

Jeff wobbled—woozy. Alex pushed him to the side and crawled out from under him and the blade. Jeff dropped the knife. Matt kicked it away from Jeff's reach. Jeff lay on his side, then staggered to one knee. A river of blood flowed from his head wound.

Harvey sat on the floor, hunched forward, moaning and holding his midsection. His hands were slick with blood. Alex stood next to Matt who wore identical latex gloves and a black knit cap.

"You okay?" Alex asked.

Matt nodded. "Yeah. Are you?"

"I think my right eardrum's busted, but, other than that, I'm fine."

Matt held out the gun with the barrel down. "Here's your gun."

Alex took the gun and pointed it at Jeff, Harvey, then back to Jeff. "What happened?"

"I don't know," Matt replied. "I tried to get the gun, and it went off. I think Harvey was shot in the stomach."

"Hospital," Harvey said, his voice strained.

"He's gonna die if you don't get him to the hospital," Jeff said, his face candy-striped where the blood flowed.

"Hospital," Harvey said again.

"You don't take him to the hospital right now, both of you are going to prison for life."

"Shut the fuck up," Alex said.

"What do we do?" Matt asked.

"I don't know."

"We're fucked."

"Matt's right," Jeff said. "You two are fucked. There's only one way we all get out of this alive and out of prison."

"I said, 'Shut the fuck up,'" Alex replied.

"Take Dad to the hospital, let me go, and we say it was an accident. You two don't go to jail, and everyone lives."

Alex glared, the gun still pointed at Jeff. "You killed my daughter."

"I didn't." Jeff looked at Matt. "Alex isn't thinking straight. It's understandable after what happened, but he's mistaken. I know you don't like me, but I didn't do this. I swear to God and my unborn child that I didn't do this. We can fix this. Take Dad to the hospital. Let me go."

Matt glanced from Jeff to Alex.

Jeff shifted from one knee to kneeling on both. He showed his palms as if he were begging for spare change. Jeff's eyes watered. He stared at Alex, past the barrel of the Glock 17. "Please, Alex, don't do this. I swear to you, I had nothing to do with Kristin's death." Tears slipped from Jeff's eyes, catching in his stubbly beard. "You're my brother. I love you."

CHAPTER 54

Alex and Blood's Thicker than Water

"I love you, brother," Jeff said again. "Please, Alex, I'm gonna be a father."

"You having a boy or a girl?" Alex asked.

Jeff paused, the wheels turning for the right answer. "Girl."

"She'll be better off." Alex squeezed the trigger, shooting Jeff right between the eyes. Jeff's body slumped to the side and convulsed with death throes.

Matt gawked, his eyes wide and mouth open.

"He killed Kristin," Alex said to Matt.

Matt nodded.

Jeff lay motionless, his eyes open and empty. The brothers turned their attention to Harvey. He sat cross-legged, hunched, his hands holding his midsection. Alex pointed the Glock at his father. Harvey raised his head, staring at Alex.

"Why?" Alex asked.

"I wasn't going ... to shoot ... you," Harvey replied, his voice strained. "I wanted ... take Jeff ... police."

"That's bullshit."

"Please, ... son."

Alex moved closer, the handgun steady, his finger on the trigger. Matt put his fingers to his ears, anticipating the shot.

"Please, … hospital," Harvey said.

Alex lowered the Glock. "Goddamnit." Alex glanced out the front window at Harvey's parked car, then looked to Matt. "I'll drop you at my truck, and I'll take him in his BMW. You were never here."

"You'll go to prison," Matt said.

"Maybe." Alex holstered the Glock. "Can you help me find the shell casings?"

Matt located the shell casings and handed them to Alex.

Alex shoved the casings in his pocket. He looked at Harvey. "Help me carry him."

Matt and Alex grabbed Harvey under his armpits.

Alex froze. "Do you hear that?"

Matt froze, listening.

Gravel crunched; engine noise increased.

Alex looked down at Harvey. "Who is it?"

"Don't answer … door," Harvey replied.

"Quick, close the door," Alex said.

Matt closed and locked the front door. Alex parted a single blind and peered outside at the incoming SUV—big and black with tinted windows. The vehicle parked alongside the cabin. Shortly thereafter, a strong knock came at the back door.

They waited. Another strong knock followed.

"Harvey," a deep voice called out through the door. "I got your package. Never been touched." Another knock.

They waited.

"Harvey, you in there?" the man asked. "You already paid for four hours." The man jiggled the handle on the back door. "I'll wait."

"If we wait for him to leave, Harvey'll be dead," Alex whispered. "I'll tell the guy Harvey's not here."

Matt nodded.

Alex walked to the kitchen and the back door. He checked the peephole of the windowless door. A large bearded man wearing a flannel stood with a tiny girl. Alex opened the door.

"You Jeff?" the man asked.

"Yeah," Alex replied. "Harvey's—"

"He told me that you'd be here." He shoved the girl toward Alex. "If you wanna piece, that's extra."

"No thanks," Alex replied, trying to sound casual.

"She's pure, like Harvey ordered. I'll wait in the truck. Tell Harvey not to go over his time. I got another appointment."

The man turned and walked back to his truck. Alex shut the door behind the girl. She stood, with her head down, trembling. She was pale. Someone had braided her brown hair in pigtails. She wore a pink coat over footed pajamas. Alex thought about Harvey and his "package." He thought about Rachel. The pieces of the puzzle started to fit. His stomach churned.

"What's your name?" Alex asked, his voice higher and softer than normal.

She glanced upward. Her eyes were blue, like the lake, like Kristin's. "Grace."

"That's a beautiful name."

Her eyes watered. "Please don't hurt me."

"I won't. I promise. Nobody's gonna touch you, okay?"

She nodded.

"How old are you, Grace?"

"Seven."

"Where are your parents?"

"It's just my mom and her boyfriend."

"Where are they? I can take you there."

Her eyes widened, and her body stiffened. "Please, I can't go there. I can't. I can't."

Alex showed his palms. "Okay, okay. Where would you like me to take you?"

She shrugged.

"Are you hungry or thirsty?"

She nodded, looking around the kitchen.

"Would you like to sit down?" Alex motioned to the small kitchen table.

She sat on one of the wooden chairs and chewed on her fingernails. They were bitten to the nub, her cuticles red.

"Lemme see what we have," Alex said, opening the fridge. It was mostly empty, except for a few beers and condiments. Alex shut the fridge and checked the cabinets. He found a box of Ritz crackers. He turned to Grace. "Would you like some crackers?"

She nodded.

Alex glanced at the expiration date. "They might be stale." He placed the box on the kitchen table. "I have some groceries in the other room. Can you wait here for a minute?"

Grace nodded again.

Alex hurried to the living room. Matt was around the corner, listening to their conversation.

"What the hell?" Matt whispered.

Alex shook his head with a scowl. "Harvey ordered a girl—a very young one."

Matt winced. "Jesus. What are we gonna do?"

Alex marched toward the front door and the grocery bags. Matt followed. Harvey still sat, groaning. A blood-streaked phone was on the floor in front of him. Alex and Matt glanced at each other.

Alex picked up the phone, his finger to his lips, signaling to Matt.

"Hang in there, Mr. Palmer, an ambulance is on the way," the 9-1-1 operator said.

Alex disconnected the call. Almost immediately it chimed. Alex powered off the phone and shoved it in his pocket.

"This is *not* good," Matt said, shaking his head.

"We need to get out of here, *now*," Alex replied.

CHAPTER 55

Alex and Harvey's Gift

Alex split a blind and peered out the front window. He turned to Matt. "Harvey got his M5 fixed. It's shielded by Jeff's truck. We might be able to get in without the guy out there hearing us."

"He'll hear the engine," Matt replied.

"Harvey left us a car with six hundred horsepower, and, like always, the prick backed into his space. We'll be gone before that guy gets his SUV turned around." Alex glanced down at their father. "We can't say he never did anything for us."

"What do we do about him?" Matt gestured to Harvey.

Alex put two fingers to Harvey's neck and carotid artery. He shook his head. "He's not gonna make it." Alex patted Harvey's pockets. He pushed Harvey over with little care to access his BMW key. Harvey groaned.

"Good riddance," Matt said, his jaw set tight.

Alex reached into Harvey's pocket and snatched his keys. Alex grabbed Harvey by the hair and tilted his head upward. Harvey whimpered. "I hope you rot in hell with Jeff." He let go and Harvey's head bounced off the hardwood. Alex turned to Matt. "We gotta go."

They hurried to the kitchen.

Alex shoved Harvey's phone in the back of a drawer, then pivoted to Grace. "We need to get going, Grace."

"Okay, bye," she replied.

"Do you wanna come with us? You'll be safe." Alex bent down to her level. "I promise." Alex stood and held out his hand.

Grace placed her hand in his, her other hand on a sleeve of crackers. "Can I take these?"

"Bring your crackers, but I need you to do something. Can you shut your eyes until we get outside?"

Grace nodded her head and shut her eyes.

They hurried to the front, Grace with her eyes shut, holding on to Alex's hand. Matt unlocked the door and opened it, taking care not to be too noisy. It was cloudy and cool, the clouds pregnant with rain. They crept to the BMW. It was a bright blue sedan with a bulging hood that housed a 4.4 liter twin-turbo V-8. The car automatically unlocked as Alex moved near the driver's side door. They climbed inside the plush leather interior—Grace in the back seat, Matt in the passenger seat.

"Everybody buckle up," Alex said, putting on his seat belt.

Matt and Grace fastened theirs.

Alex took a deep breath and pressed the ignition. The throaty V-8 roared to life. Alex put the car into Drive, selected Paddle Shift, and rammed on the accelerator. He had driven Harvey's car before. Gravel spit from the tires, and the rear end fishtailed as the BMW searched for traction. A split second later they flew down the narrow gravel drive, the forest zipping past. They turned left out of the driveway, drifting like they were in a rally race.

Alex pushed the Paddle Shifter each time the RPMs neared their limit. They were going ninety down the gravel road. Coming around a bend, the back end slid. Alex turned into the slide, the computer adding assistance, and the dashboard flashing warning signs. Alex and the engineers at BMW corrected the slide. Alex eased off the throttle. Matt looked over his shoulder periodically.

"There's an SUV behind us," Matt said. "It's gaining on us."

Alex pressed the accelerator and shifted gears again. They were going over one hundred now. The SUV disappeared in the distance. Rocks pelted the underside of the car, and they left a cloud of stone dust in their wake. Up ahead, sirens wailed. Alex slowed for a turn. The siren was closer. Around the bend, they were nose to nose with an oncoming ambulance, followed by two police cars. Alex pulled to the edge of the road to make room. The ambulance zoomed past along with a police car. The other police car turned sideways, blocking their retreat. The side of the black cruiser read Sheriff, Monongalia County. Alex stopped the BMW about thirty feet from the police car.

"Get out of the car with your hands up," the deputy said, his voice coming loud and clear from the intercom.

Alex glanced at Matt, and he nodded his affirmation. Alex mashed on the accelerator and cut the wheel, barely brushing past the police car and scraping the side of the M5 in the process. Alex zipped through the gears like Emerson Fittipaldi, leaving the police cruiser in the dust—literally.

At the end of the gravel road, they made a left onto a paved two-lane road. Traffic was sparse, the police car gone.

"Maybe he turned the wrong way," Matt said, glancing back at the empty road.

"Let's hope," Alex said, still flying down the two-lane road, the M5 very stable at 120 miles per hour.

Alex slowed the car as they neared the trailhead. He pulled the BMW into the gravel lot at the start of the wilderness trail. "We gotta switch cars, Grace."

They piled into Alex's pickup and peeled out of the parking lot, leaving the BMW and Harvey's keys on the seat.

Alex and Matt had hiked six miles to the cabin, not wanting Alex's truck to be spotted near the crime scene. They stopped on Buckeye Road, and Matt tossed the Glock into Dunkard Creek. Alex drove the speed limit to I-79, then they went south for about half an hour. The dark clouds scattered, giving center stage to the sun. They exited the highway and found the Walmart where Matt's Hyundai was parked.

Matt stepped out of the truck with his backpack.

"I'll be right back," Alex said to Grace.

She nodded.

Matt threw his backpack in the back seat of his sedan and shut the door. Matt turned to Alex and held out his hand. Alex gave his brother a hug.

"Thank you," Alex said. "I love you, bro."

"Me too." Matt wiped his eyes discreetly.

Alex said, "If they come for you, just keep quiet, and I'll take the rap."

Matt nodded. "Do you think they'll come for us?"

"I don't know."

"What are you gonna do with Grace?"

"Help her if I can."

CHAPTER 56

Alex and Emma

Alex pulled into the driveway of his soon-to-be-repoed McMansion. *Home sweet Tennessee.* Grace was asleep in the passenger seat. The garage and porch lights brightened the darkness in starburst patterns. Lights illuminated a few windows. *Did I leave the lights on?* He pressed his automatic garage door opener on the visor and pulled into the garage, stopping as his windshield touched the little tennis ball hanging from the ceiling. His full-size truck barely fit. He glanced at Emma's car next to him. *Shit, she didn't say she'd be home.* His stomach turned; his blood pressure spiked. He wasn't ready to explain. Alex cut the engine.

"We're here," Alex said to Grace.

She was unresponsive.

"Grace, wake up," Alex said.

Nothing.

Alex reached over to shake her but changed his mind. He stepped out of the driver's side and squeezed around the truck to the passenger side. He opened the door.

Grace wiped her eyes.

"We're here," Alex said. "My wife's home too. She doesn't know about you yet, so I'll have to explain, okay?"

Grace nodded, her eyes red-rimmed. "Is she gonna make me go back?"

"She's not gonna make you do anything you don't want to. Okay?"

"Okay."

"You ready?"

Grace stepped on the running board and hopped down from the truck. "Your truck is really tall."

"It takes some getting used to."

Alex led Grace inside to the kitchen. It was lit. Emma stood from the table, wearing sweats. Emma opened her mouth, but nothing came out. She stared at Grace, who stared at the hardwood.

"Emma, this is Grace," Alex said. "She needs our help. I can explain everything."

Emma stepped forward and smiled. "Hi, Grace. I'm Emma."

Grace raised her head. "Hi."

Emma looked at Alex, then back to Grace. "Are you hungry, honey? Would you like something to eat?"

Grace shook her head.

"We ate not too long ago," Alex said, then turned to Grace. "I need to talk to Emma for a little bit. Would you like to relax on the couch, maybe watch some TV?"

Grace nodded. Alex showed her to the living room and their sectional. He showed her which remote was for the TV and which was for the cable box. Grace stared back blankly. Alex channel-surfed for her until she saw something that piqued her interest. Alex left Grace with Nickelodeon and returned to the kitchen.

Emma was on him like white on rice, whispering, yet yelling—no easy feat. "What the hell is going on? I called you four times today, and you never answered. I came over because I thought something had happened to you, and I found your phone in your office. Do I need to tell you what else I found?"

Alex sighed and shook his head.

"I was gonna call hospitals and the police, but I didn't know if you were doing something ... illegal."

"I don't think ..." Alex shook his head.

Emma took a deep breath. Her eyes watered as she searched Alex's face. "What did you do, Alex? And, for heaven's sake, why do you have a little girl in pajamas with you?"

Alex rubbed his bloodshot eyes with his thumb and index finger. He opened his mouth to speak.

Emma stood with her hands on her hips.

Alex shut his mouth and hugged his wife. She was stiff as a board for a moment but quickly melted, her arms wrapping around her husband. Alex buried his face in Emma's neck. He had a lump in his throat. He cried for what he had done. He cried for what Jeff did, what Harvey did. He cried for Grace. But mostly he cried for Kristin. His investigation had kept her alive for him. Now she was really gone.

CHAPTER 57

Alex and God's Plan

It was a long night. Alex told Emma everything. He explained the corkboards, but she had already figured those out on her own. He told her what he did at the cabin and how Grace ended up in their home. Regarding Jeff and Harvey, Emma was much more an-eye-for-an-eye than a turn-the-other-cheek kind of gal. Grace, ... well, they still weren't sure what do to with her or for her.

Grace was fast asleep in Kristin's bed. Alex and Emma talked in their room, trying to keep their "discussion" to a reasonable decibel.

"Grace won't replace Kristin," Emma said.

"You think I don't know that?" Alex shot back.

"She's a child, not a puppy. We can't just decide to keep her."

"Why not?"

"Because we could get arrested for kidnapping."

"What would Jesus do? Give her to her mother so she can be sold back into sex slavery? Give her to social services so they can send her someplace shitty?"

"That's not what I'm saying. And don't bring Jesus into this."

"I'm already taking a murder rap. I'll take a kidnapping charge too. I promised Grace that I wouldn't let anyone hurt her."

"You're wrong to tell her that. That's a promise you can't keep. You couldn't even ..." Emma trailed off.

"What, Emma? I couldn't even keep my own daughter safe?"

"I'm sorry. I didn't mean it."

"You're right, Emma. I didn't keep Kristin safe. I have to live with that every day for the rest of my life. I don't care if I go to jail or die tryin', but I'm not gonna ..." Alex hung his head and rubbed his temples. "I'm not gonna break my promise to Grace."

"I'm sorry," Emma said, wrapping her arms around him and kissing him. After a moment, they separated. "If she wants to stay with us, how do we enroll her in school? How do we do anything?"

"We could homeschool her. I mean, we couldn't actually get her credits, but we could teach her everything she needs to know to get her GED. Then, when she's eighteen, it won't matter. She can use her identity to go to college or whatever she wants to do. We don't have to legally be her parents at that point. She can live wherever she wants."

"What about going to the doctor? Doesn't she need therapy after what she's been through?"

"I don't know. I mean, her family must've been pretty awful, but thankfully she never was, never ... you know." Alex clenched his jaw. "Harvey was supposed to be the first one."

"I still can't believe he was gonna ..." She trailed off. "It's pure evil."

"I know."

"Thank God she was spared."

Alex nodded, yet thought God wasn't in that cabin.

"She'll still need help."

"Maybe we could get her a fake identity, or we could just pay cash for her, use a fake name. I don't know. I haven't worked all this stuff out. I wasn't expecting to find her."

"I know." Emma took a deep breath. "I think we should get to know her better and see what *she* wants. Maybe this is God's plan."

* * *

Alex woke, a beam of sunlight touching his face. His eyes fluttered. He reached for Emma, but she was gone. He sat up in bed and checked the alarm clock on his bedside table to see it was 10:43 a.m. Laughter came from downstairs. A girl's laugh. He smelled bacon. Alex put on sweatpants and a T-shirt and went to the bathroom. He peed, washed his hands, and gargled with mouthwash. He ran his hand through his disheveled hair. Alex leaned on the sink and stared at himself in the mirror. *This is the litmus test, right? Can you look yourself in the mirror after what you did? Yes, I can. And I'd do it again in a heartbeat.*

Alex followed the smell of bacon and the sound of laughter into the kitchen. Emma was making molded pancakes, shaped like animals. Grace had a horse and a rabbit on her plate. Emma had made smiles with chocolate sauce and eyes with blueberries.

"Aww, they're cute. I feel bad eating them," Grace said.

"Good morning," Alex said, smiling.

"Hi, Alex," Grace said, grinning. "Emma's making pancakes. I love pancakes."

"Me too." Alex looked at Emma. "Need any help?"

Emma turned from the griddle. "Sit, honey. You've done enough." Emma served pancakes, bacon, and orange juice.

The three of them sat and ate.

"Would you like to go shopping for some new clothes today?" Emma asked Grace.

Grace glanced down at her dirty pajamas. "Okay."

Alex's cell phone chimed. He glanced at the screen and looked at his wife. "It's Cathy."

Emma nodded, knowing this phone call was coming.

Alex stood from the table, grabbed his phone, and swiped right as he walked into the other room.

"Hi, Cathy," Alex answered, trying to sound cheerful.

"Alex, … I have terrible news," Cathy said, barely audible.

"What happened?"

She sniffled. "Jeff and your dad were … killed."

* * *

After breakfast and the phone call, Alex went to his office. Emma took Grace clothes shopping. Alex thought about the pain he'd caused Cathy, by killing her husband and her only son. *Did she know what Harvey was doing to these girls? What Harvey had done to their own daughter? How could Cathy not know about Harvey or Jeff or Rachel?* Alex opened his laptop and did a Google search—Murder, Monongalia County, West Virginia. Alex's eyes were like saucers. The story had already been picked up—nationwide. He clicked on the *Washington Post* article.

Multiple Murder in Monongalia
By William Leonard
11-11-2018

At 10:27 a.m. on Saturday, November 10, 2018, Monongalia County 9-1-1 operators received a distress call, citing a gunshot wound and multiple unnamed assailants. Monongalia County Sheriff's deputies and an ambulance were dispatched to a remote cabin near Mooresville, West Virginia.

According to the Sheriff's Department's reports, deputies encountered two vehicles fleeing the scene. The first vehicle, a high-powered BMW, managed to evade deputies in a high-speed chase that reached speeds over one hundred miles per hour. The second vehicle, an SUV, rammed a sheriff's car that blocked the narrow road. The driver was fatally shot by a deputy.

Two more gunshot victims were found in the cabin. Both victims were dead at the scene, one of a single gunshot wound to the stomach; the other, an execution-style shot to the head.

The Monongalia County Sheriff's Department has not released the names of the victims or the driver, nor have they named any suspects in the double homicide. They have not confirmed or denied the fleeing driver's connection to the crime.

CHAPTER 58

Alex and Popping Bubbles

Alex and Emma spent the next two weeks waiting for their bubble to pop. Emma took her vacation time and then some. Grace never wavered. She wanted to stay. It surprised Alex how quickly she latched on to Emma. The girl needed a mother, and Emma was a damn good one. Emma had a close friend who was a therapist. It was asking a lot of her friend to help Grace. "I could lose my license," she had said. Ultimately, they paid cash, and the therapist didn't keep records of Grace's visits.

Alex spent his days mining his network for job opportunities. Most people never bothered to return his emails and phone messages. The ones who did just apologized as they said no, often referencing the poor economy. Alex's heart skipped a beat every time his cell chimed, hoping it was a job, but worried it was the police.

He sat at his desk, checking his email on his laptop. His office felt large without the corkboards closing in on him. He had stripped them clean, filed the information away for safekeeping, and put the corkboards in the garage. He did keep one board for job offers. It was still empty.

There was a knock on his open door. Grace stood wearing sweats and a small grin, her pale skin radiant and clear. Her features were so tiny. Delicate hands and feet, a button nose. Her brown hair was freshly cut and tucked behind her ears.

She stepped forward, holding a drawing. "Mom—I mean, Emma, said you might like this." Grace held out the turkey, detailed, drawn freehand, and meticulously colored. The header read Happy Thanksgiving in big cartoon-style letters.

Alex stood and walked around his desk. He took the picture and examined it carefully. "It's beautiful, Grace. Thank you."

She blushed.

He walked to the solitary corkboard and tacked it up dead center. "I'm gonna hang it here, so I can see it all the time."

She smiled. "Emma said we're gonna have three different pies tomorrow. You know what kinds?"

"Pumpkin?"

"And cherry and apple. I can't wait." She turned on her heels and gave a quick wave. "Bye, Alex." She ran down the hall, back to Emma and their lessons.

Alex returned to his desk and his laptop. His cell phone chimed. He glanced at the number, and his heart pounded. He accepted the call.

"Sheriff Franklin," Alex answered.

"Alex. How've you been?" Sheriff Franklin asked.

"Fine. How 'bout you?"

"I just got off the phone with Sheriff Gallaher from Monongalia County, West Virginia."

"Okay," Alex replied, trying to sound casual.

"I'm assumin' you heard about Harvey and Jeff?"

"I did."

"I'm sorry for your loss."

Alex huffed. "The world's better off."

"I thought you got along with your daddy?"

"He was a piece of shit."

"That's a helluva thing to say about your daddy who just died."

"I think he abused my sister Rachel when she was a child."

"What kind of abuse?"

"The worst kind," Alex replied.

"Where were you on Saturday, November 10, at 10:30 a.m.?" Sheriff Franklin asked.

"Probably here by myself, but I couldn't say for sure. Who the hell remembers specific dates like that?"

"By yourself, huh? Emma not been around?"

"We've had a tough time since ... She's here now."

"That's good. I don't want you to lose what you got, Alex."

"Neither do I."

There was an uncomfortable silence. "I've been doin' some diggin' since the last time we talked. Somethin' was gnawin' on me. You ever hear of Ted Bundy?"

"Yeah, he was a serial killer, right?"

"Yep. Good-lookin' guy. He'd wear a fake cast and ask some young woman for help. Used that fake injury to appear harmless, so the girls wouldn't be suspicious. When Jeff came to my office in crutches, somethin' didn't seem right. I watched him on those crutches. I watched him all the way out. You ever see someone open a door on crutches?"

"Yeah," Alex replied.

"Then you know what a pain in the ass it is to open the door and shimmy through without the door jammin' against your crutches. When Jeff got to the door at my offices, he glanced around, then put both feet down and walked out like he was perfectly healthy."

"You believe Jeff ... did it?"

"I do believe you were right about Jeff. I found a few more cases that fit the MO, and I did some investigatin'. Apparently, Jeff goes on vacation and pays in cash, doesn't use his cell or allow Gwen to use hers. I searched hotels and even made a few cross-country trips. I got eyewitnesses who place Jeff in these places. Flora says hi, by the way."

Alex's stomach churned. "I don't know what you're talking about."

"Don't bullshit me, Alex. I know you went to Jackson Hole. You be honest with me, and I'll be honest with you."

"Fair enough."

"I think Jeff killed at least seven girls between 2006 and 2018. There are gaps of inactivity within that time, and they coincide perfectly with his deployments. I bet dollars to doughnuts that there's a trail of dead girls in Afghanistan. It's a sticky situation. Men are in prison for his crimes—men doin' hard time in places they don't belong."

"Are you gonna do something about it?"

"I'm workin' on it, but they're not in my jails. The FBI's involved since the killin' took place over several states. The individual authorities have been notified too, the jails as well as the investigatin' departments."

"When will these guys get out?"

"I don't know. The wheels of justice grind slow, and they don't work so well in reverse. Detectives, prosecutors, judges—nobody wants to admit a mistake—especially one that ends in a lawsuit. I'm doin' what I can."

Alex clenched his jaw. "So they just rot in prison?"

"I didn't say that. I'm sayin' it's an uphill battle. If these departments don't make it right, I'm prepared to go to the press."

"That's good."

"Evidence is a funny thing, Alex. As an investigator, it's easy to have a suspect and to make that evidence fit. If you don't have any suspects, a lot a times that evidence don't mean squat. Apart from that piece-of-shit child trafficker, they don't have any suspects in Monongalia County. What do you think would happen if I gave Sheriff Gallaher *your* name?"

"I don't know."

"What you did was stupid and dangerous, but I get it. I have daughters. I prob'ly would've done the same thing if I was in your shoes, so I ain't even gonna ask you about Jeff, but I gotta know why you killed Harvey."

Alex's heart pounded, his stomach turned upside down. "He was a child rapist. Get the FBI to check his computer. Why do you think that child trafficker was there?"

"I think you went to that cabin to kill Jeff, but Harvey was there.

Maybe you got the jump on them, held them at gunpoint. They tried to get your gun, didn't they? That's how Jeff got that glancin' blow under his armpit. Then what? You got control again, right? I think you executed Jeff first—right between the eyes. That was the easy choice. Harvey prob'ly tried to talk himself out of it. Maybe the child trafficker showed up with a girl for Harvey. Why not shoot Harvey in the head, like you did Jeff?"

Alex was quiet.

"Was Harvey's shooting an accident? Self-defense?"

"Both, but I left him there to die."

"The FBI found child pornography on Harvey's computer. They also found that he had accessed the dark web to arrange for sex with underage girls."

"If you already knew about Harvey, why … ?" Alex trailed off.

"Why would I wanna know your intent?" Sheriff Franklin asked.

"Yeah."

"Because intent matters. I can't in good conscience let this go if you murdered Harvey in cold blood, but, if it was self-defense, then you let him bleed out because you saw what he was? Is that what happened?"

"Yes."

The sheriff took a deep breath. "Okay. I can live with that. That leaves one more loose end." Sheriff Franklin paused for a beat. "Where's the girl, Alex? Is she okay?"

"She's safe and sound and exactly where she wants to be," Alex replied.

The sheriff went silent again.

"Sheriff? You still there?"

"Yeah. Tell Emma I said hello. Stay out of trouble, all right?"

CHAPTER 59

Alex and Blessed

Alex leaned forward and cranked the throttle. His electric motor-cycle zipped forward on the narrow country road, not making a sound. The wind whipped around his helmet, and the forest blasted past in an amalgamation of green. For a moment, he felt the same sense of freedom he had felt that day—that day he had driven like his life and his brother's life had depended on it.

He eased off the throttle and turned into his driveway. The house was a one-story brick rambler—solar panels on the roof, a sprawling garden in the front yard, and fruit trees on the side. Alex parked in the two-car garage. Emma's little Honda was parked in the spot next to him. He took off his helmet, plugged the bike into the wall, and stepped inside—into the mudroom.

Daisy the Boston terrier barked and ran to Alex. She looked up at him, her ears perked and her tail wagging. Alex bent down to pet her head. "Hey, girl," he said.

Alex hung his helmet on the wall hook. He removed his padded jacket, exposing his uniform underneath. He wore a blue button-down shirt with a logo over his left pectoral that read Ashe County Ambulance, North Carolina. He walked into the kitchen, his boots heavy on the hardwood, Daisy following him. Emma flipped through the mail on the center island.

Grace was on him like bees on honey. "You didn't forget, did you?" she asked, grinning.

Alex looked down at her with a smirk. "Were we supposed to do something today?"

Grace frowned with her hands on her hips. Even though she was eighteen now, most people thought she was much younger. She was short, 5'2", with a button nose, bright blue eyes, and skin like Snow White.

"Gimme a minute, okay? I'm starving," Alex said, moving toward Emma and kissing her on the cheek.

Emma smiled and handed him a novel with a Post-it note on the cover. "Matt sent his book."

Alex glanced at the bold lettering that read *Thicker than Water*. The Post-it note instructed him to *Open to the bookmark*. Alex opened the book to the marked page. Dead center of the page read For my big brother, Alex.

"That's nice," Emma said, looking over his shoulder.

Alex nodded.

"What's nice?" Grace asked.

"Uncle Matt dedicated his new book to your dad," Emma said.

"What's it about?"

Alex read the blurb on the back and paraphrased. "It's about two brothers who take the law into their own hands."

"I wanna read it," Grace said.

Alex handed her the novel. "It's all yours. I'll listen to it." He removed his cell phone from his pocket. "I should call Matt." He pressed the Matt icon from his Contacts list.

"Hello?" a little boy answered.

"Hey, Tommy," Alex replied. "It's your uncle Alex. Is your dad around?"

"Hi, Uncle Alex. He's writing a story, so he can't talk to anybody, not even my mom. I'm 'posed to answer the phone 'cause I'm his helper."

"You are?"

"Yep. I'm a good helper."

Alex chuckled. "Can you tell your dad that I called?"

"Okay."

"Talk to you later, buddy."

* * *

After a quick snack, Alex and Grace went to the garage.

"You pull it out of the garage," Grace said, looking at Emma's Honda. It ran on compressed natural gas.

"You can do it," Alex said.

They entered the Honda—Grace on the driver's side, Alex in the passenger seat. Grace inched the car out of the garage, her hands gripping the steering wheel. She turned around in the driveway— an eight-point-turn so she didn't drive on the garden she had worked so hard to cultivate.

"Make a right," Alex said, pointing.

Grace turned out of their driveway and followed the country road, going five miles *under* the speed limit.

"How am I doing?" Grace asked.

"You're doing great, honey," Alex replied.

The country road gave way to a small highway, then to the suburbs, and finally to an abandoned high school parking lot. The massive high school was too expensive to run—most students now taking a combination of online, homeschooled, and nontraditional classes.

The parking lot was vast, but filled with potholes. They found an area toward the back that was relatively safe for the Honda's suspension. Grace worked on parking—front first, backing in, parallel parking.

"I don't understand why I need to know how to do this," Grace said. "The car can park itself."

"It's still on the driving test," Alex replied. "Plus, we're gonna buy you an old beater that you have to park yourself."

Grace smiled as she eased into the space. "That's fine. I can do it."

She put the car in Park and turned to Alex. "An old car's better than no car."

Alex stared into her blue eyes—blue eyes like Kristin's, blue like the lake. He experienced a déjà vu moment—Kristin in the driver's seat, the same driving lesson, eleven years ago.

"Dad, are you okay?" Grace asked.

Alex blinked, Grace coming into focus. "Yeah, I'm great. I'm blessed."

"Me too."

If you enjoyed *What Happened at the Lake*, you'll love …

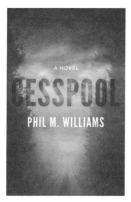

Link: https://philwbooks.com/books/

Would you become a criminal to do the right thing?

Disgraced teacher, James Fisher, moved to a backwoods town, content to live his life in solitude. He was awakened from his apathy by a small girl with a big problem. James suspected Brittany was being abused and exploited by his neighbor. He called the police but soon realized his mistake, as the neighbor was related to the chief of police.

Most would've looked the other way. Getting involved placed James squarely in the crosshairs of the local police. James lacked the brawn or the connections to save himself, much less Brittany. The police held all the power, and they knew it. But that was also their weakness. They underestimated what the mild-mannered teacher and the young runaway would do for justice.

Buy Cesspool today if you enjoy vigilante justice page-turners with a side of underdog.

FOR THE READER

Dear Reader,

I'm thrilled that you took precious time from your life to read my novel. Thank you! I hope you found it entertaining, engaging, and thought-provoking. If so, please consider writing a positive review on Amazon and Goodreads. Five-star reviews have a huge impact on future sales. The review doesn't need to be long and detailed, if you're more of a reader than a writer. As an author and a small businessman competing against the big publishers, every reader, every review, and every referral is greatly appreciated.

If you're interested in receiving my novel *Against the Grain* **for free and/or reading my other titles for free or discounted, go to the following link:** http://www.PhilWBooks.com. You're probably thinking, *What's the catch?* There is no catch. If you'd like to browse my other titles, go to this link: https://philwbooks.com/books/.

If you want to contact me, don't be bashful. I can be found at Phil@PhilWBooks.com. I do my best to respond to all emails.

Sincerely,
Phil M. Williams

GRATITUDE

I'd like to thank my wife. She's my first reader and always will be. Without her support and unwavering belief in my skill as an author, I'm not sure I would have embarked on this career. I love you, Denise.

I'd also like to thank my editors. My developmental editor, Caroline Smailes, did a fantastic job finding the holes in my plot and suggesting remedies. As always, my line editor, Denise Barker (not to be confused with my wife, Denise Williams), did a fantastic job making sure the manuscript was error-free. I love her comments and feedback.

Thank you to Deborah Bradseth of Tugboat Design for her excellent cover art and formatting. She's the consummate professional. I look forward to many more beautiful covers in the future.

Thank you to my brother Chris for exposing me to stunning Norris Lake, and for his encouragement and advice. His ideas were instrumental in the formation of the plot. Denise and I've enjoyed many Norris Lake vacations with my brother and his wonderful family.